THE OTHER SIDE OF THE MOON

By
EDMOND HAMILTON

I0616711

ARMCHAIR FICTION
PO Box 4369, Medford, Oregon 97504

For more information about Armchair Books and products, visit our website at...

www.armchairfiction.com

Or email us at...

armchairfiction@yahoo.com

INVASION FROM THE DARK SIDE...

As a team of geologists explored deep in the Yucatan jungle, they found themselves near the ruins of an ancient Mayan temple. It was an amazing sight. But what they didn't understand about these crumbling ruins was that they were also the site of an ancient alien spaceport—a spaceport that was still active. They soon found themselves attacked by alien raiders from the dark side of the moon! One of the geologists, Richard Carson, had hidden in the shadows, barely escaping with his life. He watched, horrified, as his colleagues were all horribly slain, with one lone survivor, Dr. Howland, being taken prisoner by the alien beasts. Howland then found himself with a one-way ticket back to the moon, where a lost race of turtle-like moon beings planned the eventual conquest of the Earth, a planet they had once ruled, eons in the past.

FOR A SECOND COMPLETE NOVEL, TURN TO PAGE 145

ABOUT EDMOND HAMILTON...

Edmond Hamilton was born in 1904 in Youngstown, Ohio. A child prodigy, he completed high school and entered into college at the age of 14 with the dream of becoming an electrical engineer. Unfortunately, the age discrepancy between Hamilton and the other students made it difficult for him to adapt to his new surroundings and he never completed his degree. He flunked out during his third year and took a job with the Pennsylvania Railroad while he tried to figure out what to do with the rest of his life.

Although he had never shown any inclination towards writing before, he decided in the mid 20s to be an author. Whether this decision was just an intellectual exercise or was born out of necessity is not known. From the 20s to the mid-40s, Hamilton worked solely as a freelance author and was very prolific, often writing several short stories, while working on a novel-length serial.

He also established a number of firsts during this extremely fertile period, including the first use of a space suit in science fiction, the first space walk and the first use of an energy sword, the prototype for what George Lucas, a Hamilton fan, would later dub a light saber. He also found time to travel during this period, often in the company of his friend, author Jack Williamson.

By the early to mid 70's he was under constant medical care and eventually passed away in 1977.

CHAPTER ONE
The Howland Sensation

IT IS ONLY now, in beginning this record of our great adventure, that I realize at last how fragmentary and incomplete such a record must be. For it is only now, looking back upon the thing, that I perceive how much of it remains, and will forever remain, unknown. Even I, Martin Foster, who was one of those to penetrate into the very center of that eon-old menace that gathered out there on our moon's far side, can offer but few explanations of what I experienced and saw. It is because of that, therefore, that this record must remain a purely personal one, from the first.

It was the Howland sensation that was the first of it, to me that astounding blotting out of Dr. Herman Howland and four fellow-scientists in the interior of Yucatan, which flamed from the newspaper headlines for days. It was a sensation that was intensified at Mid-Western University, where Howland had held the chair of Anthropology, and where I was a humble chemistry instructor. There were investigations, discussions, rumors, a flurry of general excitement, which swept across the campus for weeks. Yet all of this yielded, in the end, no more information really than had the first sensational newspaper accounts. And it is in those accounts that one finds, now, the most clear and comprehensive presentation of the tragic affair's main features.

For several years, as those accounts stated, Dr. Howland had been engrossed in a new theory of anthropological origins which he had formed and which he was endeavoring to prove. It was his belief that a great island-chain had in prehistoric times connected what is now Central America with northwestern Africa, and that it was by way of this chain of islands, of which the West Indies and the Azores were the remnants, that human and animal life had poured into the American continents. To support this theory he had made a number of fieldtrips to Central America, especially to Yucatan, and had collected a mass of evidence tending to establish that region as the first center of life in this hemisphere. This evidence, consisting of the resemblances of human, animal, plant and even insect life in that region to those of northern Africa, had impressed his fellow-anthropologists in spite of their general hostility to his theory. And it was Howland's contention that a comprehensive scientific survey of the Yucatan region would prove his theory beyond any shadow of doubt.

It was from Mid-Western University that such a survey expedition was finally sent forth, early in April. Dr. Howland, despite his youth, was named as its head, and it included five of his scientific associates whose combined knowledge, it was believed, would enable him to cover the field completely. These were Dr. Erasmus Willings, who held the University's chair of General Biology; Dr. John Borkoff, zoologist; Professor Alexander Grant, internationally-known botanist; Professor William Glitz, entomologist; and young Dr. Richard Carson, geologist, who was a personal friend of Dr. Howland, and of myself. Such an array of scientific talent, it was felt, could not fail to unEarth whatever scientific evidence as to the truth of Dr. Howland's theory which could be found, and when the party sailed in April for Yucatan, it seemed certain that it would return with conclusive proof or disproof of that theory.

It was in the latter part of April that news reached us that the party had reached Progreso, on the Yucatan coast, and was preparing for its journey into the little-known interior. The expedition planned, it was stated, to make its way up the winding Carajos River as far as possible by means of native canoes and paddlers, establishing successive camps as it progressed inward and using these as bases of investigation. This first message from the Howland party was received with great interest at the University, especially by myself and by my fellow chemistry instructor, Harlan Trent, who, with Howland and Carson, had made up for some time a close quartet of friends. That first message, though, proved the only news we were to receive of the party for some time, since a few days later came word from Howland that the expedition was on the point of starting up the river, which automatically cut off their communication with us and with the world.

Thus Howland and his five associates, with their dozen native paddlers, departed up the Carajos from the village at its mouth, passing up into the dark depths of the tangled Yucatan jungles, which even the natives feared. Three weeks then passed with no word from Howland and his party, weeks in which it could only be guessed that they were pushing on into the interior, through the low blue mountains against the currents of their jungle-bordered waterway. Then at the end of those weeks there came news, abrupt, astounding, news from the village at the Carajos River's mouth, a short, staggering message. Dr. Richard Carson, that sensational message stated, had been found unconscious, drifting down the Carajos in a single large canoe which was loaded with the dead, shattered bodies of four of his associates, of Willings and Borkoff and Glitz and Grant. Of Howland or the party's natives there was no sign, nor had Carson yet recovered from the complete coma in which he had been found.

THAT BARE first announcement of the tragedy catapulted the hitherto unnoticed scientific expedition onto the front pages of the world's newspapers instantly, and struck Mid-Western University and us of its staff with staggering shock. Within ten hours had come a second message that heightened the sensation. The still unconscious Carson and the bodies of his four friends had been removed from the village to Progreso, it was announced, and physicians there had made a careful examination of the four bodies. They stated that those bodies, shattered as they were, had not been crushed in the least from without, but had apparently exploded from within, an *outward* shattering of their bodies that seemed utterly inexplicable. Only some terrific and unpredictable force could ever have shattered them thus, they stated, and so the thing had to be put down, for the time being, as a result of circumstances and forces unknown, which only Carson could explain.

Carson, however, suffering from the horror and shock of whatever tragedy it was that had occurred there in the dark Yucatan jungles, did not regain consciousness until two days later. When he did recover he cleared up the mystery in a few incoherent words. For almost two weeks he and the party had progressed up the river, Carson stated, making camp at intervals along its banks, and it was at the fourth or fifth of these camps that the catastrophe had occurred. Carson, with his geological passion uppermost, had wandered away from the camp to examine some great boulders farther up the river, he said, making his way clearly by the light of the full moon that swung overhead. He had finished his inspection and was returning toward the camp, he stated, when there had come a terrific flash of brilliant light stabbing down into the camp ahead. He had rushed forward to find the camp a scene of death, the shattered bodies of his four friends and of the dozen natives sprawled about, while tracks by the river's edge showed that Howland had been struck there by the same death and had fallen into the waters and had been carried away. Carson, knowing that a giant lightning-bolt had suddenly wiped out all the party but himself, had loaded the bodies of his friends into one of the canoes, had scooped a grave in the soft sand for the natives, and then had pushed off and with horror-numbed brain had pressed down the river, losing consciousness wholly after days of such horror-driven progress, to be found when his canoe and its terrible cargo drifted down to the village at the river's mouth.

Carson's story thus explained the whole apparently inexplicable matter, to the satisfaction of all. The freakish effects of lightning strokes on human bodies were well known, and it was only such a freak of forces that could explain those bodies' condition. Carson's explanation, therefore, was officially adopted by the authorities at Progreso, and forwarded by them to the Mid-Western University officials. It was suggested by some at Progreso, indeed, that a body of investigation be sent to the scene of the tragedy, but the suggestion was not adopted, either by Carson or the officials. Nothing further could be learned from such an arduous journey, it was pointed out, and it would be impossible to recover Howland's body from the swirling depths of the Carajos. Also the natives' superstitious fear of the interior jungles had been so enhanced by the tragedy, that none would accompany a party on such a trip. So, with the matter explained to the satisfaction of most, the Progreso officials rested and Carson sailed for home.

By the time that Carson arrived, the sensation, which had been headlined by the nation's newspapers for a week, had lessened greatly in importance. The mystery of the deaths of Howland and his friends explained, the press quickly forsook the matter, with perfunctory expressions of regret for the loss of five such brilliant scientists. Even at Mid-Western

University the first shock and excitement of the tragedy had passed, and though it was still discussed, it was no longer the sole topic of conversation. It seemed assumed, even by the University's officials, that the Progreso officials were right in stating that nothing more could be done about the matter. So that by the time Carson arrived, though there had been resolutions of regret and the like on all hands, none had considered it as a subject for further action.

To Harlan Trent and to myself, though, the conclusion of the tragedy seemed unsatisfactory enough. From the first stunning report of the matter we had followed it intently through the lengthy press-articles and it seemed incredible to us, who with Carson had made up Howland's three closest friends, that the matter could end thus, that Carson could return without further efforts to discover his friend's fate. Because of that we were full of questions we desired to put to him on his arrival. It was not until some twenty-four hours after Carson's arrival, though, when we three were smoking silently in my rooms with the smoke of our pipes mingling with the scent of the warm May night that came through the open windows, that we put to him any of those questions.

For a moment after our queries he was silent, his strong face thoughtful, his eyes looking far away. Then, at last, he turned toward us.

"No," he said, in answer to our first question. "Howland's body could not be found." He paused, his eyes strange, and then added: "It could not, because Howland still lives."

We stared at him in utter astonishment for moments, and then Trent, his voice strained, was speaking.

"Howland lives!" he repeated. "But why did you leave him then, Carson? And where on Earth is he?"

Carson did not answer, for the moment, gazing at us for but a moment, then turning to the open window beside him. Outside lay the warm darkness of the May night, the dark masses of trees and buildings looming deeper in that darkness. Above, swinging down toward the western horizon from the zenith, hung the crescent moon, a great sickle of shining silver in the heavens. For moments Carson gazed up toward its gleaming crescent in silence, then turned about to where we stood wondering beside him.

"Howland is not on Earth at all," he said, quietly. "Howland—tonight—is somewhere on the moon!"

CHAPTER TWO
The Moon Raiders

"ON THE moon!"

The exclamations of Trent and me came together, as we stood there all but stupefied by Carson's statement; but he nodded calmly.

"There is much to tell you," he said, "much that I could not tell when I came back to consciousness there at Progreso, that I dared tell only you two, who know me and can believe. It is unbelievable, almost, but I think that you will believe. Had I told this to the villagers at Progreso, they would have deemed me mad, would have accused me, I think, of the murder of my own friends. So for my own sake—and for Howland's—I caused them to think what all now think, that a lightning-bolt had struck and annihilated our party. But it was no lightning-bolt that did so! It was a power greater and more terrible than the lightning, one of which I alone on Earth know, and of which I dared tell no one else.

"The story that I told at Progreso was correct, up to a certain point. We did, as I said, progress up the river in stages, making camp at regular intervals along the river's bank and using these camps as bases for our investigations. At each one we would set out on our studies, Borkoff and Grant were busy with the fauna and flora of the region, classifying and noting unusual characteristics which might prove connecting links with similar animal and plant forms of Africa. In the same way Glitz, the entomologist, was collecting and classifying species similar to African insect-forms, while Howland, and Willings, received and classified in importance the evidence the others brought in. My own work, as geologist, was intended to be the study of any geological formations which might indicate that sometime in the past a subsidence of the level of the Yucatan region had taken place. Such a subsidence, if it could be proved to have taken place, would help to prove that a similar subsidence of the island-chain between Yucatan and Africa had taken place also. We each were busy with our work, therefore, and Howland, as we pushed farther up the river, became more and more enthusiastic over the prospects of proving his theory.

"Four such camps we had made within the first twelve or thirteen days, and it was at the end of two weeks of progress that we made our fifth camp. Our journey up the river, until then, had been the usual one of Central American travelers, an unceasing and toilsome progress against the stiff currents, between banks that were impenetrable walls of jungle vegetation, with the blue mountains glimpsed now and then in the distance. I think that in those two weeks we had progressed not more than sixty miles, but it might have been six hundred for the utter wildness of the region. During the last ten days we had met not even an Indian, and as we knew that above the first score or so of miles the Carajos had been little explored by white men, we were not surprised at the region's wildness. Our own paddlers, though, were becoming more and more unwilling to progress further up the river. We attributed their unwillingness at first to the stiffening currents which we were now fighting in the narrowing river, but they finally informed us that they feared to go farther, because the upper reaches of the river were the haunts of evil spirits, and had been shunned since time immemorial by the natives of the region. By means of increased wages we induced them to keep on, and so at last made our fifth camp.

"It was in a small clearing in the jungle at the river's bank that we made that camp. Back from that clearing there sloped upward the side of a great, jungle-covered mound, perhaps a thousand feet in height, a squat, cone-like hill, at the foot of which stood the clearing, Howland, I remember, was very elated on the night that we camped there, since already, as he believed, we had collected enough scientific evidence almost to support his theory. At this camp, he told me, we would perhaps be able to collect enough to make that proof conclusive, and would not need to press farther up the river. To Howland, and to the rest of us, it seemed that we were on the very threshold of complete success. And then, on that same night, there struck—the terror.

"It was some hours before midnight that the thing came upon us. Darkness layover the world by then, a darkness that was stygian in the jungle's depths about us, but the clearing, in which our camp stood, was bathed in the silvery light of the full moon, climbing up toward the zenith. Howland, Willings and Grant, in one of the tents, were going over some of their specimens by the light of a gasoline lantern, while in another Borkoff and Glitz were mending some of the torn clothing of the party. Our paddlers had gathered, as though for protection, about a fire near the clearing's edge. Gazing about, I remembered a curious formation of boulders which I had noticed a little way up the river after we had camped, and as the full moon's light was very bright, thought to stroll up toward them for a preliminary investigation. So, calling out to Howland what I intended to do, I set off along the river's edge, following the clear strip of sand along the water.

"THE moonlight was so brilliant that I had no difficulty in finding the rocks I sought, and then for perhaps a half hour I examined them, moving around them. When at last I turned from them, and started back to the camp along the bank, I noticed that the moon had now reached a position directly overhead, a great shining shield hanging there above me. I moved on, toward the camp, and in a minute more could hear its sounds, the high clear voice of Howland, the low murmurs of the natives grouped around the tire. A moment more would bring me within sight of it, I knew. But in that moment, before I could take another step, there came the light.

"It was like no light ever seen by man before. It was a gigantic shaft of blinding brilliance, a mighty beam of pure, concentrated and dazzling white light, hundreds of feet across that stabbed down toward us from directly overhead! A colossal brilliant ray that shot downward from the heavens and vanished, in a single instant, all but blinding me even as I shrank back stunned. I had seen, though, that that mighty beam had struck the top of the great mound behind our camp, lightning-like. I had sensed, rather than seen, something that had seemed to flash down before that beam. Stunned, eyes blinded from the brilliance of the terrific light, I stood dazed for a moment, hearing the excited cries of Howland and the others, the sudden wails of the natives. I sprang forward, was at the clearing's edge in a moment, saw Howland and the others running toward the great mound excitedly, saw the natives huddled in fear apparently at the clearing's edge. I was about to spring after my friends when I saw them, at the foot of the great mound's slope, stop suddenly short. And then the next moment I too had stopped short, there at the clearing's edge, was gazing like Howland and the others up toward the great mound's summit.

"For from that mound's summit had come suddenly a strange sound, a great muffled clang of metal. Astonished, I stood there, gazing toward the mound, while Howland and the others at the mound's foot gazed up likewise, while the natives crouched fearfully in the clearing. Then from the mound came other sounds, a low muffled throbbing of power that grew quickly louder, and then burst suddenly upon our ears. And at the same instant that it did so I saw rising from the interior of the mound itself, apparently, a half-score of dark, flat shapes of great size, great flat circles or disks, their diameter a hundred feet approximately, with a low protecting wall around their edges, from which the throbbing came and which were floating smoothly up into the air above the mound! They floated up, hung there for a moment in the brilliant moonlight, and then as though they had glimpsed our camp, were suddenly slanting downward from the mound's summit toward our clearing!

"It was that that broke the spell of astonishment that had been laid upon Howland and the others there who watched. Howland himself still stood utterly dumbfounded, but the others, sensing peril, had uttered sharp cries, were leaping back, away from the mound, toward the river. Within another moment those flat great circles had shot downward through the moonlight, above the clearing, and then there was a hiss of suddenly released force, and from the hovering circles' sides there stabbed downward a half-dozen broad beams of pale and misty green light. Down those beams shot toward the running Willings and the others, toward the fear-crazed natives leaping to the river, and as they struck through the air, a swift succession of terrific detonations struck my ears. Then, as I stood there still inside the jungle's edge, spellbound with horror, I saw Willings and the others stagger and fall as the pale green beams struck them, saw their bodies swell out, shatter, *explode!*

"Even in that horror-stunned moment I guessed, I think, what it was that I was seeing, what terrific weapon it was that was embodied in that misty pale green ray. It was a vacuum-producing ray, I saw even then, one that destroyed instantly whatever atmosphere or air it touched, without affecting other matter. It was thus, I guessed, that the green rays had slain Willings and the others, but even as the thought flashed across my brain it passed, since now the great flat circles were dipping toward the clearing's surface!

"HOWLAND had stood in that dread instant of death in his tracks, motionless with astounded horror as I was, and because he had not fled, the rays had not stabbed toward him. The circles were swooping down toward him, their throbbing loud in my ears, and for the first time my own peril came home to my terror-dazed brain and I shrank back into the jungle at whose edge I stood. There, crouching in the thick vegetation, I gazed with pounding heart out into the moonlit clearing as the circles slanted downward. I saw them land swiftly about Howland, saw that they were grouped in a ring about him there on the ground, great flat circles of metal gleaming in the moonlight, noticed scores of vague shapes upon the surface of those circles, about a central mechanism that seemed to propel and guide them. Then, as I crouched there, there slid aside sections in the protecting walls of the circles, and out of them upon the ground there stepped a score or more of shapes toward Howland, shapes at sight of which a cry of horror all but escaped me. I had, unconsciously, looked upon these terrible attackers as human, at least, but it was not human shapes that stepped forward into the moonlight. They were not men at all, as we know them. They were—turtle-men!

"Turtle-men! It is only by that term that I can describe them, since the bulbous, upright body of each, some four feet in height, was encased completely in thick, dark shell. From the lower part of that shell-cased body projected two powerful thick limbs ending in broad-webbed and taloned paws, while similar shorter limbs or arms jutted from the body's upper portion. There was an opening in the body's case of shell at the top, and from that opening there projected upward on a flexible, snake-like white neck, the tapering, turtle-like head, its two lidless eyes set on either side with the narrow mouth between them. So grotesque were these turtle-creatures in their mingled familiar and unfamiliar appearance that I felt my senses reeling as I gazed upon them. Then I gripped myself, saw that some of the turtle-men held weapons or instruments of gleaming metal in their grasp, small metal hemispheres to whose curved side a handle was attached and whose flat side they kept turned upon Howland, who stood still swaying in spellbound horror before them.

"A moment they faced him, holding those gleaming hemispheres which were apparently containers of the deadly vacuum ray, and then one spoke. His voice was not loud but was of deeply vibrating chords, a deep bass so low that many tones in it were but barely caught by my ears. It was to Howland that he had spoken, apparently, though his meaning was of course totally unintelligible to him. Howland, though, spoke back in answer, his voice unsteady, apparently to show the creatures that he was intelligent also. They regarded him again in silence, held for a few moments a deep-toned conversation among themselves, and then, still threatening Howland with the hemispheres, came closer to him, examined the clothing he wore, his general appearance, then stepped back from him. Then one, apparently the leader, uttered a deep order, and at once two of the creatures behind him had stepped forward and had secured Howland's hands behind him with swift-clicking metal bonds of some kind, had secured his ankles likewise and were carrying him to one of the flying-circles resting upon the ground behind them, into which they placed him. Howland was a prisoner!

"All this had taken but moments to enact, there in the brilliant moonlight of the clearing, and now, with Howland disposed of, the turtle-men turned their attention to the camp itself. Swiftly they began a thorough examination of all in it, of the bodies of the scientists lying not far from them, of the natives lying beyond, of the tents and of all in them. I shrank back into the protecting darkness of the jungle vegetation about me as they came nearer, and heard their deep tones only yards away from me, as they carried on their examination. Brain whirling, I watched them. From whence had these turtle-men come, who had emerged from the great mound to pour death upon our camp? Could it be that they had come up from unknown depths in Earth's bowels to pour it out upon us? But what of that mighty flash of light that I had seen, that had stabbed down toward the mound from the heavens overhead?

"Once I saw a group of the turtle-men, in the midst of their searchings, stop to gesture up toward the silver shield of the full moon, that was sinking now toward the west with the swift passing of the night. They all gazed up toward it for a moment with their unwinking eyes, then turned back to their search. It flashed across my brain, then, that when the great light-beam had shot down to the mound, the moon had been directly overhead, and for a moment I wondered if there were any connection between that and the appearance of these strange raiders. Then such speculations passed from my mind as, fascinated with horror, I watched the activities of the turtle-creatures, watched them examining all in our camp. All the books, written records, and gathered specimens and notes in the tents they transferred at once to the flying-circles. The same was done with all tools and apparatus and mechanisms of any kind, which they found. I saw some of them with strange little mechanisms engaged apparently in compressing air into small metal containers, storing them in the circles also, saw others do the same with the waters of the river, storing away similar samples of that water. It was a scene of extraordinary activity, there in the moonlit clearing, and I watched it fascinated until the sinking of the moon and the growing pale light in the east warned me that day was dawning. Then I shrank back further into the thick vegetation.

"DAY BROKE, but the turtle-men in the clearing continued their examination and inspection of all things about them with unabated vigor. I dared not venture closer to the clearing in the revealing light of day, but I could see them moving about, could hear their deep tones, and see Howland sprawled out and bound inside the wall of one of the flying-circles. It was that last sight that occupied me most, for my first horror of the turtle-men had passed somewhat, and I thought only of rescuing Howland from their grasp. It seemed death to attempt it, though, since about the flying-circles there moved unceasingly the turtle-creatures, a full hundred in all, and more than half of them were armed always with the hemispheres that held the deadly vacuum ray. So through all that day, hour after endless hour, I crouched there in the thick jungle, with the blazing sun beating down above, thirsty, fearful, watching and waiting.

"Night came at last, and as its first hours passed, it was evident that they were ending their activities. They had collected samples or specimens of almost all things about them, of air, water and Earth, of the animals they had seen in the jungle, penetrating almost to my place of hiding in pursuit of the latter. Birds, too, and insects, and plants they had gathered and placed in the flying-circles, and it flashed across my brain that these raiders, from wherever they had come, had come to reconnoiter Earth only, to collect specimens of its life, to ascertain its condition, and that Howland, to them, was simply another such specimen! The thought spurred me on to attempt to free him, yet the turtle-men moved in numbers about the clearing so that such an attempt would have been suicide. At last, though, my chance came, a chance so slender that it seemed none. The turtle-men had brought their work to a close, and now as darkness fell swiftly over the land, and as the moon's silver disk again swung up toward the zenith, they had moved toward the edge of the clearing and were gazing up toward the moon's brilliant circle. For the moment the flying-circles were left unguarded, and in that moment I slipped noiselessly out of the jungle's darkness into the moonlit clearing, toward the flying-circle in which Howland lay.

"A few low bushes grew here and there in the clearing, and it was from one to another of these that I now dodged, screening myself as well as possible in their shadow, moving swiftly and with pounding heart toward Howland and the flying-circle on which he lay. I was nearer to it, was crouching for a moment in the shadow of a small shrub not thirty feet from it, and the turtle-men had still not turned from the clearing's edge where they stood. My hopes ran high in that instant, and I slipped quickly on, and saw Howland, roused by some sound I made, struggle up on his elbow and recognize me with wide eyes as I slipped toward him, then saw him turn in startled manner, and heard an agonized whisper of 'Back, Carson!' from him. For at that moment, at the clearing's edge, the turtle-men had turned and were coming straight toward me!

"A MOMENT I seemed to see death loom close, then instinctively I shrank back and downward, into the scant shadow of the small bush behind me, while the turtle-men came on across the clearing. They had not perceived me as yet, but in the scant shadow in which I lay I knew that it would be a miracle if they failed to see me now. They came closer while I crouched there, my heartbeats racing. The strange creatures seemed all about me, their deep bass voices vibrating on all sides; they were all but treading on me as they moved toward and into their flying-circles. I saw the sections of wall at the edge of these snapping shut, saw the great circles lift smoothly and suddenly upward, as there came from them a sudden throbbing of power, and then knew that they had not seen me. Above me the great circles were massing, dark disks in the light of the moon overhead, and then they were moving away, were slanting back up toward the summit of the great mound! They were going back to the place, from which they had come, and were taking Howland with them!

"As that thought burned across my brain I lost all caution, and rose erect, ran recklessly across the clearing toward the great mound, struggled up the side of it through the thick vegetation that clothed that side. Half-mad I toiled upward, saw above me that the flying-circles had massed above the mound's flat summit, and seemed to be sinking one by one down into that summit. One by one they sank from sight above me, while I toiled frantically upward, their throbbing suddenly muffled as they disappeared, until in a few moments more all had disappeared, while I was still but halfway up to the summit. I struggled frenziedly on, brain on fire, staggered up at last through the last detaining growths, and out on the broad flat summit of the mound. Out across it I stumbled, then suddenly stopped, reeled back. For there before me, yawning in the summit of the great mound, was a mighty shaft-like opening, hundreds of feet across, a great well, whose sides were lined with smooth metal and which extended down into the mound and the Earth beneath it for a depth of thousands of feet!

"The full moon was almost directly overhead, now, and its light struck down into that mighty shaft to show me that far at its bottom, thousands of feet below, there gleamed a floor of metal, a metal floor at the center of which was set a great flat circle of black, shining matter like black glass. Upon this circle there stood a giant cylinder that almost covered it, a great metal cylinder more than a hundred feet in diameter and fully three hundred in height. The top surface of this cylinder was slid outward in two sections, to either side, and down into its hollow interior, one by one, were floating the flying-circles of the turtle-men, stacking one above the other inside that cylinder! One by one they floated down into it until all were within it, until the great cylinder seemed filled with them, and then, with a great clang of metal, the two sections of the top slid back into place, closing its top!

"There was an instant then in which stared down in utter astonishment, and then, as understanding of it all flashed suddenly across my brain, I staggered to the great shaft's edge, cried out hoarsely, cried out madly to Howland who had vanished with the turtle-men inside that cylinder. But even as I cried out, the end came. The full moon, creeping westward across the zenith, reached a point directly above me, above the shaft, that great shaft aimed upward toward the moon's silver disk like the barrel of some great gun. The next instant there came a clanging great bell-note from near the black-shining disk on which the cylinder rested, a humming that held for a moment, and then suddenly up from that disk there stabbed toward the zenith, toward the full moon overhead, a terrific column of blinding white brilliance, a giant beam of dazzling light that leaped up from the great shaft in the mound and reached out toward the moon's bright disk! And even as that blinding beam had flashed and vanished before me I had perceived with a sense almost other than sight that the great metal cylinder beneath had flashed up with it!

"Blinded, stunned, I staggered to the great shaft's edge, gazed down into it. The great humming beneath had ceased, and I could make out the black-shining disk far beneath, but there was no cylinder upon it. There were big shapes about it, there were other great cylinders grouped here and there around it, but the cylinder that held the turtle-men and Howland had vanished, driven out by that blinding beam, I knew, out toward the moon itself Driven out toward the moon's bright disk that swung still overhead, out of the great shaft in the mound in which no life was now, out by the beam from the black-shining disk below! Projected out through the gulf of space in their great cylinder by that awful column of brilliance, out from Earth to moon!

"The moon! I saw it all then, as I swayed there with its bright disk above me. The moon! It was from there that the turtle-men had come in their cylinder, shot across the gulf from moon to Earth by a great propelling beam of brilliance, landing there in the great shaft of the mound and pouring out from their cylinder, in their flying-circles, to descend upon our camp. For, I remembered now, it had only been when the moon had been directly overhead that that first great beam had shot downward with the cylinder before it. They had reconnoitered Earth's condition, collected samples and specimens, taking Howland himself as one of them, and then on the next night had returned to their cylinder, had waited until the moon was directly overhead once more, and then had driven out toward it, propelled by a similar brilliant beam from the disk at the shaft's bottom. Raiders from the moon, that had driven back toward it and had taken Howland with them!"

CHAPTER THREE
Out to the Moon!

"RAIDERS FROM the moon! I remember shaking my hand madly toward its calm-shining disk above me, remember stumbling, weeping with horror, down the great mound's side into the clearing. There, working as one in a daze and driven on only by some remnant of reason in my darkening mind, I loaded the bodies of my friends into one of the canoes, scooped a grave in the sand for the natives sprawled there, and then pushed off in that canoe, down the river. Down—down—days, hours, of progress that seemed but unmeasured eternities of horror to my darkened mind. Then at last consciousness completely left me, and I awoke at Progreso, learned how I had been found drifting down the river, and was told of the great sensation that had been caused by that finding. I knew, at once, that were I to tell my tale it would not be credited for an instant, would never be investigated, even, and that I would be regarded as mad and as the mad slayer of my friends. So, for that reason, I told only of seeing a great light-flash, and let them think it a lightning-bolt that had destroyed the party, explaining Howland's disappearance by stating that the bolt that had destroyed him had knocked his body into the river. None questioned my story, which to them could alone account for the strange shattering of my friends' bodies, and so I came back here, knowing that to you two, who knew Howland and know me, I could tell my tale and be believed.

"I came back, but determined to return again, to return to that great mound whose shaft holds the secret of the moon raiders, the great projector whose beam drove them outward. The presence of that projector there in that great shaft proves that it has been there since time immemorial, there in the great mound, and that in the far past, eons in the past, perhaps, these moon-creatures had established communication between Earth and moon. They had driven down from moon to Earth in their cylinders propelled by a great beam from their apparatus on the moon, I suppose, and once on Earth had placed there, in the shaft of the mound, a similar apparatus whose beam drove them back up to the moon. And now, after what countless ages we cannot guess, they have used this method once more, have come down in a raiding, exploring party to reconnoiter Earth's present condition, and have returned with Howland as their prisoner.

"They have returned with Howland to the moon, but will they come again? I think that they will; I think that these first swift raiders were but a scouting party for myriad of moon-creatures that are to follow. I think that out on our moon, a world in which existence must be increasingly difficult for them, these turtle-creatures are gathering their hordes for a descent upon Earth, which they visited long ago, and which they now intend to visit in force, to invade, to conquer. To conquer! For they will conquer, their deadly vacuum rays and swift flying-circles are weapons men cannot stand against, when that dread invasion comes. And now that the first raiders have returned to the moon, taking Howland with them as a specimen of Earth's present races, I think that it will be soon that that invasion will come, that their great cylinders will flash down their mighty force-beam to Earth, cylinders filled with countless flying-circles, with numberless moon-creatures. A resistless invasion of our world from its own circling satellite!

"But one chance is left to us, I think, to stay that dread invasion. We cannot warn the world now of the doom that gathers above it, for never would the world believe, as you know well. But if we could, in some way, penetrate out to the moon itself, to whatever part of it holds these turtle-creatures' races, could find Howland and learn their plans, their purposes, I think that we could bring back with us evidence that even the most skeptical on Earth would credit. I think that if we could rescue Howland, could bring him back, he at least would be able to convince our world of the peril that hangs above it. That is our one chance, and to accomplish it we have that great projector in the depths of the great mound in Yucatan, the projector whose beam drove the cylinder of the moon raiders out to the moon, and which can drive a cylinder of our own outward in the same way. For that is my plan; that we three go down to that mound and its projector, use that projector and one of the cylinders I saw beside it to hurl us out to the moon, and there attempt to find and rescue Howland and bring him back with us to Earth, to bring back proof to Earth of the doom that threatens it from its moon!"

CARSON'S voice ceased, and the silence that followed seemed almost tangible, broken only by the sighing of the warm night breeze outside. Trent and I sat staring toward the speaker, astounded and appalled by what we had heard. But it was Trent who broke the silence first.

"To go out to the moon—to find Howland and bring him back—" he said, unsteadily. "Carson, it seems unthinkable that we could do it, that there are such creatures on the moon who have captured Howland and taken him back there!"

Carson gazed somberly toward him. "But it is so," he said, his eyes brooding. "They captured Howland—and tonight he is out there on the moon with them."

"But creatures from the moon!" I exclaimed. "Creatures from what we know is a wholly dead world!"

Carson shook his head. "We don't know that, Foster," he said. "Our astronomers know less almost about the moon than about other heavenly bodies considering its nearness. They have measured its dimensions and distances, they have weighed it, they have speculated on its origin, but what can they say with certainty as to the moon itself? What can they say as to the origin of its mighty craters, craters which volcanic origin could never have formed, and which they attribute to giant meteors striking the moon? For if such great meteors actually had caused those craters, we could discern them now half-buried in them, yet such giant meteors never have been discovered on the moon's surface! What can they say as to the great sheets of brilliant, glassy substance that glitter around the crater of Tycho and here and there across the moon's whole face? What can they say certainly about the moon, above all, when one side of its sphere has never been seen by the eye of man, turned always away from Earth, as the moon revolves about Earth? Who can say what mysteries might not exist upon that other side?

"And these moon-creatures; these turtle-beings who came down from moon to Earth in their cylinder on that beam of force, is it wholly incredible that such creatures should inhabit our moon? Once that moon was as inhabitable as Earth, we know, and if then these turtle-creatures rose to intelligence and power, why should they not have been able to preserve themselves through the centuries as their world died about them? Their power, their science, was great, we know, since ages ago it must have been that they visited Earth, built that projector in the mound here on Earth, and with that power and that science could they not continue their existence on the moon, perhaps within its depths, perhaps upon the other side? To creatures who could contrive the great projectors whose beams drove their cylinders from moon to Earth and back, the contriving of artificial supplies of atmosphere and water would not be hard.

"Powerful and intelligent, those moon-creatures have never made attempts to communicate with us on Earth, have never, through the ages, made use of the projector which they set here on Earth long ago, have never until now revisited Earth, thinking it perhaps still uninhabited by intelligent creatures. Now they have come, though, raiders, explorers, the forerunners of the hordes that I think gather now to follow. But one thing puzzles me about these moon-creatures. They must naturally be accustomed to the smaller gravitational power of the moon upon which they live, and so should have been greatly affected by the greater gravitational power of Earth, should have been hardly able to move here on Earth because of that greater power, just as men upon the moon would be affected by its lesser gravitational power, and could with their Earthly muscles leap and step enormous distances. But it was not so with these moon-creatures, for when they emerged from their flying-circles to Earth's surface, they moved as freely and as unhampered as though they had always lived here. That alone I cannot understand. I can understand clearly the fact of their existence, and the fact that after existing on the moon for ages, unknown to men, they have now begun to look toward our Earth, to prepare for a descent upon it."

Carson paused, and then Trent, slowly and thoughtfully, was speaking.

"I understand now too, Carson," he was saying, "understand and believe that these moon-creatures have, as you say, captured Howland—are gathering to pour down upon us. Yet, even so, can we really follow them, out the projector's beam, to the moon itself?"

Carson nodded calmly. "We can," he said simply. "The great projector is still there in the shaft that has held it for ages, and beside it in that shaft, as I said, I could see other cylinders like that in which the moon-creatures came and went. How they turn on that great beam I know not, but I do know that that beam is only turned on when the projector is pointed exactly at some certain spot upon the moon, a spot toward which the cylinders are driven by the beam. For it was only when the moon was directly above the shaft on the first night that the great beam from the moon drove down, driving the moon raiders' cylinder into that shaft exactly. And on the second night, it was only when the moon's disk was exactly above the shaft again that the great beam drove up from that shaft, driving the cylinder from Earth out to the moon. Much there is that we cannot know, cannot guess, about that great enigmatic projector, which has lain there in the shaft of the mound for ages, but if the moon-creatures operated it to drive them back out to the moon, there is a chance that we can operate it and can follow them. It is the one chance given to us to rescue Howland and to stay the dark doom that is gathering above our world. And shall not we three take it?"

He was silent once more, and in that silent moment our eyes sought, held each other's, while through the window beside us there fell upon us the pale brilliance of the crescent moon, a silver scimitar sinking westward through the night. Then suddenly, instinctively, our three hands came out together, clasped tightly.

"We'll take it!" I cried. "We'll go down to the great mound and the projector inside it, and use that projector and its beam to drive us out after the moon raiders and Howland—out to the moon!"

CHAPTER FOUR
The Cylinder Starts

CARSON ceased paddling, suddenly, and pointed ahead. "The mound!" he exclaimed. "And there's the camp beneath it!"

Trent and I gazed tensely ahead. The canoe in which we three sat floated in the middle of a narrow yellow waterway, propelled upstream against its strong currents by our paddles. On either side, shading us partially from the heat of the Yucatan sun that blazed above, there rose the tangled thick green walls of the jungle's trees and brush, extending away on either side of the narrowing river for league upon savage league. Ahead though, perhaps a quarter-mile up the river from us, there rose from out the jungle's green sea the squat, great bulk of a mighty mound, like a great rough cone in shape, truncated, or flattened at the summit. Clad with thick vegetation itself, it rose like a green hill from the jungle's tangled plain, and beneath it, between its base and the river, we could discern the brown shapes of tents, pitched in a small clearing, some of them flattened by storms.

"The mound!" I repeated, gazing toward it. "And in it is the shaft—and the projector!"

For days that great green bulk toward which we now gazed had been foremost in all our thoughts. It had been days, weeks, before, that we two had heard Carson's terrible story, had agreed with him to go to this mound to carry out our great plan. We had swiftly secured leaves from the University, had left Mid-Western for New Orleans, and within another few days had reached Progreso by steamer.

There, concealing our true mission, we had stated only that we intended to take up again that scientific work of Howland's which had been interrupted by the tragic end of his party. The officials at Progreso had done their best to dissuade us, but had in the end given up, and we had proceeded to the village at the mouth of the Carajos, buying there one of the native canoes and stowing in it our equipment. We had intended from the first to make the trip up-river alone, and found that in any case none in the village would have dared ever to accompany us, so intensified were their ordinary superstitious fears by the tragedy that had befallen the Howland party. So, pushing up-stream alone in our canoe, we had progressed slowly up the river for more than a dozen days, coming at last now within sight of the great mound that was our goal.

Carson, after his first exclamation on sighting the mound, had bent silently and grimly to his paddle, and as Trent and I did likewise, we sent our slender craft spinning upward against the currents toward the camp in the clearing ahead. That clearing lay just at the river's bank, we saw, a level and roughly circular patch of open ground in the jungle, and as we swept nearer toward it we noticed that of the several tents there only one still stood erect, all the others having been battered by rain and wind, Carson, as we swept nearer, pointed mutely to the canoes still drawn up along the bank, dumb evidence of the dozen natives who had paddled them once, and who now lay buried somewhere in the sand along the river's edge. Another moment and our own canoe had shot in among them. We had stepped out and had secured it to the bank, lifting our equipment from it out into the clearing; then we stood motionless for a moment, gazing about us.

Standing there with Trent and Carson, the thing of which was most conscious at the moment was the silence of the place. A silence, a hushed stillness, seemed to lie over it, which the monotonous sound of the flowing waters behind us seemed only to intensify. Brilliant birds flashed now and then across the clearing from the encircling jungles, and there was an occasional rustle of some small animal in the vegetation, but the main impression was of a silence and stillness unnatural and foreboding, Carson, beside me, suddenly pointed silently down to the clearing's surface, and as we looked across the soft sand, we saw that upon it were many tracks, some of them tracks of human shoes and feet, but most of them great, paw-like tracks with four taloned toes, such as I had never seen before. At the sight, my heart raced suddenly faster and I raised my eyes to Carson with interrogation in them.

"The moon-creatures?" I whispered, and he nodded.

"The moon-creatures' tracks," he said, in the same low tone. "Everything here seems as I left it." Trent was gazing intently up toward the great mound whose summit loomed distantly up from the jungle beyond the clearing.

"The mound," he said, "we'll head for it at once?"

Carson shook his head. "Not at once," he told him. "We'll settle our equipment here first, and start for the mound at sunset. I've calculated that for tonight and several nights, a few hours before midnight, the full moon will be passing over the shaft just as it did a month ago, and I want to be at the projector when that happens, and before it. We'll have time enough." So, for the next few hours, we occupied ourselves with getting our equipment ready. Setting up our own small tent—we all had an odd reluctance toward using the tents about us—we then arranged beside it the equipment we had brought, laying aside the items which we expected to take with us on our desperate expedition. Among these latter was the rope ladder we intended to use in descending into the mound's shaft, one of a half-mile in length, almost, yet small in bulk for its length and strength. Heavy automatics that looked similar to Tommy guns, automatic pistols, and cartridge belts were to form our weapons, with the addition of sheath knives. In the light knapsacks we were taking with us, were packed condensed foods sufficient for many days, and an assortment of selected drugs. Distributed among us, too, was a compact assortment of small steel tools. Slight enough equipment it was for the most desperate journey men had ever attempted, but we had pinned all to our faith that if the moon-creatures could flash across the gulf in their cylinders without other special equipment, we could do so also.

THE SORTING and assembling of this equipment took us the remaining hours of the afternoon, and as the brilliant tropic sun slanted westward, we prepared and ate a quick meal, then started on our climb toward the great mound's summit. Carson led, choosing the easiest path through the thick jungle vegetation, while Trent and I followed, bearing the coiled rope ladder's weight between us. The sun was dipping swiftly toward the west as we pressed on through the tangled masses, and started up the great mound's slope. That slope, we found, was steeper by far than it had seemed from below, and hampered as we were with our equipment and with the weight of the coils of the great ladder, our progress was slow. By the time we had reached the mound's summit, the brilliant sunset was fast fading westward, while high in the heavens eastward the white disk of the full moon was climbing toward the zenith through the darkening skies.

We gave but small attention for the moment to these, all our interest centering on the flat summit all which we found ourselves. A fairly level circle of several hundred feet in diameter was that summit, almost barren of vegetation, but what held our eyes was the great opening that yawned at its center, taking up the great part of the summit itself. It was a great, well-like shaft, at least four hundred feet across, whose smooth metal sides sank vertically downward into depths invisible, whose gathering shadows our eyes could not penetrate, into depths that seemed to us unfathomable as we gazed down in awe into them. We could make out nothing in the shadows beneath, and at last lifted our eyes and looked toward each other. The heavens above had darkened swiftly, and now the pale light of the full moon swinging upward fell upon us, and upon all the far-reaching stretches of jungle that we could vaguely discern from the mound's summit. At last Carson broke the silence.

"Time to go," he said quietly. "We must be down at the shaft's bottom when the moon swings directly above it."

Swiftly we uncoiled the slender length of the great ladder, fastening one end of it firmly into the ground at the shaft's edge by means of stakes we had brought for the purpose. Then, letting the rest of the ladder unroll into the great well, we saw it disappear into the shadows far beneath until it hung steady, vanishing down into those shadows. Carson stepped toward the ladder, then paused, turned and gazed out once more over the distant reaches of the moonlit jungle. We stood gazing, the same thought unspoken in all our minds. Would we ever look out on that moonlit scene again? Then Carson had turned back to the ladder, had knelt and swung himself over the great shaft's edge, holding to it, and then was moving down its length, down the colossal well's side, like an insect crawling down a string.

Another moment and I had followed him, had swung over the edge of the abyss like him, gripping the ladder. As I did so, gazed down and glimpsed the vast depths that yawned beneath, disappearing down into the shadows below, a sudden nausea gripped me for an instant as I swung there dizzily. Then, clinging tightly to the rope rungs, I forced it away, began slowly to descend. Rung after rung, step after step, down the ladder I went. The smooth gleaming metal of the great shaft's wall was all that I could see as I clambered steadily downward. Gazing up, I saw Trent above, following me, his figure darkly outlined against the moonlit sky. Glancing down, I could make out Carson's shape as a deeper shadow against the shadows far beneath, caught a glimpse of his face as a white blur against those shadows as be glanced up toward me. Down—down—still downward we descended, rung after rung, yard after yard, until the mouth of the great shaft had become but a dwindling circle of pale light far above us.

The shadows about us were deepening swiftly as we descended farther into the shaft, and I judged that we had already climbed down for more than a thousand feet, yet in the deep dusk beneath was no sign that we were nearing the bottom. Down—down—a seemingly endless descent, that became soon almost automatic on my part, an unconscious and unceasing movement of arms and legs that steadily took me further down into the great shaft's shadows. Those shadows had deepened to darkness about us, by then, and by the time that I estimated our downward climb at two thousand feet, we were descending in a stygian darkness in which we could not even see the wall down which we climbed. The great shaft's mouth was now but a tiny ring of pale light far above. Continuing to feel our way, we moved down the ladder, until there came a sudden exclamation from Carson, below me, which halted Trent and me.

"The ladder!" he exclaimed. "I've come to its end, and it doesn't reach to the shaft's bottom!"

"The end!" I cried. "Can you see how far the shaft's floor is beneath it?"

"I can't even guess," he said. "This darkness is so thick, it may be one foot or a hundred. And we daren't wait here until the moon comes above the shaft and lights it, for then it will be too late for us to use the projector!"

WE HUNG silent there a moment, a silence akin to despair, clinging there to the ladder, hanging against the smooth wall of the great well whose depths extended for an unguessed distance into the utter darkness beneath us. Then Carson's voice came calmly up to us through that darkness.

"I'm going to let go," he said. "The shaft's bottom can't be but a little beneath us, and I'll take the chance."

Before we could cry to him to wait, the rope ladder had twitched suddenly in my grip as he released his weight from it beneath me, and then the next moment had come a light thud, seemingly just beneath. And then, inexpressibly welcome to our strained ears, came the sound of Carson's voice.

"It's all right," he was saying. "The shaft's floor is only a few feet beneath the ladder's end!"

Swiftly I climbed downward, reached the last rung of the ladder's length in another moment, and then for an instant hung from that rung, hesitant. The darkness about me, impenetrable and enveloping, made the space beneath me seem an abyss, but I released my hold, shot downward, and in an instant had struck a hard, smooth floor not a half-dozen feet beneath me, I felt Carson beside me in the darkness, and in another moment there came another thud and Trent dropped down beside us. Then, joining hands so that we might not lose each other in the blackness there at the shaft's bottom, we waited for the coming of the light, which would illuminate the shaft. Its mouth far above was a small circle of pale light in the blackness, and it was up toward that circle that we gazed as we waited. Moments passed thus, moments in which we were aware only of the smooth, hard floor upon which we stood, and then across the edge of the pale circle above there drifted slowly the shining disk of the full moon. As it did so, there poured down into the shaft, reflected downward by the metal walls with surprising strength, a flood of pale light which illuminated, in misty fashion, all things about us.

We were standing at the edge of the level metal floor of the mighty shaft, that floor being a great circle of the same diameter as the shaft's mouth. At the center of this metal floor, taking up almost half the shaft's bottom, the metal gave way to a tremendous disk of smooth black substance, shining, as Carson had said, like black glass, which seemed inset in the floor. On the other side of this disk there were ranged along the floor a regular row of some twenty mighty cylinders of metal, vague great shapes that gleamed dully in the misty light from above. Save for these and for the great black disk, there was nothing visible at the bottom of the great well. The disk glittered brilliantly even in the pale light that filtered down upon it, but there layover all things else the thick dust of endless centuries.

Carson led the way at once toward the great cylinders ranged at the glittering disk's edge. A hundred feet in diameter each, three hundred in height, they loomed giant-like before us in the misty light. We seemed but three pygmies as we gazed up toward them. They stood upon a narrow, deep slot in the metal floor, perhaps six feet in width, and this slot led across the metal floor and across the black material of the disk to its center. The great cylinders themselves seemed quite without break in their gleaming walls, and to slide open their great tops as the moon raiders had done would be impossible for us. But as we walked around the nearest of them. Trent's quick eyes detected a stud set in its surface, and swiftly he pressed it. At once, smoothly and noiselessly, a square section of the great cylinder's curving wall slid upward, and we could see that that wall was a yard in thickness, formed of alternating layers of gleaming metal and gray insulating material, shielding its interior from the terrific cold of outer space.

Through the doorway we stepped, and found ourselves in the gigantic cylindrical chamber that was the cylinder's interior. But now we saw that its great flat top and flat bottom, and sections of its curving sides, were quite transparent from within, though opaque from without. At the center of the cylinder's floor stood the only object in it, a solid little pillar of metal bearing on its top a number of small studs. Carson pressed one of these studs experimentally, and the door through which we had entered clicked hermetically shut behind us. He touched another and the cylinder began to move, to slide smoothly and noiselessly along the slot above which it rested, until it had slid upon the black disk, stood at its center, covering almost all the disk's surface!

CARSON clicked open the door again, then pointed out through it. There at the great black disk's edge, rising from the metal floor but a few feet from the door of our cylinder that rested on that disk, stood another short pillar of metal, bearing on its top a small metal disk and a white-handled lever that could be thrown down upon its upper surface.

"The switch that turns on the great beam!" Carson exclaimed. "I see it all now. That switch out there turns on the mechanisms beneath which generate the great beam, and whose humming I heard, a humming that lasts for a moment before the beam drives upward. In that moment, after turning on the switch, I must leap back into the cylinder and click shut its door before the beam drives it upward through space."

"But when?" Trent asked. "How can we know at what exact moment to turn it on?"

"The moon raiders turned it on when the great bell-note sounded," Carson said, "so that bell-note must be the signal that sounds automatically here to mark the moment when the moon is directly overhead, when the beam must be loosed and the cylinder driven moonward!"

Gazing upward, we saw that the silver shield of the full moon was creeping almost across the center of the shaft's circular mouth far above, and Carson strode out to the pillar-switch beside the disk, while we stood at the one inside the cylinder, ready to snap shut the door when he should have turned the switch outside and leaped within. There were no other preparations to make, none that could be made. The great beam of light, which we knew must drive the cylinders out by means of light-pressure, intensified in some way, must drive them at almost the speed of light itself, we knew, and so if we succeeded, our cylinder would be hurled across the gulf from Earth to moon within moments, seconds, the speed of light being some 186,300 miles a second and the approximate distance to the moon but 238,840 miles. If we made it, we knew we would make it in seconds, and so would have no need for air-supplies or other special equipment during the moments that we would flash outward.

If we made it! Yet it seemed incredible now, as we waited, that we could do so, that we could hurtle across the awful gulf toward the calmly shining disk above us. Gazing up toward that disk, waiting with taut nerves for the great bell-signal that would mark the moment when we must drive out toward it, Carson outside and Trent and I inside the cylinder regarded it with pounding hearts. I could make out upon that silver moon-disk the dark blotches of its seas, the *Mare Serenitatis* and the *Mare Nubium* and the rest, the brilliantly shining region about Tycho, toward the lower limb, and the more central dark circle of Copernicus' mighty crater. Within moments more the cylinder in which we stood would be driving out toward that shining sphere with all the pressure of the awful beam behind it. What was awaiting us there? Would our cylinder be shot unerringly upward and into a shaft like this on Earth, that would in some way automatically cushion and halt our great flight, or would we crash in instantaneous death against the lunar crags? What strange cities of unhuman hordes awaited us, what hopeless search for our captured friend?

Tensely, silently, we waited, and I think now that those moments of waiting were the most terrible of all, those moments in which we waited for the signal that would send us flashing out with all the great beam's awful power and speed into that gulf, where never men had flashed before, into that great void of airless space between Earth and moon. Nearer the moon's circle was creeping toward the center of the cylinder's transparent top, above us. Carson's hand was tightening on the great switch outside, the switch that we knew would be thrown automatically back again after our cylinder had been shot forth by the beam. My own hand was on the stud that closed the mighty cylinder's door, and tensely through that door I watched Carson outside. And nearer— still nearer—toward the center of the circle of pale light far above crept the shining moon. Creeping steadily westward still-nearer—nearer—

Clang!

The mighty note rang suddenly out from somewhere far beneath us, mighty, compelling, like the note of an inconceivably titanic bell, and at the same instant Carson snapped down upon the little metal disk's top, the white-handled lever in his grasp! There was a tremendous clear humming from beneath, and as it sounded, Carson leaped toward us, through the cylinder's door, which a moment later snapped shut as I pressed on the stud I held. Then the next moment blinding, dazzling light was stabbing up from beneath and all about us, a colossal ray of inconceivable brilliance that seemed to grip the cylinder, to stab upward with it in its grasp at velocity inconceivable, all things that we could see vanishing instantly from about us, save the moon's bright disk above. Our moment had come at last, and at almost the speed of light itself we were flashing out into the void of space toward that disk—out from Earth to moon!

CHAPTER FIVE
The Other Side of the Moon

NEVER ARE the following moments more to me than a swift succession of lightning-like impressions. At the instant that the beam had shot upward with our cylinder, we had been pressed against the floor for a split-second with enormous force, and then that pressure had as instantly lessened. That instant of pressure passed almost unheeded by us, though, because at that terrific moment all was to us but a mighty blaze of brilliant light that flooded about our cylinder and through its transparent floor and windows as we flashed up and outward. Clinging to the central pillar on the cylinder's floor, Carson and Trent and I were aware for that first instant only of the blinding ray that had caught and flung us outward, and then in the next flashing moment I had seen the moon's bright sphere swiftly growing in the black heavens before us!

Thrilled through and through every atom of my body by the awful velocity at which we were racing through the void, brain whirling as we clung there to the pillar, I glanced back and below us, caught for an instant through the brilliance of the great beam the dark, dwindling shape of a brown sphere that I knew was Earth, with to one side and beyond it the blazing disk of the sun, adorned with vast streamers of flame and blazing toward us through even the blinding brilliance of the great beam! Beyond and all about us, too, I had a momentary impression of thousands of stars, brilliant, terrible, burning with undimmed splendor there in the awful void through which the cylinder that carried us was leaping at almost the speed of light!

All of this, the wild flash outward with the great beam about us, my glance ahead and behind, all had taken but a moment of time, and then, even above the wild thrumming sound which our cylinder gave forth beneath the awful pressure of the beam, I heard a hoarse exclamation from Carson who clung there beside me, turned my gaze upward to see that even in that single moment that we had been flashing outward, the moon's great sphere had grown to giant proportions before us, filled now a third of the heavens, a half, two-thirds! A huge world it turned before us now, leaping closer and growing larger with inconceivable rapidity. I caught a glimpse of the vast dark upper plains of its great seas, the brilliance that flared toward us from about Tycho, the great towering ranges of the Carpathians and the Appenines, all growing enormous, with the passing of each fraction of a second that we hurtled toward them! Then straight before us, at the center almost of the great moon-disk that now filled all the heavens before us, I discerned a gigantic circular crater whose awful towering walls formed a colossal ring miles high and dozens of miles across, a giant jagged crater toward the center of which our cylinder at all its immense velocity was rocketing!

"Copernicus!" It was Carson, shouting in my ear in that mad moment. "We're going to smash inside Copernicus' crater!"

Even as Carson cried out there beside me, the jagged floor of the mighty crater seemed to be rushing lightning-like toward us, all the brilliant, bare and savage outlines of its rocky surface photographed upon my brain in that instant, and then the crater's floor was full before us, looming like a giant wall before us as the cylinder rushed at its awful speed toward it! I knew it was the end; in that wild moment, we seemed to cling there and stare fascinated toward it in that instant that we rushed to death. And then, in the brilliant-lit rocky floor of the great crater just before us, in that giant wall across our path, a tiny black dot had appeared, a dot that in even the fraction of a second that I had caught it, had grown swiftly to a great black circle, the opening of a great shaft in the crater's floor, a shaft whose black mouth loomed for an instant full before our flashing cylinder, and then into which our cylinder had hurtled, and into the dark depths of which we were racing on at the same terrific speed!

On—on—it could hardly have been for more than a moment that we flashed on through the great shaft's dark stygian depths, with our great driving beam brilliant still beside and behind us, yet that moment seemed to us to be a time of unmeasured length. The thought flashed across my spinning brain as I clung there, that we were speeding into the very bowels of the moon, on through that great shaft, I had a lightning-like vision of tremendous, rocky, cavern-like spaces through which we clicked like light, spaces illumined for that split instant by the brilliance of our great driving beam, and then seemed to see before us, across the shaft, a great metal barrier which with the speed of light itself split open before us and closed shut behind us. Then I was aware simultaneously of a point of brilliant light in the darkness ahead, a point that even as I saw it had grown and seemed to rush toward us with a speed as great as our own, a giant beam of brilliant light-force like that which drove us on, and which in the next instant had met our flashing cylinders, blinding us completely for an instant by the dazzling glare from the great beams ahead and behind!

Then we were aware suddenly that the cylinder was slowing with unbelievable quickness and yet smoothly and noiselessly, was slowing as the beam that drove us forward was opposed and balanced by the beam that drove toward us from ahead! The brilliance about us was lessening swiftly, and as we opened our eyes and looked forward, we saw that the cylinder was gradually decreasing its terrible speed; we could see another point of white light ahead, a soft white light utterly unlike the brilliant beams. Toward that point the cylinder swept smoothly, and then as the point loomed and grew before us, the cylinder had plunged suddenly up from the shaft into it, up from the shaft's dark depths into a great space lit with soft white light! We saw before us a great black-glittering disk, set above us, that seemed very familiar in appearance, saw a great framework of metal girders set beneath that disk, which seemed imbedded in the great room's ceiling. Then the cylinder had swept up into that framework and had halted against the disk. There was a great clicking of metal from the framework about us, and our cylinder hung motionless, suspended beneath the disk. Our terrific journey was ended!

CARSON was the first to stagger to his feet. Half consciously, I heard his voice, and then Trent and I released our grip upon the pillar's metal handholds to which we had clung, and staggered up beside him. He was gazing eagerly through the transparent sections of the cylinder's sides, and now as we gazed out with him, we saw that the cylinder hung in that great metal framework from the ceiling of a great chamber of vast proportions. That chamber, cube-like and with sides and floor and ceiling of metal, was more than a thousand feet wide and long, and was lit by circles of soft light inset here and there in walls and ceiling. At the center of its floor there yawned the black circular opening of the great shaft up which we had come, and above which the cylinder now hung. Just above that shaft, and above our cylinder, was inset in the chamber's ceiling the great black-glittering disk we had been watching, and beneath which our cylinder was suspended.

I knew it had taken us only moments to flash across that titanic gulf through which we had come, though our swift-succeeding and unforgettable impressions in those lightning-like moments had made it seem much longer. I remembered now, though, as with Carson and Trent I gazed forth in awe, that when we had first flashed into that great shaft in the moon's side, in Copernicus' crater, we had seemed to be driving straight forward, but that when we had shot up into this soft-lit chamber, we had seemed to rise straight upward. It came to me, though, that our direction was the same but that our sense of direction had changed as we had reached the moon and our terrific speed had lessened at the great shaft's end. Nor did I doubt longer the way in which our awful velocity had been lessened and halted so swiftly, knowing that our cylinder's approach had somehow automatically turned on an opposing beam from the black disk before us, which had swiftly neutralized the drive of our own outward beam and had slowed and halted us here. These things, though, flashing across my mind as they did, were yet nothing to it at that moment, beside the intent interest that held us as we gazed eagerly forth from our cylinder, through the transparent sections of its sides.

"Cylinders!" Carson was exclaiming. "Cylinders like this one—and in hundreds!"

We turned to the place from which he was gazing, and then saw that at that side of the vast chamber in which our cylinder hung, there was a great corridor or passageway opening from its wall, and that in that mighty passage stood a great row of huge cylinders like our own, a row that led directly to the framework of metal in which our own hung. It was apparent that these could be moved forward at will into that framework, and shot by the disk through the great shaft to our Earth, and as I saw that, a sudden chill passed over me, a wave of fear that was not for myself, but for my world. With these cylinders massed here, extending back into that great corridor in unguessed hundreds, thousands, perhaps, what great invasion of Earth did not their silent presence here portend? I had a momentary vision of them flashing down to Earth from the disk above us, hundreds, thousands of them, filled with tens of thousands of the great flying-circles, and a countless horde of the monstrous creatures who had gathered them here!

But that swift vision passed from me in the excitement of the next moment, for Trent was pointing now to a narrow little metal bridge that led from our cylinder's door to the floor of the room, and to the edge of the circular abyss above which we hung. We could see at the great room's far end, too, a metal stair that led steeply upward, and afire with eagerness gazed out toward it. I think that in that moment we all believed ourselves somewhere in the moon's interior, since there was no natural light about us, only the soft glow of the inset circles. We knew, too, that in the moments before our cylinder had halted, it had flashed for a great distance into the moon's heart through the great shaft, and now were eager to discover our whereabouts. I turned swiftly to Carson.

"There must be air in this great room!" I cried to him. "For this must be where the moon raiders left their cylinder!"

He gazed doubtfully forth. "If there were air here it would rush down that shaft," he objected, "out through it into the void of airless space—instantly."

I shook my head. "Didn't you see the great metal barrier or door across the shaft, that split open before our cylinder and closed behind us as we flashed on?" I asked. "That must have been a great gate or valve that opened automatically at our coming, and closed behind us, a valve that keeps the air here from rushing out as you say."

HE GAZED forth a moment still, perplexed, then silently nodded and turned toward the door-stud. As he placed his hand upon it, we waited tensely, silently, for we knew that if there were no air outside, or if there was but air of great rarity, we would die within the next few moments. But Carson pressed the stud without hesitation, and as the great door clicked upward in the cylinder's side we stood motionless. As there came no rush of air either outward or inward, we turned, gazed at each other with eyes alight, then turned toward the door. A moment later, holding to the cylinder's side so that our efforts might not send us soaring upward by reason of the moon's weaker gravitational power, we stepped out upon the little bridge outside, the air without seeming exactly like that within. But as we stepped out, we stopped short on the bridge, astounded.

For the steps we had taken had been the same as though taken on Earth! Knowing that because of its smaller mass and weaker gravitational power that our weight should be but one-sixth its normal figure on the moon, we had expected from the first plans of our trip to have to overcome this disadvantage. Had half-expected, even, that the sudden and great change in gravity would prove our deaths at once, since such a change might be expected to have fatal results upon the body's internal organs. We had counted upon taking that chance, though, had braced ourselves as we made our first moves outward from the cylinder against the weaker gravitation we supposed to exist, and now we had found that that gravitation, apparently, was exactly the same as on Earth!

"The gravity!" Carson was exclaiming, startled more than by anything that had gone before, as we all were. "It's the same as on Earth—yet it's impossible!"

A thought flashed across my brain. "The moon raiders!" I cried. "You remember you said when they came to Earth they walked about on it as though quite used to its gravitational power!"

Carson nodded quickly. "They did," he said. "And we know the reason for it now. Yet how can the moon's gravity be the same? It's against every law of science!"

But now, even though stunned by the inexplicable equality of the moon's gravity with that of Earth, we were gazing eagerly about us. The steep metal stair we had caught sight of from the cylinder lay before us, and as we looked upward we saw that it led up to the great chamber's ceiling, and further upward and outward through a great circular opening in that ceiling, an opening through which we could see a vast, dim-lit space above, a gleaming far above it that puzzled us. Without words, moving like men in a dream, we strode to that stair, were climbing up its steep slant, up and up until we were almost to the opening, could see more of the mighty space above, could hear a faint sound of throbbing that was beating in our ears from somewhere above, and that came and went.

Hearts pounding, we slowed our upward climb now, moving more stealthily toward the opening just above. As we neared it we saw, set at the edge of that opening, a short metal pillar, which seemed familiar in appearance. Carson pointed to it, whispering, "The switch of the great disk on the moon!" I nodded. It was a duplicate of the switch on Earth; a small metal disk mounted on the pillar with a white-handled lever swinging at its edge. But this lever, I noticed, could be swung not only to the metal disk's lower side, to send the great beam driving downward, down through the great shaft to Earth, but could be swung to the metal disk's upper side, too. Could it be that the great beam here could be driven upward, too, from the disk's upper side? Only momentary was the wonder that flashed across my brain, as we stole upward past the great switch, for none of us dreamed, then, of the cataclysmic thing that was to take place upon these steps, at that great switch which we passed unheedingly.

Upward we crept, Carson ahead, Trent and I just below him, and then as his head came above the last step, as he peered forth into the great space above, gazed about and upward, I saw a look of awe come on his face, awe and amazement inexpressible, as though his eyes gazed upon something which his brain refused to credit. Staring forth, it was as though for the moment he had forgotten the existence of Trent and myself, and we glanced toward each other, and continued to creep silently after him. We reached him, raised our eyes carefully above the level of the last step, above the edge of the great opening in the big chamber's ceiling. Then, as our eyes too took in what lay about and above us, we too were stunned into unbelieving silence.

We were gazing out into a great space whose very dimensions and existence were incredible to us, a far-reaching vault of space that extended, lit with soft white light, as far as the eye could see. The first thing about it which caught and held our eyes was that which lay above it, a great vault of blackness, of night, in which burned the familiar stars, yet which seemed closed out from the space about us by a barrier that we could scarcely realize, a gleaming yet transparent material that stretched far away, over all the great space about us, and that was only visible by reason of the light dimly reflected upon it from beneath! A titanic, unbelievable transparent roof, stretching away as far as the eye could reach, miles above the great space that surrounded us, closing in that space from the blackness of the outer night and from the burning stars!

OUR DAZED eyes, moving from that gigantic transparent roof to the vista about us, we saw that there stretched away in all directions to the horizons a smooth level plain, a great plain that was covered as far as the eye could reach by buildings! Buildings of metal, buildings like none that man had ever looked upon before, surely; buildings that towered for thousands of feet, many of them, through the dusk toward the transparent roof far above! Buildings that were many-sided, angle polyhedrons, that were like great faceted diamonds of metal, that were like giant metal crystals ranged in rows and streets! In their angled, faceted sides were set circles of soft glowing white light, light that changed this lunar city's night into a dim, twilight dusk.

And that strange, great city swarmed with life! For here and there across and above it there flitted smoothly in ceaseless swarms scores and hundreds of great flat circles, throbbing from building-roof to roof, circles upon which we could see dark figures. Figures erect and bulbous, their bodies cased in shells, their short limbs ending in webbed and taloned paws, their great heads reptilian and tapering, borne on snake-like necks! Turtle-figures, turtle-men like those who had raided down to Earth in one of their great cylinders on the mighty beam, and into whose city we had won, at last, in our search for Howland! Far away reached the crystal-like buildings of that city, the streets between them swarming too with turtle-creatures, but in the mass of those buildings lay a great central plaza, or circular clearing, in which was the great opening through which we gazed. And set in the metal floor beside our opening, we saw, was the black-glittering upper surface of the great disk, the disk whose lower surface was set in the ceiling of the great chamber beneath us. Could it be, then, I asked myself, that my inference on seeing the switch had been right, and that the giant beam was shot upward from this great disk's upper side also? But that was but a passing thought across the stunned awe that filled us now as we gazed forth.

"The city of the moon-creatures," Carson was whispering, as we gazed out. "The city of the moon-creatures, and it is here where we never dreamed that it might be—on the other side of the moon!"

The other side of the moon! For we saw now, knew now, that it was there that this city about us lay, it was there that we now stood. Our great cylinder, flashing into the mouth of the great shaft there in the crater of Copernicus, had rushed on at its titanic speed through the moon's depths, not halting in those cavernous depths as we had thought it might, but going on through the moon itself, to its other side! Flashing on to this other side that never had been seen by anyone on Earth, turned always away from Earth as it was, and that yet held upon its surface this giant, transparent-roofed city, whose masses of colossal angled buildings, held within it the unguessed-myriad of the turtle-creatures' hordes, stretched all about us as far as the eye could reach! For it was here that the moon-creatures had existed—for how many ages?— unsuspected by any on Earth. They had pierced their great shaft down from this side through the very center of the cold moon itself, down and out the moon's earthward side, so that their cylinders might be driven by the great disk's beam down and out that shaft, through the moon and across the gulf to Earth, just as our cylinder from Earth had been driven lightning-like out toward the moon's earthward side and through the great shaft there to this other side, straight through the moon!

And in this mighty city about us, this great turtle-city that lay now beneath the darkness of the moon night, two weeks long, even as the moon's earthward side lay in the lunar day of two weeks, the moon-creatures could change their night to dusk, at least, lighting it by their great glowing circles inset in their buildings. Shielding it from the awful cold of space, from the airless void, by the giant transparent roof far above it, which we knew must cover all the moon's far side, a great airtight shield, which made existence here in their city possible by means of an artificial air supply. For well we knew that without that shield above it the air about us would rush forth into the void instantly and leave this far side of the moon as dead and cold and barren as the earthward side! Here in their great shielded, airtight city on the moon's one side dwelt the turtle-hordes, yet why had they built this city upon one side alone, upon the side never seen by Earth?

BEFORE MY whirling brain could suggest any explanation of this, though, Carson had gazed about, had drawn himself up through the opening to stand upon the surface of the great plaza itself. No turtle-shapes could we see through the dusk upon all that great clearing, though in the city's streets that we could glimpse through the dusk we could see great masses of the turtle-creatures moving busily to and fro, hordes of flying-circles that throbbed to and fro over the city and from building to building. Standing there in that strange soft dusk, shielded by it from the eyes of the turtle-creatures in the city about us, whom our own Earth-sharpened eyes, accustomed to the deeper natural night of Earth, could easily make out, we paused. Gazing with awe about us, at the giant shapes of the great buildings looming in the dusk all around and beyond us, we came back suddenly to realization of our own purpose as Carson turned toward us.

"Now is our best chance to search for Howland in this lunar city!" he exclaimed. "For with this dusk lying over it we have a chance to evade the turtle-creatures for a time, at least, to escape discovery long enough to find some trace of Howland!"

"But where would they take him?" asked Trent. "This city must stretch over all the moon's far side, and how can we find him in it?"

"It's our one chance to do so, in this dusk of the lunar night!" Carson declared. "Twenty-four hours from now Earth will have revolved again, so that its shaft there in Yucatan will be in line with this shaft down through the moon, and when that occurs we must go back—back to warn our world. But during those twenty-four hours there is a chance, a million to one chance, I admit, that we may be able to find Howland here, to escape discovery by these swarming turtle-creatures, and to take him back with us!"

"But to venture into this city around us—these streets crowded with turtle-creatures—is death!" I exclaimed. "Even now it is a miracle, that even through this dusk we haven't been discovered on the plaza, at the city's center!"

"We must risk it," Carson said. "Some of the streets in the city around us, you can see, are hardly used by the turtle-creatures, while others are swarming with them. Well, if we can make our way through these comparatively deserted streets, in this dusk, we can perhaps evade the turtle-creatures long enough to find some clue to Howland's fate."

Gazing about us again, straining our eyes through the dusk across the great plaza's surface, we could see that Carson was right and that some of the narrow streets that branched from that plaza were almost empty of turtle-creatures, while the other and broader ones were filled with masses of them, apparently most of them carrying with them tools or instruments of one sort or another. All this we could only perceive as through a misty screen, through the dusk that lay unchangingly over all this lunar city. Yet we were puzzled by the fact, thankful as we were for it, that no turtle-creatures moved upon or across the great plaza at whose center we stood. It was evident, to us, after a moment's thought, that only those came out on the plaza who wished to reach the chamber beneath it, through the opening by which we stood, and as none were desirous, apparently, of reaching that great chamber now, the great plaza was deserted.

Pausing there, peering about, we stood for only a moment longer, and then Carson, with a silent gesture, was leading the way across the plaza, through the soft thick dusk toward its edge, toward one of the narrow and almost empty streets that branched from that edge. Before us as we moved on, hearts beating rapidly with every step, the gigantic crystal-like building loomed larger, and to our ears came louder the sounds of activity from the thronged broader streets, the deep bass note of many turtle-voices, the throbbing of many flying-circles that sped past in the dusk high overhead. Even through the shrouding dusk it seemed impossible that we could move nearer toward the great buildings without being discovered, but Carson was leading the way straight toward one of the narrower and emptier streets, a mere crevice between the great towering metal buildings, and once we reached its deeper shadow we might elude the creatures without great trouble, I knew. On we crept through the dusk toward it, then suddenly flung ourselves flat, as a flying-circle throbbing by overhead dipped suddenly close toward us!

Lying there with pounding heart, it seemed impossible that we had not been seen by those on it, but in a moment it had passed, and with the next moment we were up again, moving on through the dusk toward the deeper dusk of the narrow chasm-like street that opened through the looming buildings before us. We were almost at that opening now, but a few yards from its welcome deeper shadow. We were within yards, feet of it, of the great plaza's edge, when we stopped abruptly and recoiled! For into that narrow opening just before us, from one of the great buildings beside it, had emerged a dozen or more dark, upright forms conversing in deep bass tones that came clearly to us through the dusk, and moving straight toward the great plaza's center and ourselves! Dark, bulbous turtle-forms, who, before Carson and Trent ahead or I behind could leap back, were within yards of us. Grotesque great shell-cased creatures who stopped short as they caught sight of us, stared toward us for a moment with lidless eyes, and then were rushing forward upon us!

CHAPTER SIX
The Battle of the Flying-Circles

AS THE dozen or more great turtle-creatures ahead rushed toward us, I seemed to stand for a moment in a stunned paralysis of inaction, then saw Carson's automatic leap from his side, heard the swift crack of it and saw two of those onrushing creatures stumble and fall, saw another collapse as Trent's gun spoke in his hand. My own weapon was now in my grasp, and I was leaping forward, hearing from all about the plaza and all across the giant city a sudden wave of sounds of alarm. But before I had leaped more than a step forward, Carson had cried out to me over his shoulder.

"Back, Foster!" he cried. "They've got us, but you can get away! It's the only chance now for Howland and us—for one to stay free!"

Even in that agonized moment, as the great turtle-creatures rushed forward unchecked upon Carson and Trent ahead, I knew that Carson's cry was truth, that if we all were captured there would be no chance, but that one free might save the rest, might escape back from moon to Earth to warn our world, at least. I stood hesitant for an instant, weapon in hand, torn by my desire to rush forward beside my two friends, and then had turned, and was running backward through the dusk across the great dear plaza's surface, back toward the opening in it up through which we had come.

Behind me I heard the crack of the automatics of Carson and Trent suddenly cease, heard a quick scuffling, a babble of deep-toned cries and hoarse shouts, and knew that the moon-creatures had rounded up my friends. From all around the great plaza it seemed that other moon-creatures were pouring forth from the mighty buildings in answer to the alarm, and at top speed I ran on through the dusk toward the great opening through which we had come.

A moment more and I was at that opening, but now I could discern, far across the plaza through the thick dusk, a half-score of great turtle-forms that were running toward it! They had not as yet caught sight of me, I knew, but as I flung myself down the metal stair into the great cube-chamber where our cylinder still hung suspended above the abyss of the great shaft, I knew that within minutes they would reach that chamber. Frantically I gazed about for some place of concealment, but in the great, metal-walled and white-lit room there seemed none. I jumped to the bridge that led to the open door of the suspended cylinder, some wild idea of hiding in that cylinder flashing across my mind, but as I reached the bridge I stopped, gazing up at the mighty metal girders about the great cylinder, which supported it there, beneath the disk and above the shaft's circular abyss. Two of those giant girders crossed at right angles just above me, and in the next moment I was clambering upon them, lying along the horizontal one and praying that its broad surface might shield me from the gaze of anyone beneath. Hardly had I reached that precarious place of concealment, the dark mouth of the bottomless shaft down beneath me, when there burst into the great room from above a group of a dozen turtle-creatures!

All, I saw, were armed with half-hemispheres of metal like those Carson had described to us, containers of the deadly green vacuum ray, and I held my breath as they burst down the stair, calling to each other in deep tones and gazing eagerly about the room. None looked up toward the great girder on which I lay prone, and they seemed reassured by the emptiness of the great place. For a few moments they conversed in their strange vibrant tones, glancing about them, a dozen inconceivably strange great-shelled turtle-creatures, and then as one of them glanced toward the cylinder that hung suspended beside me he uttered something and all moved toward it, to cross the bridge just beneath me.

As they came across that bridge, halting beside the cylinder's open door and peering within with hemispheres ready, I could have reached down my arm and touched the tops of their great reptilian heads, so close were they beneath me. I hardly dared breathe; I lay with muscles tense, yet with an intolerable desire to shout aloud, as they conversed there for a moment more, inches only beneath the great girder on which I lay. Then my tension relaxed as they turned to go. Hope rising in me again, I saw them turning to go across the great chamber and up the narrow stair, but then saw to my dismay that one of them had remained there in the big room, one who held his vacuum ray-hemisphere still in his grasp and who was obviously a sentinel left on guard! Despair rushed across me again as I saw the others leaving, passing up the stair and out the great opening into the plaza above, while the single one remaining paced about with lidless eyes alert, as watchful as ever.

A MYRIAD plans of escape flashed through my brain as I lay there, yet all seemed hopeless while that guard remained beneath me. At any moment I might be discovered by him, I knew, and then a flash of the deadly green ray would put an end to my existence before I could make a move. Yet somewhere in the mighty city about me, living or dead, were my two friends who were willing to sacrifice themselves to allow me to escape, and I knew that unless I could win free and find Carson and Trent soon, and with them make our search for Howland, the twenty-four hours, at the end of which we must flash back to warn Earth, would be gone. Racking my brains for some expedient, I finally chose the most desperate, for I dared not make use of my pistol. It was a slim chance, to be sure, but putting my idea into operation, I reached forth and rapped sharply upon the side of the giant metal cylinder suspended beside the girder on which I lay.

As the resonant sound of my rapping broke the stillness of the great chamber I saw the turtle-guard, at the other end of the great room, turn instantly, with hemisphere upraised, gazing toward the cylinder. Then quickly he was coming across the great floor toward it, toward the little bridge of metal that jutted out from the great shaft's edge to the cylinder's open door. He came slower as he reached that bridge, standing there at the very edge of the abyss and gazing forward into the cylinder with ray-container still ready for action. Silently I gathered myself, and then as he stepped just beneath the great girder on which I was, I threw myself down upon him!

Even as I had leaped down upon him the sound of that leap had brought his deadly hemisphere flashing up toward me, but he was a moment too late, for in the next instant I was upon him, had crumpled him down to the surface of the little bridge, and we were struggling madly upon it. Gripping each other with the utmost of our powers, we struggled there upon that narrow little strip of metal, and beneath us was the mighty depths of the giant shaft, that led down through the whole sphere of the moon itself! Twisting, turning, with the turtle-creature who gripped me striving above all else to bring his hemisphere up against me, while I strove to prevent it, we rolled there on the little bridge in as silent and deadly a conflict as I have ever experienced. Endeavoring in vain to get a hold upon that grotesque, shelled body, I felt my strength leaving me fast; I felt the great paws that held me dragging me inch by inch toward the bridge's side, toward the abyss!

Another moment and we were rolling at the very edge, and then I felt myself being drawn irresistibly over that edge by the great limbs that held me, saw beneath me, as though from a great distance, the black depths of the great shaft into which I was being propelled.

A sudden mad frenzy of strength surged through me at the sight, a wild accession of sudden strength with which I thrust blindly out at the monster who held me. That fierce thrust, unexpected as it was to him, knocked him suddenly away from me, to the very edge of the bridge, and then he was toppling over that edge, hurtling down into the great shaft's depths. A deep wailing cry came up to me for a moment, and then all was silence!

I stumbled to my feet, across the bridge and to the solid metal floor of the great chamber, toward the stair that led upward. But before I had taken a half-dozen steps I stopped once more and gazed upward. From above had come a growing throbbing sound, a throbbing that was rapidly increasing in intensity, that was nearing me! Only an instant I heard it and then saw, through the great round opening in the big room's ceiling, a dark circle that was coming down toward that opening from high above through the dusk. It was one of the great flying-circles, and it was coming straight down toward the opening above me, straight down toward the great chamber in which I stood!

Spellbound with horror I stood there for a moment as the great dark shape swept downward, and in that moment it had reached the great opening in the ceiling, was floating smoothly down through it. But as it did so I had turned, had leaped backward, I knew even in that moment of deadly peril that I had no time to reach my former place of concealment on the girder, that I would be seen before ever I could reach it. The great suspended cylinder lay before me, its open door just across the little bridge on which I had battled, but neither could I take refuge in it, and for an instant I stood in an agony of indecision. Then even as the great flying-circle shot down into the big chamber I had made my decision, had leaped to the edge of the great shaft before me and had lowered myself swiftly over that edge, hanging from the rim of the abyss with all its terrific depths beneath me, and with only my fingers now visible on the rim to which I clung!

EVEN AS I had lowered myself into that desperate place of concealment, I had heard the great flying-circle sweep down through the opening above, to the great chamber's metal floor, coming to rest there with its throbbing of power ceasing. I heard the deep vibrant voices of turtle-creatures then, many of them by the sound, as they emerged from the flying-circle to the room's floor, and I prayed that they might not see my clutching fingers there on the great shaft's rim, since a slight push would send me hurtling down into the awful depths beneath me after my late antagonist. The creatures above seemed to halt upon emerging from the flying-circle, and I heard one passing across the narrow little bridge to my right, peering into the cylinder, apparently, and then returning without having seen my clinging shape in the shadows of the great shaft's depths. But now my hands seemed going numb with the strain of holding me there from the shaft's rim, and I felt my grip upon that rim slowly slipping!

There was an agonized moment in which the turtle-creatures above conversed in their deep tones, while my grip continued to relax in spite of all the efforts of my will. I knew that a moment more would mark the limit of my endurance, would see me hurtling downward, but as I gave up all hope, I heard the sound of heavy footsteps on the metal floor above, and I knew that the turtle-creatures were moving around the great shaft to the room's opposite side, were passing apparently back into that great corridor which opened from it and in which the long row of cylinders was ranged. Hardly had the sound of their voices receded into that corridor than I was endeavoring to pull myself up over the rim from which I hung. For a moment my numbed muscles refused to obey the commands of my will, my aching limbs seeming incapable of further effort, and panic shot through me as I found myself unable to draw myself up. That very panic, though, served to spur me to a greater effort, and at last with a wild convulsion of my muscles, I had scrambled up over the great shaft's side and lay panting beside its edge.

For a while I lay there in utter exhaustion, then staggered to my feet. The great flying-circle of the turtle-creatures lay on the big room's metal floor not far from me, but none of the creatures themselves were in sight, all having passed into the corridor on the other side, from which still came the faint vibrations of their voices. I sprang across the room, toward the stair that led upward, but at the foot of that stair I halted, gazing back toward the silent flying-circle, a sudden thought occurring to me. Could I but operate that flying-circle it would enable me to make a survey of the great moon-city, which I could accomplish in no other way. Afire with the idea, I leaped back toward the great craft.

It was simply a great flat circle of smooth metal, a low retaining wall of metal perhaps a foot high around its edge. The circle, like all the others I had seen, was fully a hundred feet in diameter, and at its center was the mechanism by which it was propelled. This mechanism, whatever its nature, was cased in a low flat cylinder or raised circle, upon the top of which was a bewildering series of studs, and oddly charactered dials, all grouped about a single central upright lever or handle. I flung myself down beside this switch-cylinder, pressed swiftly upon the studs in turn, but without result. The voices of the moon-creatures, back in the great corridor, seemed nearer, louder, now, and I knew that they were returning, would in a moment more be emerging into the great chamber, so frantically I pressed and twisted at the studs before me. Then as my fingers fell upon the studs in a certain order, something clicked beneath them and there came instantly a smooth, powerful throbbing from the circle's mechanism. At once I grasped the central handle, and as I did so, felt the circle rising smoothly up from the floor toward the ceiling, a section of the circle at the center being transparent for downward vision.

A moment's experiment showed me that the central handle was the one control of the circle's direction, the great disk veering to whichever side that handle was inclined, descending when it was pressed downward and rising when it was pulled upward. Clumsily I guided it up toward the great opening in the ceiling, maneuvered for an instant beneath that opening, and then had risen up through it, my great circle throbbing smoothly upward into the dusk above the great moon-city! All about me there stretched into the thickening twilight that seemed never to change the great masses of the strange faceted buildings, seeming as I soared up above them like giant crystals of metal, angled and regular-sided, cast down into geometric, neat formations. I could glimpse through the dusk many other flying-circles that were coming and going from roof to roof of the great buildings, but for the moment paid these small attention, sending my own circle soaring across the great plaza beneath me to the spot where I had last seen Carson and Trent.

AS I reached that spot, I halted the circle's progress, hanging motionless a few hundred feet above the plaza's smooth surface and gazing down toward it. Nothing lay beneath me, though, but the smooth metal, stretching away to the great buildings at the plaza's edge. There was no sign of Carson or Trent beneath, no loitering turtle-creatures, even, and it was with heart sick with despair that I gazed about on every side in search of them. Nowhere were they to be seen, no shapes were moving across the great plaza, though masses of the turtle-shapes moved in the streets of the city about me, and swarming circles throbbed by all about me in the dusk of the lunar city's night.

Despairingly I stared around, for where in this mighty, dim-lit city could I hope to find my friends? The proverbial needle and haystack seemed easy beside my own problem, but I knew that never could I rest until I had discovered my friends' fate. I had seen no bodies or blood stains below, so it seemed logical to hope that they still lived. Grasping the control of my flying-circle again, I sent it slanting up above the great city again, out now over its strange massed buildings and swarming streets at a height of a hundred feet or so, peering down through the dusk at buildings and streets for some trace of my missing friends. Nothing could I see of them, nothing but the giant buildings, inset circles of glowing light and small triangular windows alternating in their sides, the metal streets below in which the hordes of the turtle-creatures surged with their never-ceasing gathering of instruments and materials, their great preparations that seemed never to end. Down among the buildings I slanted now and then, hanging beside their small triangular windows and peering inside, but the darkness of their interiors baffled me, made me slant upward again.

I continued to drive across the city, peering down into it with the hopelessness of my search growing more and more complete. From the turtle-creatures who moved in masses below me I had no fear of discovery, but the flying-circles that swarmed thick about me, I twisted and turned unceasingly to avoid, knowing that if those creatures on them discovered my human form through the dusk, it would mean the end. But the turtle-creatures on those swarming circles ignored me.

The city, I could see now, stretched from horizon to horizon, covering all the moon's far side, without a break. Long before the great plaza and its opening had vanished in the dusk behind me, but still far above I could see the faint gleaming of the mighty transparent roof, which shielded this airtight lunar metropolis from the airless void of space. Through that roof, and through the dusk beneath it, I could make out the familiar stars, the great constellations unchanged in form or position, and the sight sent a poignant Earth-sickness sweeping through me for an instant. Then I snapped back to sudden attention, fear stabbing me in the next instant, for a great flying-circle, which I had not seen approaching had swept only a score of feet above me!

I turned, saw it soaring on a little distance behind me, then saw that it had stopped, turned, and was coming back toward me. The turtle-creatures on it had seen me! Straight toward me it was flying, but in the next instant I had grasped the control of my own circle, had sent it zooming upward, throbbing with power, up over the city at a greater height and away from the following circle. Upward I shot steeply, clinging to the circle's center, and then as I glanced back saw that the other circle was following, was slanting up after me with the dozen turtle-creatures upon its surface plainly visible to me, gazing toward me as their craft shot up on my track. They were pursuing me!

Something of panic filled me as I realized the fact, but I gripped myself, sent the flying-circle on which I crouched slanting higher, higher until the city beneath was fading from sight in the thick dusk. Yet the pursuing craft came on, and because its drivers could maneuver it more skillfully than I, was rapidly overtaking me! Up and outward, up until the great massed buildings beneath had passed completely from sight in the dusk, pursued and pursuing circle fled, my heart racing as the gap between us steadily lessened. It had been my hope to lose the pursuing craft in the dusk, but turn and twist as I might, I could not shake them off, and rapidly they were drawing within yards of me. I could now see the gleam of the gigantic transparent roof, not far above, and knew that in my flight I had risen far above the moon city, was almost against the great roof. Then, just as I turned to glance back again toward the pursuing circle close behind me, I saw a great ray of misty green light, driving straight toward me, from a large hemisphere set at that circle's edge.

Instinctively, in that instant, I jerked the handle in my grasp, sent my flying-circle rushing sidewise to avoid that misty ray. The next instant the green ray had struck through the air where I had been, and as it did so, the sharp thunder of a great detonation sounded in my ears, while my fleeting circle reeled beneath a swift and sudden rush of air about me! I knew it was the deadly vacuum ray that Carson had seen, the green ray that destroyed all atmosphere about what it struck, creating a perfect vacuum by annihilating the air in its path, and thus slaying any living thing within its range by that vacuum. Even as I had rushed sidewise, through, to avoid that deadly ray, the pursuing turtle-creatures had swerved their racing circle likewise, and in another moment another shaft of the green ray stabbed toward me.

AGAIN I swerved, dipping downward, but this time the misty ray had driven past but a few feet from my circle's edge, and the resulting stunning detonation beside me had all but upset my flying-craft. Clinging desperately to its controls, twisting and turning in a vain effort to escape these merciless pursuers whose deadly shafts were flashing about me, I felt my blood rising in swift, burning anger, looked swiftly about and then saw that at my own flying-circle's edge was attached one of the big metal hemispheres like that from which they loosed their ray. I saw, too, that on the side of the switch-case before me was a green stud that I had not noticed before, and with sudden resolution I swerved my fleeing circle swiftly about upon my pursuers, the hemisphere on its edge turned toward them, and then pressed the green stud. At once there leaped back from the hemisphere at my circle's edge a shaft of misty green light, stabbing toward my pursuers and past them at a short distance. As the sharp thunder of its detonation came to my ears I saw the pursuing circle dip and reel suddenly as the ray created a vacuum beside it.

Still it drove on toward me, and then as I sent my own circle rushing straight back toward it, our two deadly rays crossed and clashed there in mid-air, both of us swerving instantly to avoid the opposing ray. Circling, dipping, striking, we hung there beneath the giant transparent roof, high above the great moon city that lay in the dusk far beneath, engaged in what was surely as strange a battle as ever was fought. I knew, though, that that battle could not continue for long, for my opponents were very skillful in handling the great flying-circles, and it was only by superhuman efforts that I had been able to avoid their leaping shafts of green light as long as I had. Those green shafts striking from our circles produced a swift succession of great thundering detonations about us, and I knew that should the sounds be heard in the city far beneath, it would be a matter of moments before other flying-circles would be racing up also. Knowing that, I decided to risk all on a desperate expedient which had occurred to me, and which would give me a chance, at least, of destroying my pursuers.

Driving my circle toward the hovering circle of my enemies, I waited until their green ray had leaped lightning-like toward me, cleaving the air but a few feet above me as I dipped from it, and then as the thunderous detonation of that ray sounded, I collapsed suddenly, went limp there on the surface of my flying-circle, its control loose in my grasp. It went whirling downward through the dusk without my guiding hand, while I clung to it. I saw the rays of the enemy circle cease as it did so, saw them driving smoothly down after my falling circle, as though to inspect it more closely. Swiftly they slanted down after me, while I clung frantically to my own circle's surface. Then as they swept nearer toward my tumbling craft I grasped its control, righted it with one swift motion, and before the driving circle beside me could swerve away had pressed the ray-stud and had sent a shaft of the green ray stabbing toward the group of moon-creatures at its center!

As that green ray struck them I heard the rocking detonation of it loud in my ears, and in that moment, while their circle drove beside my own, I saw the creatures upon it suddenly collapsing and staggering and falling, falling to death as their bodies swelled, broke, and exploded before my eyes! The next instant, with no living hand at its controls, their great flying-circle was driving crazily down toward the shrouding dusk beneath in a long slant, disappearing in the dusk in another moment as it plunged to destruction! Then, with my own flying-circle speeding smoothly on through the dusk, I lay for a few moments motionless at its center, filled with the sick horror that had flooded through me as I had seen the turtle-creatures explode beneath my ray, forgetful for the moment of all save the hideous form of death that had overtaken them in the green shaft of light that I had loosed upon them.

When I overcame that horror and came back to a complete realization of my position, I found my circle still soaring smoothly onward through the dusk which veiled all things about me. Now I sent the strange great craft slanting downward again, down through the thick twilight until the gleam of the transparent roof had receded again to far above me, until I could make out again the masses of faceted buildings and thronged metal streets of the great moon city beneath. As I drove cautiously down over it, avoiding with utter care the flying-circles, swarming here and there above it, I became convinced that the battle which I had fought high in the dusk above had aroused no attention here in the city below, since no alarm had been given. Flying-circles still swarmed across the city from roof to roof, and in the metal streets the turtle-creatures continued to throng, but there was no evidence that any had heard the detonations of our combat.

Satisfied that this was the case, I gazed about me to ascertain the direction of the great plaza from which I had come. But now I saw that the great buildings and the streets, above which I moved, were so similar in appearance to each other that there was nothing by which I could remember the way I had come. Swift panic shot through me, as I comprehended suddenly that my circlings and turnings in the battle high in the dusk overhead had hopelessly confused all my direction-sense, and that, without any landmarks to remember in the great moon-city beneath me, I had no idea where the great plaza, with our cylinder beneath it, might lie! I was lost—lost there above the great city of the moon-creatures!

CHAPTER SEVEN
Through Strange Perils

A COLD, uncontrollable terror gripped me as I realized that I had lost all idea of my whereabouts, that I might wander through the dusk over this colossal moon city until some unavoidable accident would inevitably discover me to its hordes beneath. Then, forcing myself to consider my situation calmly, I strove to remember in what direction I had come from the great plaza, but found the effort in vain, my twistings and turnings aloft having hopelessly confused me. To rise higher for a wider survey of the great city was useless, since the higher one went, the more difficult did the dusk make such a survey. I came to the conclusion, finally, that my best hope was to move on over the city in search of Carson and Trent as I had been doing, trusting that my search might bring me within sight of the great central plaza.

So, sending the great flying-circle down toward the huge, crystal-like metal buildings, I began again to soar smoothly above them at moderate speed, watching intently for some sign of my friends, scanning the crowded streets and the great buildings carefully for some trace of them. On and on, over the weird seemingly endless city of the moon-creatures I went, but all its vast expanse seemed the same, geometrically patterned rows of giant buildings, their inset circles glowing with soft light; the ways between them crowded with the never-ceasing throngs of the turtle-creatures, and the air above them swarming with great flying-circles like my own, among which I desperately twisted and turned in the dusk. On I went, and had been engaged in this seemingly fruitless survey for some two hours, had begun to think that after all my quest was useless and that Carson and Trent had been slain in the struggle there in the plaza. But the sight of a gigantic building of the same shape as all the others of this strange city, but immeasurably larger than any I had yet seen, drove all such thoughts from my mind.

A single titanic crystal of metal, with many angles and faceted sides, set with glowing circle and triangular window, it loomed giant-like among the smaller faceted crystals that were the buildings about it, its own vast bulk lifting for fully two thousand feet toward the transparent roof far above. I sensed, immediately, that this was some center of the moon city's activities, the more so because its great flat roof was alive with flying-circles landing and departing. To venture near it, I knew, was to risk instant discovery, so swarming with life was the air above it and the streets about it, yet hope was rising suddenly in me, and I drove the flying-circle down toward the great building's faceted side, partly hidden by that side and by the thick dusk from the masses of flying-circles arriving and departing above. Then, gazing forth with hope-quickened eyes, I began to move slowly with my great flat craft about the mighty structure's side, gazing tensely toward its triangular windows as I passed around it. And then when I had passed around half the giant building's bulk, I stopped my throbbing craft suddenly short in mid-air, gazing through the dusk toward a window above me, with heart suddenly racing.

I had seen a face there, a half-discerned face that, in the moment I had seen it, had appeared to be white, *human!* For but a moment that face had showed at one of the triangular little windows set in the mighty building's side above me, but that uncertain glimpse through the dusk had given me sudden new hope. Quickly I grasped the control of my flying-circle, began to move up toward that window. The next moment I had swerved outward again from it, for glancing down, I noticed a number of turtle-creatures standing motionless at the mighty building's base among the surging throngs about it. Apparently they were guards, and they were gazing up toward me through the dusk! I dared not loiter longer outside the great building's side lest their suspicions be definitely aroused, and with something like despair I sent my flying-circle driving upward instead.

As I shot upward, though, above the level of the great building's roof, I saw that which suddenly renewed my hope. The masses of departing and arriving circles had ceased for the time being on that roof, and amid the flying-circles resting on it I could see a round opening and a stair leading downward. Gazing across the great roof, hovering in the dusk beside it, I saw then that there were guards upon it, a half-dozen turtle-guards armed with ray-hemispheres, but that they were moving toward a great flying-circle, which had landed upon the roof's far side a moment before, one that was loaded with many strange machines. Not only the guards were moving toward it, but up through the opening from the great building's interior were pouring several scores of turtle-creatures who were heading toward that newly landed circle, preparing apparently to unload from it the mechanisms it carried.

Within a moment all had hurried toward that disk, far across the great roof, and as I peered through the dusk toward it, I saw that the opening leading downward was quite unguarded. A moment I hesitated, then abruptly sent my flying-circle throbbing smoothly downward toward that opening on the roof. Down I slanted, the circle coming smoothly to rest in a moment on the flat roof beside the opening, and then I had sprung from it to the roof, gazing fearfully across it through the thick dusk toward the group of turtle-creatures about the newly landed circle at the edge, hundreds of feet from me. They had apparently not noticed my landing circle in the deep twilight, and at once I sprang toward the opening leading downward, pistol in hand, and was creeping silently but swiftly down the narrow stair that led into the mighty building's interior.

DOWN—down—step after step I crept, silently as possible and with pistol ready, down until I saw that the stair ended a dozen feet below me in a wide corridor from which opened many doors. From those doors came sounds of activity, humming of machines and deep tones of turtle-creatures, and I gripped my weapon tightly as I crept toward the nearest of them. In a moment I had reached it, was silently drawing myself to its edge, peering inside. There was a great room inside, duskily illuminated like the broad corridor by a few circles of glowing light. Within it were great, looming mechanisms, moving cogs and bars and chains which were mysteries to me, tended by a score or more of turtle-creatures who appeared to be shaping upon them hemi-spheres of metal that recalled to me instantly the deadly ray-hemispheres. Only a moment I peered inside, thankful for the deep dusk of the great building's interior, then with beating heart silently pulled myself past the open door, unobserved by the busy monstrous shapes inside, and was moving on down the corridor.

Past other open doors I crept, all opening into great dusky rooms filled with humming machines and with turtle-creatures. In the shadowy corridor I had met none of them, so far, but knew that not for long could my good fortune thus continue, knew that with the return of those who had poured out upon the roof, the corridors would be filled with them. Swiftly and silently I crept on, toward a stair that I could see now leading downward from the corridor, a metal stair, down which I crept as I had descended the first, to find myself in a long corridor almost exactly like that which I had just left. From it too opened many doors, but through the deeper shadows of that corridor I crept toward the continuation of the stair, almost without seeing the interior of those busy rooms. It seemed incredible that I had progressed even so far downward without discovery, but I knew that the level of that window, in which I had seen the face that had brought me down into the great building on this mad quest, lay considerably lower.

Down another stair I crept, and another, and another—shrinking back as I came down the third to see a half-dozen turtle-creatures approaching me along the corridor beneath, bearing some machine with them. But though I crouched on the stair with pistol gripped tightly, they did not come that way. Instead they passed along the dusky corridor beneath, and as their footsteps on the smooth metal receded, I was down into the hall, moving through its dusk toward the next stair to take me to the level below, which I estimated to be the level I sought. Down that last stair I moved, but when I reached its bottom I stopped abruptly short. For though it ended in a corridor like those above me, that corridor had a metal wall on its right side only. On its left side was sheer space, and as I crept to that side and gazed downward, I saw that there dropped downward the great emptiness of a titanic room, a vast, circular hall that was hundreds of feet in diameter and in height, and near whose curving ceiling I was crouching, only a low rail separating the floor of the corridor in which I crouched from the great room's emptiness.

A great, soft-lit hall it was that must have occupied a half of the giant building's interior, and peering down, enthralled, I saw that upon its circular floor were ranged thousands of low metal seats, empty now, their emptiness making the room seem greater. At their center, though, was a round clear space and there, about a small triangular metal table, sat three turtle-creatures, three monsters who seemed silently examining a litter of thin metal sheets and a mass of small models or mechanisms before them. Quite silent they sat, at that vast fane's center, yet seemed strangely to dominate it, fill it. For a while I gazed at them, then, recalled to realization of my own purpose and peril by some sound above, turned swiftly, I was on the level I had sought, I knew, and I knew that the room whose window I had noted lay somewhere to the right from me. So, hastening along the dusky corridor, the gigantic soft-lit hall's depths still to my left, I felt my heart beat with hope again, as I saw before me another branching corridor turning to the right from the one I followed. In a moment I was at it, hurrying around the corner into it. And as I turned that corner, flinging myself recklessly forward by then, I collided full with a great turtle-creature who had been coming round it toward me!

The great monster and I had crashed together at the same moment that I caught sight of him, and then before I could raise the pistol in my hand he had grasped me, knocking it from my grip, and we were straining there together in a death-grip! Even as the great taloned paws had closed about me, as I had been pulled in toward the hideous, shell-cased body, I realized in a flash that a single cry from the creature would sound the alarm, and so had grasped his snake-like neck just beneath the reptilian head, in a throttling grip into which I put all my power. Thus for a moment that seemed endless to me, we stood there together, silent, almost motionless, locked in a death-grip in the corridor's shadows, the great taloned limbs crushing about my body with inconceivable force, even as my own hands closed tighter about the snaky throat. I felt my strength going as the relentless crushing grip about me held, but heard too strangled cries from the creature whose throat I held, and then felt his grip on me relax as he struck out with all his force to free himself from me and from the grip that was throttling him. Whirling me about with terrific power, he strove to free himself, yet his struggles were weakening and dwindling, as I held fiercely on. Another moment and with a sudden collapsing movement, the creature had slumped downward. A moment I retained my grip, then satisfied that the monster was dead, I straightened, looking wildly about me.

NOTHING disturbed the dusk of the corridors about me, no alarm having sounded, but now the sounds overhead were nearing me and I knew that the creatures on the roof were pouring back down into the building. Swiftly I glanced about, panting still, then moved forward down the corridor into which I had been turning, toward the right. The body of my late antagonist I left where it had fallen, perforce, though I would have wished to conceal it lest the first passer in the corridor discover it and comprehend what had happened. Down this new hall I went, and found that though doors opened from it, the rooms held no humming machines or turtle-creatures like the others I had seen; these seemed dark and empty. A few moments more and the end of the corridor loomed before me, a blank wall. But to one side of the hall near its end was the last of the open doors, and one that I judged must lead into the room whose window I had seen from outside.

Cautiously, though, I crept toward that open door, disregarding in my excitement the nearing sounds of the coming of the turtle-creatures from above, creeping toward that door until I was at its edge, peering with beating heart inside. So dark was the room's interior into which I looked, that for the moment I could make out only the triangular section of dusky light that was its window. I took a step forward toward the open door, another—and then sprawled on the corridor's floor as though knocked back by some giant invisible hand from within! Even in the instant that I fell, I knew what had happened, knew that across that apparently open door there stretched a sheet of invisible force through which no matter could penetrate. But even as I fell, then even as I rose swiftly to my feet, I noted a stir of movement inside the room's dark interior, saw dark figures within rushing toward the invisible door, toward me, the dim light of the corridor falling upon them through that door as they did so, erect, dark figures at sight of which I gasped aloud.

"Carson—Trent—*Howland!*" I exclaimed, and at the same moment heard a cry from the foremost of them.

"Behind you—quick!" cried Carson.

I whirled around, and behind me stood three of the great moon-creatures! Even as I whirled and saw them I knew that they had found the body of their slain fellow in the corridor, had searched after me to overtake me at the very moment that I had found my friends. Even as I turned toward them their great arms had swung up above me, the ray-hemispheres in their grasp. I flung up my arms toward them in that flashing moment, but was too late to ward off their blows, for the next instant one of the metal weapons had descended upon my head with crushing force. I felt myself swaying, stumbling and falling before them, and then they and all else about me vanished from my mind as darkness overwhelmed me.

CHAPTER EIGHT
Howland's Story

CONSCIOUSNESS came back to me through fiery mists of pain, consciousness in which my first sensation was of a throbbing ache that beat through my brain like the dull beat of a great machine. Moving about somewhat exploringly, I became aware that I was lying on a smooth, hard floor, and that there was a similar smooth wall beside me. Then with an effort, I opened my eyes. I was lying in a small, almost dark room, its metal ceiling a half-score feet above me. A triangular window opened upon a great soft-lit, dusky space outside. Then, as I stirred, I heard movements on the room's other side and in a moment there had come toward me and were bending over me three figures at sight of which I caught my breath, remembrance of all that had happened rushing over me.

"Carson—Trent—Howland!" I exclaimed again. "I've found you then, Carson—and you've found Howland!"

Carson nodded silently, and then Howland, who was bending down with keen, eager face to help me to a sitting position, spoke.

"Carson and Trent and you have found me," he said, "have come from Earth to moon to find me—but only to be imprisoned with me!"

I turned to Carson. "Then you and Trent were captured in that fight on the plaza—brought here and imprisoned?" I asked. He nodded.

"Captured there and brought here and imprisoned with Howland, only a few hours ago," he said. "But you, Foster?"

Swiftly I explained to him how I had managed to escape the moon-creatures, when the alarm had been given, by concealing myself in the great chamber of the cylinder, beneath the plaza; of how I had slain the guard in my battle over the shaft and had stolen a flying-circle to soar up over the moon city in search of my friends; of how on that flying-circle I had ventured across the great city, had fought my wild battle with the flying-circle of the turtle-creatures who had discovered me, high in the dusk above the city, and of how, after finding myself lost over the city, I had stumbled upon the gigantic building in a window of which I had glimpsed the face that had made me dare all risks to venture down into that building in search of my friends, only to be discovered, stricken senseless, and imprisoned with them. When I had finished, they sat for a time in silence, and I saw that Howland's face was working.

"I did not dream that Carson and Trent and you might ever follow me here, through all these perils," he said, slowly. "I never dreamed that any there might be who would venture from Earth to moon after the moon-creatures who captured me."

"It was Carson's plan," I told him. "It was he who saw you captured, there in the camp at Yucatan, and it was he who suggested that we follow—out to the moon—to rescue you and to take back to Earth proof of the doom that Carson thought hangs above it."

"You thought that, Carson?" asked Howland, turning quickly toward him, and when the other had nodded, his eyes grew brooding, strange. "Then you have divined the truth. You know now that within hours these countless millions of moon-creatures, who fill the mighty city about us, will be starting to leave that city, will be starting to leave the moon, forever—will be launching their first hordes, their first terrific attack, against the Earth to seize it for themselves, and to wipe from existence for all time all the races of man!"

He was silent again for a moment, gazing out through the little window and across the great, unearthly city of faceted metal buildings, of swarming flying-circles and turtle-creatures that lay in the dusk about us and then he turned again toward us.

"Carson—Trent—to whom I've had time to tell nothing in the hour or so you've been here, hearing your own tale," he began, "and you, Foster—you three know how I was captured by the moon raiders there in our camp at Yucatan, Carson has told you how Willings and the rest were slain, how I was captured by the turtle-creatures and taken down into their cylinder on the next night, how that cylinder was driven out through the gulf when the signal note sounded, out to the moon itself on the great beam, out at awful speed and through the moon's shaft, like your own cylinder, to come to rest there beneath the plaza's disk. Then the cylinder's bottom was opening, and the packed flying-circles inside it were emerging, with myself on one of them still, moving up through the great opening and above the great lunar city itself.

"OVER THAT colossal city, lying in dusk beneath the lunar night, our flying-circles drove, a city that I recognized was built upon the far side of the moon from Earth, and which amazed me utterly. Why had these turtle-races built their tremendous, airtight city on the moon's far side alone, where it could never be seen from Earth? Was it for that reason that they had built it there? That thought startled me, but before I could consider it farther, my captors had sped across the great faceted buildings of the city and had reached their goal, a single greater building, hugest of all I had seen, this building in which we now are, and which is the great center of government for the moon-race. Down toward its roof our flying-circles slanted, coming to rest on that roof, and then after being challenged by guards upon the roof, we were passing down into this great building's interior.

"Down through corridors and stairs and halls we went until we had reached the colossal hall that occupies most of this great structure, and that was filled then with a full three thousand of turtle-creatures ranged in regular rows of seats about it. At its center sat three others, about a triangular table, and I saw instantly that this was the great council that ruled the moon, and that the central three were, without doubt, its heads! Toward those three I was immediately led by my captors; who then made swift explanations, in their deep tones, to the three and to the thousands about them. Then, the center of interest for all the grotesque turtle-creatures massed about me, I stood there, wondering, awe-stricken, until the bass voices of the three leaders recalled me to myself.

"Just as I had done the first time, I replied in English, convincing them that my speech was wholly different from their own. They pondered a moment, then gave brief orders. At once I was hurried out of the great hall, back up into the building to this cell, one whose open door was closed upon me by a sheet of force projected across it, a sheet of force quite transparent to the vibrations of light and heat and so forth, but utterly impervious to matter-vibrations, thus forming a door more secure than steel. The window was quite open, and is still, but escape by it is impossible, because it is set in the sheer walls of the great building and lies hundreds of feet from either ground or roof. Then I was given food, a semi-liquid food that tasted like some chemical to me, and that was obviously artificially made by the synthesis of organic compounds directly from their original elements.

"Left alone for a time, I endeavored in vain to comprehend the strange situation in which I found myself; the purpose of these monsters in raiding Earth; the presence of the great shaft and disk there on Earth; the Earth-like gravitation here on the moon; the gigantic preparations and activity going on all about me. My thoughts were soon interrupted by the arrival of three turtle-creatures who, I found, had been sent by the great council to instruct me in their language. Pointing to objects outside, they called them by name in their strange tongue, I repeating after them as best my human voice could. In this way I gradually acquired a few words of their strange language, and soon picked up the rudiments of that language, could express myself haltingly to them, and could understand a great deal of their conversation.

"Day after day, hour after hour, they kept at me, until I could exchange ideas with my teachers with some fair success. They informed me, partly by gestures, that they had been ordered to instruct me in the moon-creatures' tongue so that I might be questioned by the great council, which I had already seen. That council was called the Council of Three Thousand, while the three leaders of it, which I had seen, were called the Council of Three. The great council represented the whole moon-creature race, as I learned, with the Council of Three acting as executives. Learning this, I strove to learn more, questioned my instructors as to the reason for my capture, for the moon-creatures' raid to Earth. And, because they had been given no orders otherwise, they told me readily enough. And in that telling, in the eon-old history of these moon-creatures, which they laid bare to me at last, I saw at last the true colossal solution of the great enigmas that had puzzled me, and saw too what gigantic doom it was that was hanging above our unsuspecting Earth! Learned what I had never dreamed before, learned that these moon-creatures had not always dwelt here upon the moon but that they had come here eons in the past, *had come here from our own Earth!*

"Yes, from our own Earth! For eons ago, Earth was far different from the Earth we know. It was a young planet, a planet covered almost completely by its great seas that now have receded, seas which covered almost all its face, leaving but small sections of land here and there. And in those seas, as we know, began Earth's life. Starting from the first crude jelly-like forms at those seas' bottom, climbing up the great ladder of evolution through invertebrate and vertebrate forms that life developed—developed into the prehistoric armored fishes, into the great crustaceans, into the great shell-coated sea-monsters, at whose size and ferocity we can but guess. Life swarming and abundant, life developing through thousands of different forms, but all life in or about the sea! For in our Earth's youth, ages were to pass before the first landforms were to appear, before the first land-creatures that were to develop into the mammals and into man had come to exist.

"Out of that great swarm of different forms of life, sea-life and amphibious life, there developed finally a single race or species of more intelligence than any of the rest, which rose slowly to dominance above the rest. A race of amphibious beings it was, armored with thick shell and with great taloned limbs, with snake-like neck and reptilian head, a race seeming like great turtle-creatures to us, yet which were in reality far, far different from any crustacean forms, or any other forms of which we have knowledge. A race of beings out of the world's dim, forgotten youth, all memory of which has passed on Earth. Yet there, in the long-dead past, these turtle-creatures had risen to power above all the other reptilian and amphibious and sea forms about them, by reason of their great intelligence, their reasoning power. They had climbed upward to the supreme position in their world just as man, ages later, was to climb, and so at last developed a civilization equaling and surpassing the later one of man.

"Cities they built across the Earth's surface, strange amphibious cities built along the sea's shores, inhabited by that strange, amphibious turtle-people. As the seas on Earth slowly receded, though, they lost their amphibious nature, became wholly land-creatures, though unchanged in appearance. And in their great cities their power and their knowledge, their science, rose ever to greater levels. They discovered the forces of the world about them, of electricity and radium and heat, built cities ever more gigantic, came at last to have all the Earth beneath their sway. From icy pole to icy pole the turtle-creatures reigned supreme. They even penetrated into the depths of space, with the great telescopes that they had constructed. And, peering out across those depths, they made a great discovery; they discovered that Earth's moon was inhabited as well as Earth itself!

"Earth's moon was inhabited, and had been inhabited for eons before Earth itself. This, of course, is not surprising, when we consider the origin of Earth and moon. We know, thanks to Chamberlin and Moulton, who first promulgated the theory, that in the remote past, the sun was but a single great fiery ball, spinning in space without accompanying planets; that some other sun, some other star, passing close to it through space, set up in our sun great tidal waves of its fiery self, great waves that instead of receding broke loose and burst out from the sun, forming into smaller fiery masses that fell into orbits about it, moving around it in regular order and forming the eight major worlds of our solar system. Some of these worlds, in turn, due to unstable conditions, threw off in turn smaller fiery masses which were to become their moons. The fiery mass that was Earth thus threw off a smaller single mass that was to be our moon. This the turtle-creatures knew to be the history of the solar system's formation.

"They knew, too, what is evident to all, that the smaller of such fiery masses cooled and solidified far more quickly than did the larger. For that reason, the smaller flaming mass that was the moon had solidified and cooled long before the Earth. Its molten mass had cooled into rock, its elements had condensed into great seas that covered the greater part of its surface, and following the usual evolution of worlds, those seas, with their erosion and the added erosion of wind and weather, had worn away the barren rock partially into small particles, into soil, so that finally the moon's surface was much like Earth's is now, a surface mostly covered with its great oceans, but with continents also, with great mountain ranges and deep valleys.

"All of this the turtle-creatures, reigning on Earth, had guessed, but now as they peered out toward the moon they found that it was inhabited by a strange race of great black worm-beings, like huge worms in shape, but of intelligence and knowledge of science greater even than their own. By means of great light-signals they were able to communicate across the gulf with these beings, and from them learned how they had arisen on the moon long before. For when the moon's surface had cooled, had formed great continents and seas, life had arisen upon it also, life that had changed through a myriad alien forms of its own, there on the moon, while Earth was still a fiery mass upon which nothing might live! And on the moon too, long ago, one form had become dominant above all others, a race of great black worm-folk whose strange shapes and swift movements were the result in some way of the moon's gravitational power, so much less than that of Earth. These worm-folk had risen to supremacy on the moon, by their own science and power, while Earth was still but a molten ball, and as the ages had moved on, their science and their power had steadily increased.

"But at last there loomed before them a situation which required all that science and power to overcome. The moon had cooled quickly, had solidified quickly, in accordance with the law of the evolution of worlds, but in continued obedience to that law it was still cooling, was growing colder and colder. Soon, the worm-folk knew, its fiery heart would have become completely cold, and then life would become impossible upon the moon, since as it cooled, its air was deserting it. Its great seas had dwindled and vanished long before, though this meant nothing to the worm-folk, who by their science could produce artificial water supplies. But if their world grew completely cold, if its atmosphere left it as they knew it would soon do, nothing could prevent their extinction. So all the great scientists of the worm-folk met to find some means of staving off the doom that hung over them.

"IT WAS impossible for the worm-folk to migrate to Earth, since Earth had just begun to solidify, to cool, and was still a great ball of half-liquid lava. It was true also of the other planets, so they knew they must meet their problem on the moon. Thereupon, they devised a tremendous plan by which they might save themselves. And this plan was none other than to enclose all the moon's surface, all its sphere, with a great transparent and airtight covering, or roof. Beneath this covering they could live comfortably and safely enough, for it would not be difficult to construct great plants to supply their airtight city with an artificial atmosphere. It meant a titanic labor, even for the powerful worm-folk, to adopt this mighty proposal, but it meant too that they could thenceforward live upon their world unthreatened by any danger. They set to work upon it at once.

"It had taken them an age to complete that gigantic task, an age throughout the years of which all the millions of the great worm-folk had labored upon it. At last it was completed. They had erected, several miles above the moon's surface, a mighty transparent roof, which was of a transparent alloy of metals, stronger than any we know, and which admitted unchecked the sun's life-giving light and heat but which was completely airtight. Then they had constructed their giant atmosphere—plants, plants that functioned automatically, replenishing and purifying the atmosphere of the great airtight space, and which made the air question of no further danger to them. Their great transparent roof was so supported by great pillars placed at a few strategic places that there was no danger of it ever falling or breaking.

Outside the last remnants of the moon's natural atmosphere had left it, leaving but a perfect vacuum outside the airtight roof, but inside it the worm-folk had in plenty the air, which they required like most creatures for life, and so could live on unharmed in their airtight city that covered all the moon.

"For age upon age they had lived on thus, in that strange and mighty hermetically-sealed city, while the Earth was cooling, and forming its continents and seas as the moon had done once. And swiftly on that Earth, as I have said, life had arisen in a myriad swarming forms, life that had produced at last the great race of turtle-creatures who had become dominant and who ruled by that time over all the Earth. And, as I have said, these turtle-creatures, with their growing science, had peered out and discovered the strange worm-folk whose mighty city lay beneath the moon's great gleaming roof. They had, by means of their light-signals, managed to communicate with them, and let them know that there was now an intelligent race on Earth, also.

"The worm-folk, in their great moon city, were surprised to learn that such a race of intelligent beings had arisen on Earth, for long before they had lost interest in Earth and its savage creatures. Now, though, welcoming the event as a break in the monotony of their lives in their airtight world, they communicated at length with the turtle-creatures on Earth, and finally began to devise a plan by which members of the two races might visit one another, by which they might cross the gulf that lay between moon and Earth. And finally the worm-folk, whose science was greater far than that of the turtle-creatures, devised a plan by which that gulf could be crossed, almost instantly and without danger. Communicating their plan and its details to the turtle-creatures on Earth, both races began to construct the apparatus that would enable them to cross the void.

"That apparatus, which the worm-folk had devised, was a great disk which shot forth a beam of terrific power, a beam whose pressure and power were due to the phenomenon of light-pressure. You know that light exerts a considerable pressure upon objects, which it strikes. You have seen the various methods by which physicists have measured this pressure, the various small mechanisms such as radiometers and the like which they have claimed to be driven by that pressure. Well, the disks, which the worm-folk had devised, shot forth a great light beam generated by mechanisms, which concentrated the pressure of a vast amount of light into one single, terrific beam. The worm-folk constructed a disk like that in a deep, vertical shaft on the moon's surface, while the turtle-creatures, following their communicated instructions, constructed a similar disk in a similar shaft on Earth. Then came the first trip across the space, made by a score of the worm-folk.

"These entered a cylinder specially made to insulate them against the cold of space, an hermetically tight cylinder which they placed upon the great disk in the shaft on the moon. This shaft was in the side of the moon, which is always turned toward Earth. They waited then, all but one in the cylinder. That one remained at the switch outside. Finally there came a great bell-signal, one which told them automatically that the two shafts, the one on the moon and the one on Earth, were facing each other exactly at that moment, pointing straight toward each other like two great cannon. As that signal sounded, the one at the switch threw that switch and leaped inside the cylinder, closing it. The next instant the great beam had driven up from the disk, had driven them up and outward, through a special valve-opening they had placed in their great transparent roof, out across the mighty void between moon and Earth. And that great beam, driving the cylinder before it by its own light-pressure, drove it on through space at almost the speed of light itself, just as an empty can, driven forward by the stream of water from a hose, will drive on at almost as great a speed as the stream about it rushes.

"Propelled through the gulf by the great beam at that awful velocity, it took one instant to flash the great cylinder from moon to Earth.

"From moon to Earth they flashed, and straight into the great shaft in the Earth's surface, down into that shaft. As they went down, the approach of their cylinder automatically turned on an opposing beam from the disk beneath them, which brought them swiftly and smoothly to a stop.

"Then the worm-folk emerged from their cylinder, the first travelers across the void, the first moon-beings to venture to Earth, and they were greeted by the turtle-creatures who had gathered about them in great numbers.

"The gravitation power of Earth, of course, was far greater than the gravitation power on the moon, but this did not trouble the worm-folks. They had devised something which would easily overcome that difficulty. As they came out from the cylinder, they boarded a small craft they had brought with them for the purpose, in which was embodied a mechanism that could increase or decrease the gravitational force about it at will, by either intensifying or weakening (whichever the circumstances demanded) with its own vibrations the vibrations of gravitational force. The worm-folk, therefore, could move freely about the Earth in their craft, and could inspect the cities of the turtle-creatures.

"After that first visit, many such visits were made, worm-folk flashing down to the Earth on the beam in their cylinders, while turtle-creatures flashed up to the moon in their cylinders on the beam from their shaft, in the same way. And the great worm-folk, whose science was so much greater than that of the turtle-creatures on Earth, taught them, instructed them, generously and unselfishly, gave to them out of their stores of science and knowledge, without suspicion or reserve. And ever the turtle-creatures learned from these mighty beings whose civilization had been great on the moon while Earth was still a fiery mass, learned and learned. Turtle-creatures flashed to the moon in numbers to inspect the great wonders of the airtight city that covered all the moon, to learn from the great worm-scientists the secrets which they had discovered, the control of nature's forces which they had attained to. While down to Earth from the moon came numbers of the worm-folk to help and to instruct the rising races of the turtle-creatures. An intercourse it was between Earth and moon, between two mighty and intelligent races of unlike beings, taking place eons, ages, before man or the forerunners of man had ever arisen on Earth!"

CHAPTER NINE
A Saga of Worlds

"SO THE two great races had dwelt together, one on the moon and one on the Earth, the older race of the worm-folk on the older world of the moon, and the younger turtle-creatures on the Earth. Following out the things they had learned from their instructors on the moon, the turtle-creatures reared greater and greater cities, came to greater and greater power. It must have seemed to them, indeed, that they were lords of Earth beyond any shadow of question, that none upon Earth dared doubt their will. But fate, if there is a fate that smiles grimly above our tiny worlds, was even then preparing a great catastrophe that was to rush upon them, a giant blind and brutal force of nature against which all their science and power could not stand. And that cataclysmic force that crept at last upon them with the thunder of doom was—the glacier.

"The glacier, mightiest of all forces that move upon this Earth, shaping Earth's very face with its slow, resistless movement! A gigantic tide of ice, sweeping southward and northward from the poles, across the face of Earth. Sweeping southward and northward at eon-long intervals as Earth's poles incline toward the sun, sending the giant polar ice-masses creeping across Earth's face toward the equator. Giant floods of irresistible ice, marching inexorably out across Earth from the polar regions and only receding from Earth's face when Earth's poles tilt away from the sun once more. The glacier, that carves the very mountains of Earth from out its surface, with grinding, inconceivable power—and that was the colossal icy doom that was creeping forth now upon the world of the turtle-creatures!

"Startled as they were by the first alarm, they rallied at once to repel this cataclysmic doom that was marching southward and northward upon them. Their first move was to devise great heat-producing mechanisms, mechanisms that shot forth giant rays of intense heat, and with which they sought to melt the oncoming glacial floods. But though these mighty rays instantly melted the ice-masses that they touched, those melted masses froze again when the heat rays were turned off. Also the great melting ice-masses soon flooded them so that the operation of the mighty ray-mechanisms was impossible, and they saw now that such rays could never hold back the glacial masses, even though they were kept constantly trained upon them, since resulting floods would sweep away the mechanisms, and then with their passing would freeze again to ice. Discarding this method, therefore, the turtle-creatures sought for others. They could not ask the worm-folk on the moon for aid in this, their great extremity, since they had become with passing ages proud of their own science and power, had rejected those who had been their teachers, so that the once great intercourse between moon and Earth had almost entirely ceased. They must fight their great battle alone, and they fought desperately.

"Their next move was the construction of a mighty moat or ditch across the glaciers' path, one that was miles wide and many miles deep, and which they hoped might stop the oncoming icy floods. Using great vibrations which broke down matter by destroying the chemical affinity between its atoms, separating those atoms from each other, they blasted, completely around the north and south polar regions, a giant moat that was a score of miles in depth and of equal width. The great ice-masses rolled on toward those giant moats, and into them, pouring into their great depths, so that for the time it seemed that their plan had been successful and that the march of the great glaciers had been halted. But still, steadily, slowly, remorselessly, those glacial floods were grinding on, on until soon they had filled even the great moats before them, were pouring on unchecked toward the equator.

"NORTHWARD and southward they swept, unchecked, and then the turtle-creatures saw at last that all their efforts were in vain, that there was no way by which these resistless icy floods could be halted in their titanic march over Earth's surface. Already their northernmost and southernmost cities were being overwhelmed by the giant ice-masses, those great ice floods surging across their cities, grinding into fragments their soaring structures, the great, many-sided and faceted buildings that made up those cities. From north and southward the turtle-creatures were fleeing from those cities, and it had now become evident that the great glaciers could not be stayed, and that the turtle-races could only stave off annihilation by flight from Earth, across which the great ice-floods were grinding! And there was but one place to which all the turtle-hordes could quickly flee, and that was to the Earth's moon!

"Yet how, the turtle-creatures asked themselves, could they hope to find a refuge on the moon? For it was covered completely with the great city of the worm-folk, whose transparent and airtight roof covered all the moon's surface. So great in number were the worm-folk that there could never be room upon the comparatively small moon for them and the turtle-creatures also. In hundreds of millions, in billions, swarmed the worm-folk in their strange vast covered city, and for the equally great hordes of the turtle-creatures to hope to share their moon-world with them was out of the question. There was but one chance left for them, the turtle-creatures decided, and that was to destroy utterly all the great worm-folk, and seize the moon-world for themselves.

"But what hope had they of doing this? They asked that question of each other. What hope had they of conquering and destroying the great worm-folk, who were farther advanced in science and power than they were, and who were equal in number to themselves? They could send invading parties of turtle-men out to the moon on the great beam, but such invaders would never return; they would be annihilated instantly by the terrific weapons, which they knew that the worm-folk possessed. It never occurred to any of the turtle-creatures that it was blackest treachery they were proposing in this contemplated annihilation of the friendly worm-folk, who had helped and instructed them through their own scientific knowledge. To the turtle-creatures' cold, unsympathetic minds, the right and wrong of the thing did not exist. Their problem was to find some way in which they might quickly annihilate the whole races of the worm-folk, and seize their world, and that problem seemed insoluble to them.

"But at last, spurred on by the cruel menace of the grinding glaciers that were marching steadily over Earth's surface, the turtle-creatures found an answer to that problem. They found a method by which all the mighty races of the worm-folk on the moon could be annihilated, in a single moment. They found a way by which, without the slightest danger to themselves, they could instantly depopulate the whole moon-world. And that method, the weapon which they could use for it, was the great beam of light-pressure that shot the cylinders back and forth to the moon, the great beam which the worm-folk themselves had devised for them!

"The center of the turtle-creatures' great plan was the fact that the airtight city of the worm-folk, its mighty transparent roof, extended over all the moon's surface. As I have said, the worm-folk, being air-breathing beings like the turtle-creatures, like ourselves, like almost every form of life, had made that great roof airtight, so that their artificial atmosphere inside it could not escape to the vacuum of outer space. For around and outside that mighty shield there lay only the utter vacuum and cold of the outer void, and well they knew that if any openings were in their great roof, all their atmosphere would instantly rush out through those openings, into the great void outside, just as a container of air, if opened within a vacuum, would instantly lose its air into that vacuum. An opening in the great roof, indeed, would mean that the moon-world beneath that roof would be stripped in an instant of all its air, and that in that same instant the whole race of the worm-folk would be demolished by the vanishing of the air that meant life. For this reason they had been extremely careful in building their great roof to make it quite hermetically sealed and airtight, since an opening in it meant instant death to them.

"The turtle-creatures knew this well, for many of them had visited the moon-world when intercourse between moon and

Earth, between the worm-folk and turtle-creatures, had been frequent. Now they remembered it; they made it the basis for their gigantic plan. That plan, which was now well formulated, was merely to suddenly puncture in many places the great roof of the worm-folk! The whole artificial atmosphere of their moon-world would instantly rush forth into space, and in that instant the worm-folk would be annihilated, and the turtle-creatures could then proceed up to the moon-world in all their hordes, could repair the punctured roof and take possession of the moon, and live upon it in safety while the great glacial tides rolled across their own world of Earth!

"Such was the plan of the turtle-creatures, and they only needed a weapon with which to put it into effect, to puncture the great roof of the moon-world. And, in the great light-pressure beam that had driven their cylinders back and forth, they found such a weapon. That great beam exerted colossal pressure, pushed forward with terrific force, due to the vast amount of light whose pressure was concentrated within its ray. The beam's pressure they had used to drive their cylinders back and forth from Earth to moon, but now they planned to use it for their great plan, to use it to puncture the moon-world's mighty roof. For they knew that the great beam's awful pressure and force would, if turned upon that roof, drive through it as a stream of water from a powerful hose would drive through paper.

"THUS DID the turtle-creatures plan to annihilate at one stroke the worm-folk in all their millions, and now at once they began to put their plan into effect. Concealing completely their preparations and intentions from the worm-folk on the moon, with whom their intercourse was now very limited, they prepared hundreds of great disks capable of shooting forth the mighty light-pressure beams, placing them in great batteries over one side of Earth, aiming them all toward the moon. Swiftly they completed and placed these masses of mighty disks, while ever southward and northward toward them the menacing glaciers came over the land. At last all the disks were ready, and they waited only until a few nights had passed, until the moon was full, that they might stab their hundreds of great beams upward with greater accuracy. They knew that even a single great puncture in the moon-world's roof would slay instantly all its inhabitants, but they desired to take no chances, and so had prepared the hundreds of disks that they might puncture that roof simultaneously in hundreds of places.

"The few nights of waiting passed soon enough. At last the full moon rose and the turtle-creatures knew that their moment had come. A moment it must have been in which all the universe held its breath, a moment in which the one great race on Earth, prepared to loose annihilation upon the other great friendly and unsuspecting race on the moon. Upward toward the zenith rose the full moon, the great gleaming roof over it gleaming now in splendor for the last time, while the turtle-creatures, in grim masses, stood waiting about their great batteries of disks on Earth. Stood waiting until the moon was almost directly overhead. Then across the whole side of Earth flashed a signal, and in the next moment the hundreds of waiting disks had loosed their brilliant beams, had sent those awful beams of force driving straight toward the moon and the great gleaming roof that covered it!

"The turtle-creatures, watching from Earth with their great telescopes, saw those beams strike the moon's face in hundreds of different places across its circle, saw them drive in through the great airtight roof and into the moon's surface with terrific power. And as they did so, as they shattered the mighty roof before them, they perceived with their instruments that out from beneath the shattered roof there rushed through the great openings within an instant all the moon-world's artificial atmosphere shown by clouds of vapor, knew that in that instant all life upon the moon had perished! Knew that their giant beams had indeed punctured and broken the airtight roof of the moon in hundreds of places, and that all the worm-folk races had gone to instant death, when their atmosphere rushed out into the void! The turtle-creatures had with their one mighty stroke annihilated the life of a world!

"The giant beams that they had shot forth in hundreds had indeed crashed through the great transparent roof, but so terrific in power were they that they had driven onward with unchecked force, had driven with all their awful force into the face of the moon itself And blasting into the moon's surface with all the terrible power that was theirs, they had instantly gouged great circular holes or craters out of the moon's surface in hundreds of places, just as a stream of water shot forth at great force against a level surface of Earth will gouge in that surface a great hole or crater.

"It was thus that the hundreds of great craters that pit the face of the moon, that looks towards the Earth, came into being, craters that have always puzzled the science of us humans. You know that it has been suggested that great meteorites striking the moon caused those craters, but that was impossible, for if those bodies had struck the moon when it was solid, the meteorites themselves, though half-buried perhaps, would still be visible at the center of the great craters, and no such meteorites can be seen. If, on the other hand, they struck the moon while it was still semi-liquid at the surface, the craters they made would have closed up, flowed together smoothly again. It was not volcanic activity or meteorites that had formed those great craters, but the hundreds of giant beams from Earth, gouging out those craters with inconceivable force, but leaving no trace of themselves.

"The turtle-creatures, however, were triumphant over the complete success of their mighty plan, and at once began to prepare to migrate in all their hordes to the moon, for it would not be long before the great glacial tides closed ever in upon them. Their first move was to send up a party of turtle-creatures to the moon in cylinders, driving them up with the beam here on Earth, and equipping their cylinders with special apparatus to allow them to land safely on the moon, since the other transportation disk on the moon had of course been destroyed by the cataclysmic power of the hundreds of beams that had struck the earthward side of the moon. These first turtle-creatures reached the moon's earthward side safely, and found it a scene of terrific death. Beneath the punctured and broken roof, amid the giant craters that had been gouged from the earthward surface, lay the millions of the worm-folk, slain instantly when their atmosphere had rushed forth into the void through the openings in their great roof. The exploring turtle-creatures, protected from the vacuum about them by special airtight craft, moved around to the moon's other side and found the city there filled with the worm-folk dead, too. The great roof was intact on that other side, and there were no giant craters, since it was only toward that side of the moon visible from Earth that the great beams had stabbed.

"THE TURTLE-CREATURES on Earth, after hearing the signaled news from the party they had sent to the moon, began preparations for the great migration of all their hordes, but before doing so they reached a momentous decision, namely, that they would settle only upon the other side of the moon, and not upon its earthward side at all, because, they reasoned, we of Earth have slain all on the moon by stabbing with our beams at its earthward side and puncturing the great roof there. If we settle over all the moon, they said, rebuild that great roof on the moon's earthward side, we will be laying ourselves open to the same terrible fate. For if any other race of intelligent creatures ever rose on Earth in the future, they could slay all the turtle-creatures on the moon by the same method that we used to eliminate the worm-folk. But if the turtle-creatures settled only upon the moon's other side, which was turned always away from the Earth, it would be impossible for any on Earth to reach them or puncture their roof with rays, or even to know of their presence.

"For these reasons, therefore, the turtle-creatures decided to settle upon the moon's other side only, and they made that decision the more willingly since the moon's earthward side was torn now with gigantic craters that their beams had caused. Sending a larger party of thousands up to the moon, then, these thousands prepared for their coming. They first closed in the great transparent roof, which still stretched unbroken over all the moon's other side, building transparent walls from it down to the moon's surface so that the whole other side was completely enclosed, the earthward side broken and shattered and neglected by them. It was not exactly half the moon's surface they enclosed in that other side, since a little more than half can be seen from Earth. It was just a little less than half, the limiting walls of their great roof being placed on either side just far enough around the moon's other side so that they could not be visible at all from our Earth.

"This done, the turtle-creatures working there put into operation the great atmosphere-plants, which again turned forth their artificial atmosphere, serving now but half the moon, yet maintaining within the transparent and airtight roof of that half a breathable and perfect atmosphere. The turtle-creatures had by then destroyed completely the strange subterranean cities of the worm-folk and their dead millions, themselves constructing in place of them giant crystal-like buildings of metal, angled and faceted and strange, like those of the turtle-creatures on Earth. They then set themselves to overcome the last obstacle that remained to prevent the turtle-hordes from moving to the moon, that obstacle being the difference in gravitational power between moon and Earth.

"For the gravitational power of the moon was, as I have said, one-sixth that of Earth, and the turtle-creatures, accustomed to the greater gravity of Earth, could not live long on the moon, the weaker gravity there affecting their internal structure fatally. The visitors who had gone from Earth to moon formerly, though, and those of the worm-folk who had come from moon to Earth, had overcome this change of gravitational power in the way that I have already described, by using craft in which were mechanisms that altered the gravitational power about them at will; increasing that power by generating a vibration which was tuned to increase the intensity of the vibrations of gravitational force; and decreasing that power by generating a vibration tuned to dampen or decrease the vibrations of gravitational force.

"It was by means of these generating mechanisms that the turtle-creatures had visited the moon in the past, had sent their thousands of workers there now, increasing the moon's gravitational power by means of those mechanisms until it was, in their craft, the same as on Earth. Now they began to build similar generators, but of gigantic power and size, mighty generators that would be able to change the gravitational power on the moon's whole other side, increasing that power there until it was the same as on Earth! They built these great generators, then buried here and there beneath the surface on the moon's other side, generators that functioned automatically and unceasingly and that made the moon's other side the same as Earth, as far as gravity was concerned. The turtle-creatures could walk about that surface at will, unhampered, and without ill effects; they could live there as they did on Earth.

"All was ready; the great airtight city that covered almost all the moon's other side, the artificial atmosphere that was maintained within it, the change of gravity that had been made. All was ready to come to the final step of their gigantic plan, to bring the hordes of the turtle-creatures from Earth to moon. They must be brought soon, for by this time the great glaciers had covered almost all the Earth; yet here the laboring turtle-creatures upon the moon met another obstacle. How were they to bring those vast hordes from the Earth to the other side of the moon? They could not drive them up in cylinders straight toward that other side, since that other side was never turned toward Earth. Neither could they bring them up to the moon's earthward side, a barren and airless desert of great wreckage, and transport them around in airtight craft to the other side. They had done that with their first thousands of workers, but could not hope to do so with all the turtle-creature millions on Earth, in the limited time that was left. Pondering this difficulty, the turtle-creatures on the moon again brushed aside all difficulties to solve the problem in the most direct manner.

"THEIR SOLUTION of that problem was a truly titanic one. They planned to pierce a great shaft clear through the moon, from its earthward side to the other side. That shaft, with an airlock, opening in the heart of their great airtight city on the other side, would enable them to bring their hordes straight from Earth to that other side, across the gulf of space in the great cylinders, driven by the mighty beam, and on through the great shaft, through the moon, to emerge into the airtight city on its other side. So the turtle-creatures on the moon commenced work at once upon that great project, and in heated frenzy they labored upon it to complete it in time to bring their races from Earth. Using the great vibrations they had used before, which destroyed matter by destroying the affinity of its atoms, they steadily blasted a great circular or cylindrical shaft straight through the moon's sphere. That shaft opened on the moon's earthward side in the great crater that we now call Copernicus, while its end at the moon's other side was just beneath the great plaza that lies at the center of their city.

"In that plaza, then, at the shaft's end, they placed one of the great disks to shoot forth the mighty light-pressure beam, a disk which could shoot its beam *downward*, through the shaft, through the moon and across the Earth, and *upward* toward the great transparent roof above. The beam, if turned *upward* from the disk, would crash up and through the transparent roof above, would puncture that roof and allow the great airtight city's atmosphere to rush out into space, of course, and slay instantly all the turtle-creatures as they had slain the worm-folk. They did not plan to use the beam that way, but placed the great disk there and made it possible to shoot its beam upward so that, if they wished, in the far future, to visit one of the other planets with that beam, they would be able to construct an airlock and a valve-opening in the roof just above the disk, and drive cylinders out and upward to other planets in that way. They feared, somehow, that Earth would possibly never again be fit for habitation even though the icy glaciers receded, and they desired to have some way of reaching other planets which they could not reach by sending the beam downward. This upward beam, though, was never used by them, nor was any valve-opening ever constructed above. In time they gave up the thought of reaching other planets. But the beam still could be shot upward, by means of the great switch at the opening in the plaza.

"So, having placed the disk there in the plaza, with its beam capable of being shot downward or upward, all was ready for the coming of the turtle-creatures in all their hordes from Earth. A great central disk had been prepared on Earth, in what is now Yucatan, since except for a belt of the Earth's tropical regions, the mighty glaciers had swept out by then until they covered all Earth. At the center of a great mound they had sunk their shaft, placing at its bottom the great disk, taking to it the thousands of cylinders that would be necessary to transport the races of turtle-creatures from Earth to moon. Then, when all was ready, the first of those cylinders was placed upon the disk, with others waiting beside it. Into the cylinder there went the great flying-craft of the turtle-creatures, their great flying-circles, propelled by the same method of gravitation-change they had already used, flying-circles that filled that cylinder, masses of the turtle-creatures upon them. There was a wait then, until the moon was directly overhead, the great shaft through it directly in line with the shaft in the mound. Then at that exact moment, a great bell-signal sounded automatically, the disk's mechanism was turned on, and in an instant the cylinder and its freight of turtle-creatures was driving out across the gulf to the moon.

"Out through the void it drove with lightning-speed, within instants, toward the crater of Copernicus, toward the great shaft in it, clicking on through that shaft through the moon; through a great valve or door in the shaft that opened automatically before it and closed as swiftly behind it, an airlock and valves that prevented the escape of the airtight city's air through the shaft, through the sphere of the moon itself, coming to rest beneath the great disk there in the plaza. Instantly the cylinder was snapped aside, for even as it had flashed out through the void, others loaded likewise were flashing out after it, in the few seconds that the two shafts on Earth and moon were in line.

"So each night, as moon and Earth faced each other with the shafts in each, the disks in each, in line, the turtle-creatures on Earth sent more of their cylinders driving out, until within weeks the last of all the turtle-creatures on Earth were leaving it—leaving it in the last cylinder, turning on the beam and clicking up through space from that disk in their cylinder. The whole races of the turtle-creatures had been flashed from Earth to moon on the great beam in those cylinders, cylinders that had been flashed back empty from the moon to be driven up again with new loads, until all the turtle-races had passed up thus from Earth to moon, to their airtight city on the other side of the moon. A mighty migration of countless millions of beings, from world to spinning world!"

CHAPTER TEN
To Crash Down Man Forever!

"SO AT last, at the last moment, the turtle-creatures had saved themselves from doom, had moved in a mighty mass from Earth to moon. Settling in all their hordes in their mighty city upon the moon's far side, they took up life as comfortably and as safely as on Earth. The air they breathed was made for them artificially by their great atmosphere-plants, and enclosed beneath the mighty transparent roof. The power of the moon's gravity had been increased to that of Earth by the generators beneath their great city. Nothing had been forgotten that might serve their comfort, and they had found in their mighty airtight city on the other side of the moon a safe refuge from the great glacier floods that were rolling across the Earth.

"For on Earth, as they could see now, those mighty glacial tides had forged on until all but a small part of Earth's surface was covered by them, grinding on across the Earth and obliterating beneath them the crushed and shattered cities of the turtle-creatures over which they forged. Safe on the moon's other side, though, the turtle-creatures gave but small attention to Earth, beginning again their life in that strange city. Gradually they became accustomed to the long lunar days and night, each of approximately two weeks length, and by scientifically changing some of the characteristics of their own bodies were able to live as usual through the dusk of the lunar nights, nights but softly illuminated by the circles of light they had set in their buildings' sides, and they were able also to remain in unhindered life and movement during the two weeks of the lunar day, not being bothered by the length of that brilliant day. They became, in fact, completely habituated to the moon, almost forgetting that they had ever lived upon the Earth.

"Almost forgotten, too, was the moon's earthward side, since hardly ever did any venture from their comfortable airtight city on the far, side to the airless, savage and barren surface of the near or earthward side. Upon that side still yawned the mighty craters gouged out by the great beams, and about and among those craters there lay the remnants of the great wrecked city of the worm-folk that had once covered the moon's earthward side, the remnants of the great gleaming roof that had once covered that side also. Those great gleaming fragments of the shattered roof lay most thick about the crater that we call Tycho, though they extended here and there across the moon's whole earthward side. Because of that, because their gleaming surface reflected back the sunlight brilliantly, Tycho and the brilliant-gleaming region about it were to be a great mystery to man and the science of man, who could not know that those great gleaming regions marked the last shattered remnants of the giant roof of the worm-folk, that had once extended over the moon's whole earthward side.

"Forgotten by the turtle-creatures, who could not even see it from the great city on the moon's other side, Earth worked on toward its destiny. The great glaciers that had covered almost all its surface moved northward and southward almost to the equators, lay for ages upon that surface, so that the Earth was a barren world of ice, a great frozen desert. It almost seemed that the thought of the turtle-creatures had been right and that Earth would never again be the abode of life. But at last the sun's heat falling upon its central regions, the glaciers that layover those regions began to recede. Slowly, sullenly, but steadily, the great ice-floods receded back to the polar regions to north and south, until once more the rest of Earth's surface lay warm and habitable, scarred and scored with deep valleys and great mountain ranges by the glaciers that had passed over it. The ice terror had passed and Earth was again a world in which life could flourish.

"Life, though, had been almost wholly wiped from Earth's surface by those grinding floods of ice. The great race of the turtle-creatures was gone, fled to the moon, and the other forms of life, the great reptilian forms of Earth's youth, had perished beneath the ice. Only smaller forms were left now, forms that had preserved themselves in sea and on land, and now these remaining forms began to increase and multiply as the glaciers went back and the Earth grew warm once more. Changing into a myriad protean shapes, climbing upward on the path of evolution with the spur of cruel conditions ever behind it, life surged through countless forms, from saurian to mammal, while at last, out of the mammal forms, there rose the first crude ape-like creatures that were the progenitors of man.

"So, at last, out of that ruck of changing species, of shifting forms and characteristics, there rose the races of man, moving upward with ever-increasing intelligence, from troglodyte to savage to modern man. And man had become lord of all Earth, never dreaming or suspecting that long before him there had ruled on Earth the turtle-creatures, whose civilization and science were as great or greater than that of man. For though men sent their vision searching into space, as their predecessors had done long before them, though they saw and photographed the giant craters on the moon, the strange-gleaming patches upon that moon, never did they dream of the true terrible origin of those craters and gleaming patches. Never did they guess that even then, out on the other side of the moon which man had never seen, there stretched the colossal, airtight city in which the turtle-creatures in their millions still went their ways.

"Nor did the turtle-creatures, within that city, have more knowledge of this new race of man that had risen to be lords of Earth. For long ago, as I have said, the turtle-creatures had lost all interest in the Earth from which they had come. Comfortable and safe in their strange, great moon city, they had noticed that the glaciers had receded, had supposed that new forms of life would arise on Earth, but had not been enough interested in the possibility to send even a single party of explorers back to Earth. The great disk in the central plaza of their city, and the shaft that led down through the moon from it, were unused, during all those centuries, those ages. The turtle-creatures had forgotten Earth.

"So, forgetting it, they lived on in their moon city, but at last there came to disturb their safe life the looming specter of a great menace that threatened their existence—a menace slower and subtler and less spectacular than the glaciers that had driven them from Earth, but fully as deadly. Their artificial air and water supplies threatened to fail them. For, as I have said, there was no air or water upon the moon, save a little frozen vapor lingering in its craters. Artificially, though, the turtle-creatures, like the worm-folk before them, had manufactured their own air and water supplies by the great atmosphere and water plants set here and there in their city.

"THESE GREAT plants produced their air and water by a combined process of chemical analysis and synthesis, carried on on a vast scale. Their first step was to take great quantities of certain of the moon's compounds, compounds containing hydrogen and nitrogen and oxygen. Then, by treating these in great masses with an altered form of their matter-destroying vibrations, they destroyed the chemical affinity of the atoms of those compounds, loosing those atoms one from the other, breaking up the compounds into their original elements. The atoms of hydrogen and oxygen and nitrogen thus released were drawn off from this first disintegrating process into huge underground tanks or containers in which the gases were stored.

"From these great containers the gases were drawn forth at will, and hydrogen and oxygen atoms were mixed together automatically, two atoms of hydrogen to one of oxygen, to form H_2O or water. In the same way four nitrogen atoms would be combined with one of oxygen, in vast quantities, to form air. This is, of course, but a brief outline of the turtle-creatures' process, which was in reality more complicated. From these great central mixing plants the water supplies were piped to every portion of the moon-city, while the atmosphere supplies were automatically loosed at the exact rate required to replenish the atmosphere beneath their great roof. The whole of this vast process was carried on by automatic machinery, requiring but small attention on the part of the turtle-creatures, and they saw no reason why it could not be continued indefinitely.

"But now, at last, they had come to see that soon those processes would come to a halt, for lack of the elements that were vital to them.

"More and more difficult was it becoming to procure supplies of the compounds which they disintegrated to get their supplies of nitrogen and oxygen and hydrogen, since it was but a certain number of compounds that could be used by their process with any degree of effectiveness. And these compounds were not plentiful in the moon's materials, and had already been used for ages, by the turtle-creatures and by the worm-folk long before them. Deeper into the bowels of the moon they penetrated for the compounds that gave them their water and air, but they began to see that before long those compounds would be almost wholly unavailable, and the moon would no longer be habitable for them.

"Realizing this, they began to look about them once more for a new place of refuge from the doom that was once more overtaking them. Naturally enough, they had no inclination to become a totally extinct race—at least, not without a definite struggle for survival.

"Their first thought was of the sun's other planets, since there in their central plaza they still had the great disk whose beam could be shot upward and out into space, once they constructed the necessary airlock valve in the transparent roof above it. But after considering the situation, they saw that escape to one of the other planets was out of the question, because even if there were one habitable for them, it would take a considerable time to transport all their hordes across the space from the moon to such a planet. And they knew that they did not have much time in which to work—they knew their time was very limited.

"Seeing this, they turned their thoughts, after the passing of ages, back to Earth once more, to the Earth from which they had come. Peering across the gulf toward it with their instruments, they saw that, as they had noted before, the great glaciers had long ago receded, and saw, too, that Earth had become warm and habitable. To pour all their hordes back to Earth from the moon would take little time, since the disk at their city's center could shoot their cylinders straight down their great shaft through the moon and across to Earth. The shaft on Earth, too, they thought, and the disk inside it must still be lying unharmed in the depths of what is now Yucatan, since they had sunk that shaft in the great mound where it was protected from the shifting dirt of ages, and they knew that the great glaciers had not quite reached the region in which that mound was located.

"Earth, then, was a sate refuge for them again, the more so because they had originated there and its gravitational power would be what they were always accustomed to, on Earth and on the moon.

"ONE THING, however, prevented them from pouring down to Earth in all their hordes at once. During the ages that had passed, some new race of intelligent beings might have arisen on Earth, which the moon-creatures would have to fight with, when they descended on Earth.

"They decided, therefore, to send an exploring party down in a single cylinder, to make certain of Earth's present habitable condition and to find out the power and intelligence of any race that happened to have risen to supremacy on this planet.

"A hundred or more of the turtle-creatures, therefore, rose on their flying-circles and moved into one of the great cylinders. That cylinder was snapped into the framework beneath the great disk, and the beam was turned on.

"A moment more and that beam was driving the cylinder down through the shaft, down through the moon and out its earthward side, out across the gulf once more, to flash down into the great shaft in Yucatan and come to rest within it, flying across the void from moon to Earth at the moment when the two shafts were in line as they had been before.

"Down into the shaft in Yucatan their first raiding party had dropped, a shaft near which fate had brought our own scientific party. Then out of that shaft on their flying-circles came the moon raiders, the turtle-creatures, slaying Willings and the rest, imprisoning me as a specimen of Earth's races. Swiftly and scientifically they proceeded on their survey, taking all the instruments, books and papers in our tents, taking samples of Earth and air and water, taking specimens of the bird and beast and insect life about them, gathering all the information possible from about them, to take them back with them to their fellow millions in the great city on the other side of the moon. And back to that city on the next night they had gone, back up to the moon and through it to the great moon city on its other side, back with me and with their gathered specimens and data to the great Council of Three Thousand before which I had been taken and subsequently questioned.

"Then I was imprisoned in the great Council Building, and those turtle-creatures who instructed me in their strange tongue and who told me this gigantic saga of the turtle-races, this tremendous chronicle of eons of time and vast voids of space and tremendous dooms of worlds, that I have just told to you, had come. And hearing that great tale I, Howland, understood at last the true awful significance of that swift descent on Earth by the moon raiders, understood at last what terrible doom it was that hung over the Earth now as the turtle-creatures prepared to pour down upon it once more. But then, as I learned enough of the turtle-creatures' tongue to roughly speak and understand it, I was taken again before the Council of Three Thousand for questioning.

"There, with the great Council about me and the Council of Three questioning me, they examined me as to the state of affairs on Earth. They had learned much, I found, from the books and papers and instruments that their raiders had brought back from our camp, and which they had been soon able to decipher. But when the Council of Three questioned me, I refused absolutely to answer them. Well I knew that my refusal would gain Earth no respite, that death was the doom that awaited me for such refusal, yet I would not help them in the slightest in their terrible plan that meant the annihilation of the world of man. And when the Council of Three saw this, they ordered me back to this cell, to be kept alive, so that their scientists might experiment on me, in the hope of finding some way by which human intelligence could be blotted out without affecting the human body, so that when they will have conquered Earth they could spare from the annihilation of its peoples enough humans to serve them as slaves and machine-tenders.

"It was only a few days ago that I was brought back to this cell, for while I had been held in it and had learned their tongue, the long lunar night had waned and the brilliant lunar day had waxed across the city, and had waned to give place to the dusk of night once more, the dusk of this night that is about us now. During night and day and night again, without ceasing, I had seen their great preparations going on unremittingly in all the mighty city about me, had seen their flying-circles massing their great stores of weapons and instruments and materials, preparing to pour into the great cylinders beneath the plaza, to flash down in those cylinders to Earth in their first great attack on the inhabitants of that planet.

"Within days more, as I had heard from the Council, that attack would take place, the first masses of cylinders flashing down the beam to Earth when the bell-note sounds to mark the time when the shaft through the moon and the shaft on Earth are in line. Each twenty-four hours, during the last days, I've heard that distant great note, and each one seemed a note knelling the doom of our world. Several hours ago, when I heard the note again, I knew the next time it sounded it would mean the end, for when the bell-note sounds again, when the two shafts are in line as they will be again in a few hours, the time will have come for the great attack and the moon-creatures will be pouring down to Earth on the great beam in their cylinders. I did not dream, though, when I heard that last note sound that you three were flashing up from Earth and the disk on Earth, upon the great beam in your cylinder, through the moon and out into the moon city to find me. I never dreamed that, until Carson and Trent were brought and imprisoned here with me, to serve with me, as specimens for the experiments of the turtle-scientists.

"Now, Carson, Trent and Foster, you know all; you know the great doom that's looming, gathering above our Earth. For even now, in the great city about us, the turtle-creatures are completing their last preparations, gathering together all the flying-circles and forces that will be launched down upon Earth. Within hardly more than a dozen hours the great bell-note from the plaza will sound again, will mark once more the moment when shaft on Earth and shaft through moon are in line. And when that signal sounds countless cylinders in masses, filled with terrific, irresistible hordes of flying-circles and turtle-creatures, will be driving down to Earth on the great beam! Will be pouring down to Earth to annihilate humanity as they annihilated the worm-folk, to crash down man and the supremacy of man forever, and make the turtle-creatures once more the masters of all the Earth!"

CHAPTER ELEVEN
A Fight for Freedom

"THE TURTLE-CREATURES once more the masters of all the Earth!"

Howland's words, in the silence that followed his story, seemed vibrating in the little cell about us, like the note of some great warning bell, a bell that was striking the doom of Earth. I seemed to see, in that moment, a swift succession of pictures in the dusk of the place; seemed to see cylinders in hundreds, thousands, flashing down from moon to Earth on the great beam; seemed to see those cylinders giving forth their freight of flying-circles and turtle-creatures, those flying-circles flashing north and south and east and west from the shaft in Yucatan, out over all the world of man; seemed to see dreadnaughts and artillery and airplanes vanquished and destroyed, reeling back before the swift and mighty flying-circles, the deadly vacuum rays, millions of man's great cities' inhabitants going to death beneath those rays; seemed to see Earth covered once more with the giant faceted buildings of the cities of the turtle-creatures, as it had been once long before, with those monstrous creatures ruling Earth from pole to pole and the races of man annihilated, save for a few mindless things left as slaves to the turtle-creatures!

Beneath that awful vision my brain reeled, while Carson and Trent and Howland beside me stared with brooding eyes that held a horror as great as my own. Through the triangular opening in the wall we could gaze out over the great dusky moon city, swarming still as before with turtle-creatures and flying-circles, with all the mighty hordes of the moon-creatures, gathering their forces now for their first great attack on Earth. And, gazing out across that mighty city with the titanic saga, which Howland had just related, vibrating still in our minds, gazing out across that great city that stood where eons before the strange city of the worm-folk had stood, our minds could grasp but one great fact of all that crowded upon them, could comprehend but the one great horror of what had just been revealed to us.

"The turtle-creatures once more the masters of all the Earth—and we who alone could warn Earth imprisoned here!" exclaimed Carson.

"Imprisoned here without hope of escape," assented Howland somberly. "And within hours, now, their great attack begins. When the great bell-signal beneath the plaza sounds three notes, it will be the signal for the turtle-creatures' flying-circles and forces across all the city to start toward the plaza, to enter the cylinders beneath it so that when the single great note sounds they may be shot down to Earth on the beam."

"But *is* there no hope of escape?" I cried. "Isn't there any way by which we, who alone know of it, can halt this deadly invasion?"

Howland looked at me thoughtfully. "There is a way," he said slowly, and afterward I was to remember his words, "a way by which the menace of these turtle-creatures might be removed forever, could we but escape from here. Yet how can we win free of this cell?"

Hopelessly we looked about us. The cell's door, which seemed to the eye quite open and unbarred, was in reality barred more securely than by steel, closed unchangeably to us by the sheet of invisible force across it, through which no matter could penetrate. Nor, when we turned to the window, were our hopes raised in the least. For that window, though quite open and large enough to allow us to pass through it, was set directly in the outer wall of the great building, in one of the great smooth facets of that building's side. Below and above stretched the mighty structure's wall, for it was hundreds of feet from our window to the crowded streets below, and almost as great a distance to the roof. The facet in which our window was set, too, was quite vertical, the one beneath it slanting inward and the one above it slanting inward, too, like the face of a great gem exactly. Without rope of any kind, we knew that to attempt escape from the window would be but to meet instant death.

Yet we could not give up hope of escape, hope of finding some way to escape from our prison and to get to the great chamber beneath the plaza, to get to one of the cylinders and back to warn the Earth. We examined every corner of our dusky cell, inspected door and window exhaustively, but in vain. We could find no way of escape, while through the corridors outside we could discern a ceaseless movement of turtle-figures, bearing their loads of weapons and instruments and materials up through the great building to its roof, loading them, apparently, upon the flying-circles that rested there awaiting the great signal of three notes that would send them and those from all the city toward the plaza to enter the cylinders beneath it. Soon now, within a few more hours, we knew, those three warning notes would be sounding; at the thought a rage of despair seized us. It was then that Howland, who had sat motionless, wrapped in thoughts of his own, beckoned us to his side.

"There is but one chance in thousands for us to escape from this cell," he told us, quickly. "But with only an almost certain death ahead of us, we must take that chance, and soon. Each twenty-four hours food has been brought me here by two guards, and if they come as they should again, within the next hour or so, we will have that one chance to escape."

Then he went on to explain to us the plan that he had formed, while Carson and Trent and I listened intently. Simple enough and desperate, too, was the plan he proposed, yet it was at the same time the one way by which we had even the faintest hope of escaping from our cell, so without further discussion we agreed upon it. It seemed possible that by it one or two of us, in any case, might be able to escape from the cell, and it was agreed that whoever did so should make for the roof and endeavor to steal a flying-circle and head toward the great plaza and the chamber of cylinders beneath it. The whole scheme, of course, was perhaps the most desperate and reckless one possible, yet it was, as Howland said, a chance, and as such we grasped at it eagerly. Then, since all depended upon the coming of turtle-guards with food, we waited anxiously for their coming, when we might put the scheme into effect.

NOW, LOOKING back, it seems to me that the time that followed was almost the most agonizing I ever spent—the time in which we sat motionless and silent there in the dusky cell, awaiting the coming of the two guards. Carson watching at the force-defended entrance, Howland and Trent and I seated across the room, we waited in silence. And never, surely, could there have been a stranger scene than the one we must have formed. Four men, white-faced and unmoving and silent, seated there in the dusky cell in the mighty building's side, with groups of busy and monstrous turtle-creatures pouring through the corridors beyond, with other masses of turtle-creatures surging through the streets of the colossal dim-lit city about us, with flying-circles throbbing thickly through the air, all gathering here on the moon's far side, beneath the great transparent roof that covered that side, to pour down within hours, now, upon Earth and the races of Earth.

Slowly the minutes passed, their passage unmarked by any change in the unceasing dusk of the city about us, nor in that city's activities. Would the turtle-guards not come, after all? Had we been forgotten in the great preparations going on, and was our last wild chance to be lost to us? Tensely, despairingly, we waited, knowing now that but little more than an hour remained before the three great notes from the plaza would sound, before the moon hordes would be massing toward that plaza, and the great chamber beneath it. Now we heard the activities in the city without, in the great building's corridors, slowing, ceasing, and we looked at each other with startled eyes. The turtle-creatures' preparations were complete and their first great attack was ready to be launched!

There was a sound as of many turtle-creatures moving down from the building's roof through its interior, a sound of many heavy steps and of deep, bass voices, and then these seemed to have passed, and again there reigned a sudden silence in the great building and in the city without. Gazing out from the window we could see that the great flying-circles throbbing to and fro seemed to have settled in masses upon the roofs of the great buildings, that the turtle-hordes were gathered together in crowds, surging no longer through the streets. They were waiting—waiting for the great force which within the hour would be pouring into the cylinders beneath the plaza, to flash down to Earth! As realization of all this, of our swift-waning time, struck me, I wheeled from the window with an exclamation on my lips. But before I could utter it, Carson had whirled silently from the door by which he watched, his hand raised toward us.

"The turtle-guards!" he whispered. "They are coming!"

Struck motionless and silent by his words we listened for an instant, then we heard clearly the sound of heavy steps approaching us on the metal floor of the corridor outside, of deep bass voices rapidly nearing us. At once, then, we put into execution the plan we had formed, for these coming ones could be none other than the guards, the turtle-guards with our food. Throwing ourselves upon the cell's floor, therefore, we lay there quite motionless, I near the door, Carson and Trent a little away from me, and Howland at the dusky room's other side. There, lying completely stiff and motionless, with closed eyes, we awaited with trembling nerves the coming of the turtle-creatures.

A moment more and they were outside our invisible force-door, halting there. Lying facing them, without moving a muscle of my body that might be noticed, I opened my eyes slightly and saw them through my lashes, halting outside. I saw one reach forth to touch a stud on the wall outside, heard a click, and then, though all was as before, I knew that the force-door had been lifted from across the opening. Then through that opening came carefully, watchfully, the great turtle-creatures, and as I saw them I almost cried aloud in my despair. For these were not the two guards that had brought Howland's food, and whom we had expected, upon whose coming our plan had hinged! These were five in number, four of them armed with ray-hemispheres that they kept trained upon us, the other unarmed and seeming to command them, an air of authority apparent in his tones and manner. And as I saw him I comprehended in a flash the thing that a malign fate had put upon us. These guards and that commanding one came to our cell only to take us to the laboratories of the turtle-scientists!

Utterly cold went my heart as I divined this, yet even so I moved no muscle as the four guards and their leader came in toward us. I saw them stop in amazement as they looked down upon us lying prone upon the floor, saw their weapons turned towards us still, as though fearful of some surprise. The leading turtle-creature, surveying us in something like surprise, spoke aloud to us in his deep tones, evidently to arouse us, but we didn't move. We remained stiff and motionless. He reached a taloned foot or paw toward me, who was nearest to him, stirred me with it; but despite the cruel prodding of those talons I lay limp, unchanged. Then, quite perplexed, apparently, he bent down over me, to examine me. It was the chance for which I had waited. As he bent over me, as his face came close down to mine, my arms flashed up and gripped him!

THE NEXT instant was one of such wild combat and confusion in the dusky little cell as to defy description. At the instant that I grasped their leader, the four guards had swung all their weapons toward me, but did not dare to loose their rays in that moment lest they destroy their leader, too. And in the instant that their weapons had turned toward me, my three friends had leaped up also, and were upon the guards! Then we were whirling about the little cell in such fierce, swift battle as I had never known before. Grasping still the turtle-creature with whom I struggled, I strove to attain upon his snaky neck the hold which experience had taught me was the one vulnerable point in these shell-cased monsters. Before I could gain that hold, though, his own tremendously powerful limbs had grasped my own throat with taloned paws, and swiftly then were choking me!

As I struggled madly there, I caught sight of Carson swaying in a death-grip with another, striving with taut muscles to prevent the thing from bringing his hemisphere into play; I saw Trent, who had grasped one of the creatures by the neck, send that creature slumping down in death on the floor and leaping upon another, who sought to escape through the open door; saw Howland rolling at the room's side with still another, who seemed to be overcoming him; heard the mingled sounds of deep vibrating voices and hoarse exclamations, of struggling bodies and the clang of metal, as the weapons of the guards struck the floor. Then all about me seemed to be darkening before my eyes, as I felt the relentless grip on my own windpipe tightening!

I knew that a moment more of that grip would mean the end for me! I gathered all my strength for a supreme effort, and struck out at the turtle-creature who held me with all his force. The great blow broke loose his grip from about me, sent him whirling back against the room's far side, and as he reeled back I looked sharply about me, saw that at the same moment the antagonists of Howland and Trent, beside me, had broken from them, back to the room's side with the other, the three turtle-creatures facing us at that moment with Carson struggling somewhere behind me. All this I saw as I straightened there, then saw in the same instant one of the three monsters before us reach swiftly to the floor, to something round and gleaming there, to one of the deadly hemispheres which in the next moment he had swung swiftly straight toward us!

In that wild instant I knew that nothing could halt the death from that hemisphere, the deadly ray that would leap from it toward us, yet I gathered myself even then for the leap that I knew was hopeless. But as I did so, there was a little clicking sound behind me, a broad ray of green and misty light drove past me from behind, and then that ray had struck the three turtle-creatures at the room's other side, had struck them with a detonation that in the little room was thunderous, deafening! And as it did so, I saw them swaying, reeling, falling; saw their bodies suddenly puff, swell, explode, falling in shattered, broken masses to the room's floor! I turned, unsteadily, to see that at the critical moment, Carson had overcome his own antagonist and had wrenched from him, as he slumped downward, the hemisphere whose ray he had loosed upon the three creatures opposite us!

Panting, torn, wild-eyed, we gazed unsteadily now about us, listening tensely. The detonation of the green vacuum ray had seemed titanic to us in the little cell, but apparently that cell's smallness had muffled the sound effectively, since there was no sound of alarm in the great building about us. A moment we listened, then reached toward the hemispheres on the floor, grasping their handles with our fingers on the control-buttons in those handles; then we were moving toward the door. Out that door we went, leaving the silent bodies of the five turtle-creatures in the dusk of the cell, out through the opening that was unbarred now by the invisible force-sheet, to find ourselves in the dusky corridor that led toward the left, toward the edge of the great Council Hall and the corridors leading upward.

"Less than an hour left!" Howland whispered as we crept forward down that corridor. "Pray God we get to the roof before the three warning-notes sound!"

It was a prayer echoed in all our hearts as we moved silently on. Swiftly the time was passing. The moment was approaching when Earth-disk and moon-disk would again be in line, would permit the moon hordes to flash down to Earth. So, tensely, with set faces, we crept on down the corridor, until we came at last to the place where it ran into the larger corridor, the one whose stair led upward. We had not seen any trace of turtle-creatures as yet, and the whole building seemed strangely silent about us, but as we entered the larger corridor, we gazed watchfully along its length. In it there were no turtle-creatures visible, but before us, at the corridor's other side, there yawned the depths of the great Council Hall, along which it ran. Cautiously we crept toward it, toward the low rail that protected the corridor from the great hall's depths, then peered down over that rail forgetful of all else for the moment, at the sight beneath.

For there upon the floor of the mighty, soft-lit hall, whose vast, curving walls dropped beneath us for hundreds of feet, there sat now in the myriad seats, row upon row of silent turtle-creatures! Turtle-creatures who filled those seats, in strange, silent rows, the great Council of Three Thousand who ruled all these turtle-races! Silent, listening, they sat there, far beneath us, while at the clear space at the great floor's center were the three creatures whom I knew to be the Council of Three. One of them, now, was standing, was speaking to the three thousand about him in deep, strong tones, tones that came vaguely up to our own ears.

It came to me then, as we crouched there in the narrow gallery high above the great hall's floor, that it was now, on the very eve of their titanic expedition back to Earth, that the Council of Three Thousand beneath us had been gathered. That the speaker at the room's center was addressing them, who soon would be pouring up to the roof and out on their flying-circles to the plaza, to the cylinders beneath it, that would carry them down to Earth. He seemed to be exhorting them, reminding them of the power that had once been theirs on Earth, reminding them of the doom that waited for all their races unless they conquered, unless they wiped Earth clean of the races upon it, and won it for their own. Gazing down toward them, Carson and Howland and Trent and I stared as though fascinated, as well we might be, by that strange and solemn scene.

A moment more we gazed, and then Carson straightened, motioning silently to us, and we too straightened to go, and to start up toward the roof. But in the moment that we did so there was the slightest of sounds from behind us, and then before we could whirl around we had been gripped from behind, gripped by great taloned arms that grasped us, held us fast! Even as I flung myself around with wild fury in that grip I knew that we had been discovered, that a party of turtle-guards in the corridors had found us there, and crept up behind us. I heard a choking cry from Howland, as the others struggled wildly there beside me in that moment, and then as I, too, struck out and backward madly at the monster who held me from behind, I felt him lift me swiftly in his powerful arms and swing me out over the low rail before me, to drop me to death on the metal floor hundreds of feet below!

CHAPTER TWELVE
Up the Wall

I THINK now that the terror I felt in that swift moment, when I hung above a dreadful death, so numbed me, that I was without power of motion, I remember being thrust out over the low rail, of the floor of the great room far below seeming to rush up toward me, the massed creatures upon it still unconscious of our struggle high above them, and then as I closed my eyes, and abandoned myself to my fate, I felt another grip close upon my shoulder, and after an agonizing moment felt myself being pulled back over the rail. As I touched the corridor's floor again, I saw that it was Carson who had saved me, after felling with a great blow the creature who had held me.

Beside me two others of the creatures lay still, and Howland, bleeding from a great cut in the side of his head, was raising the hemisphere in his hand to crash it down upon the head of the creature with whom he was struggling. Carson, as I found, had escaped the first grip of the creatures when they had crept up behind us, and had turned to crash down his heavy weapon upon them in swift blows that had felled two of them, Trent and Howland disposing of the other two. Luckily for us, the combat, wild as it was, had lasted for but a brief moment, because the creatures, feeling certain they would capture us, did not use their ray-hemispheres, for fear it would have sounded the alarm to the massed thousands of the Council far beneath. As it was, though, our fierce struggle had been so high above them that no sound of it had come down to them, and none had looked up toward us.

By this time we were moving forward along the corridor, toward the narrow stair that led upward to the next level, for we knew now that not many minutes remained to us if we were to reach the plaza and the cylinder beneath it in time. Carson leading, we ran toward that stair, but then stopped short as we gazed up. For in the corridor above we could discern through the dusk four more turtle-guards, lounging at the stair's top; we could see and hear other parties of them that seemed to ceaselessly patrol through the corridors and stairs clear up to the building's roof! It was apparent that we could never reach that roof, could never reach the flying-circles upon it; we could never go past the countless turtle-guards that were between us and the roof. For a moment we stood there in utter despair.

Then suddenly Carson's eyes lit up. "We can't get up through the building's interior to the roof," he whispered, "but there is a chance."

"A chance to get to the roof?" Howland asked, and Carson nodded.

"Yes," he said; "up the great building's outside wall!"

A moment we stared at him uncomprehending; then he pointed swiftly to a group of mechanisms and materials stacked along the corridor's side. We had passed them unheeding before, but now Carson's eyes were upon them.

"That drill-mechanism there," he said. "With that and the metal bars beside it we can make it up the wall!"

Then as he reached, picked up swiftly the drill-mechanism he spoke of, we understood. It was a metal affair some eighteen inches in length, the drill proper being of pure white metal much harder than the metal of the buildings and streets of the city, and more than an inch in diameter. The white drill projected from a bulbous casing on the side of which was a small control-switch, and as Carson touched this, it set the drill whirring swiftly, and he placed it against the metal wall beside us. We saw the white drill eating into that metal as smoothly and as swiftly as through wood. He pointed to the short metal bars that lay piled beyond, bars that were large enough to fit snugly into the holes made by the drill, and at once we understood his plan. Desperate as it was, we realized it was yet the one remaining chance to reach the roof, since now the minutes were fleeting fast and we could never pass through the numberless guards who filled the corridors above us.

So each of us grasping three of the short thick bars, and with the drill in Carson's hands, we raced back along the corridor, back to where the four guards with whom we had struggled a moment before still lay. One of them was stirring, showing signs of life, but we paid no attention to him in that tense moment, racing back down the branching corridor toward the cell from which we had escaped. In it lay the bodies of those whom the green ray had slain, and over them we raced toward the triangular window. Then Carson, drill in his grasp, was drawing himself up to that window, balancing there within it and drilling swiftly with the mechanism in his grasp a deep little hole in the metal of the wall just above it. In a moment that hole was made, and withdrawing the drill he placed in the hole one of the metal bars. It fitted snugly in it, as before, forming in effect a solid bar projecting outward for two feet from the great building's smooth side, above the window.

Clinging to this bar, therefore, and with feet still in the window's opening, Carson reached upward and swiftly bit with the drill a like hole a yard above the first. Into this also he inserted a bar, and then standing on the first bar, clinging to the one above it, he reached upward higher with the drill, boring swiftly a similar hole, inserting in it another bar, and moving upward thus a step on the great ladder which he himself was building in the great building's wall. Far outward and below us there stretched the great lunar city, its crystal-like buildings looming through the dusk, their roofs crowded with flying-circles and the streets crowded with turtle-creatures. These in the streets, though, could not see us through the dusk, apparently, for there came no alarm from beneath as Carson continued to creep upward.

Now Trent was following him, using his own bars in the holes which Carson had bored, creeping up the mighty building's smooth faceted side after him, inserting his bars in the drilled holes, pulling himself up from bar to bar, and then drawing up after him the bar beneath him and using it to insert in the hole above. Howland, too, as Trent moved upward, was following him, using his own bars in the same way. I waited there at the window until Howland was a half-dozen feet above me, and then with beating heart I prepared to follow him, swung myself out of the window, last of the four, and inserted one of my three bars into the hole just above the window.

The bar fitted snugly, like the others, and in a moment I had placed another in the hole above it, was clambering up onto the first bar, as the others had done, and placing the third in the hole above. Then pulling myself up onto the second, grasping the third, I reached down and withdrew the first from its hole, straightened and placed it in a still higher hole above the two to which I clung. And thus I made my way up after my three friends, Carson and Trent and Howland. We were like four great bat-like creatures, moving up the great building's vertical wall through the shrouding dusk.

UP—UP—bar after bar, hole after hole, a steady, unvarying progress that became semi-automatic to me. Once I looked down through the dusk at the crowded streets far below, the great turtle-hordes that filled those streets, then as an intolerable dizziness swept over me I gripped my bars tighter and forced myself to look upward. Above me I could see Carson, moving upward still with the drill in his grasp, boring holes in the softer metal of the great smooth wall, progressing steadily upward with drill and bars, while Trent and Howland and I followed in order beneath. And, gazing up beyond him, I could make out far above the faint gleam of the great transparent roof, the burning points above and outside it, that were the familiar constellations, the shining, unchanging stars.

Could men ever have moved upon a stranger journey than we up that mighty building's sheer, metal side? Up a building that held within it the great Council of the turtle-creatures, who when the three signal notes sounded would be massing their great forces toward the cylinders beneath the plaza, toward those cylinders which the last single-note would send driving down through space to overwhelm our Earth! Up a building set there on the other side of the moon from Earth, with far below us the unsuspecting masses of the turtle-creatures' hordes, and far above us the great transparent roof that alone shielded this air-filled world from airless space! Up—up—bar after bar, hole after hole, until Carson above had reached the point where the building's great upper facets slanted inward, until I myself was more than a hundred feet above the window through which we had come. And it was at that point, glancing downward for a moment, that I saw projecting from that window beneath me the hideous reptilian head of one of the turtle-creatures, gazing straight up toward us!

As my eyes met those lidless, unhuman ones beneath, I shuddered involuntarily, an utter cold of fear seeming to flood through me there as I clung to my bars on the great building's side. I saw, in that moment as I gazed downward, that upon the creature's head was a great wound, saw and understood at once, that this was the turtle-guard whom we had seen stirring as we had raced back through the corridor, who had revived and had come after us. A moment only the creature below gazed up toward us, a moment in which I heard exclamations of horror from Carson and Howland and Trent above as they, too, saw him. Then his head had vanished inside the window, and it flashed on me that he was sounding the alarm. But even as I thought so, he had reappeared beneath, metal bars in his own grasp like our own, bars which he was inserting in the holes beneath like ourselves, one above the other!

He was coming up the wall after us!

SWINGING swiftly up, bar after bar, from hole to hole, he was coming up beneath me, and was swiftly drawing nearer toward me, while I gazed down toward him transfixed with horror. Then the cries of Carson and Howland, above, aroused me, and I thrust my bars into the holes above me, began with frantic efforts to climb faster after them. Up— up—swiftly, frantically, I climbed, but ever closer to me drew that monstrous form beneath, thrusting his own bars in the holes and swinging up upon them with ease on his great taloned limbs. Above me I could see that Carson and the others were already passing up over the inward-slanting facet of the wall, climbing up that inward facet with drill and bars working swiftly, and I knew that once I reached its slope, instead of the vertical wall to which I now clung, I might progress up faster, might elude the creature beneath. Up—up—I dared not look down toward the pursuing turtle-creature, as with pounding heart and bursting lungs I clambered upward. At last I was but a few yards beneath the inward slope of the wall, Howland already upon that slope. And it was just then that something gripped my ankles tightly, and I looked down to see that the creature beneath had reached me and had grasped me!

As that grip tightened about my feet I dropped suddenly downward from the bar I held to the one which my feet had rested upon, and there, clinging to that bar with the turtle-creature pulling himself up, I struck out savagely at him, felt his own great blows falling upon me as he struggled up to the bar upon which I clung. There, both clinging to that single slender metal bar, projecting from the mighty building's vertical side, we swayed in such a giddy combat as few have imagined. Striking with all our power at each other, the one aim of both of us was to break the other's hold upon the bar, to send him hurtling down to death on the metal base of the great building, hundreds of feet below. And with his first blows the turtle-creature almost accomplished that, since those blows took me off balance for a moment and after tottering for an instant, I had slipped sidewise off the bar, was holding to it with but one hand.

As I dangled thus from the bar, the monster clinging to it, raising his arm for a blow that would knock me completely loose from it, I heard the horrified cries of Howland and the others above, saw them climbing down toward me with their bars, saw also the cold smooth metal at the base of the great structure, far below. Then, even as the arm of my opponent swung up for a finishing blow, I had hooked my knees swiftly up over the bar, clung with them in the next moment as we struck and thrust at each other wildly again. And even as we did so, in that next moment, I became conscious of something that made the blood run cold in my veins. The bar was giving beneath our combined weight!

The slender metal bar, strong enough to support one, was bending slowly beneath the combined weight of the turtle-creature and myself and in a moment more would send both of us hurtling downward as it gave completely. Even as it bent slowly downward beneath us, though, we two struck still madly toward each other, slipping gradually toward the bar's outer end as it bent downward, slipping until, still struggling madly, we were clinging to its very end. Then it bent suddenly, completely downward, beneath our weight and we had slipped off it, hurtling downward! Yet at the very instant that we did so a hand had reached down from above, had gripped my collar, my shoulder, and had drawn me slowly up to the bar above, while the hideous form of my opponent went hurtling downward with a deep scream!

Down, down, twisting and turning, he fell and in a moment we could see him strike the bare stretch of metal at the building's base, unobserved it seemed by any in the masses that filled the streets beyond. I turned, trembling, to find that it was Howland who had saved me, who had clambered down from above to catch me just as the bar gave way. Now he removed the strain upon the bar on which he had pulled me by climbing to that above, and then, Carson and Trent above glancing down to assure themselves of my safety, we resumed our climb up the wall. Within moments, moving up in the same order and by the same method as before, we had passed up over the slant of the wall, and were climbing more easily up the hundred feet or more that remained between us and the roof.

Up and up still we went, Carson above boring steadily with the drill, we moving up after him with our bars, moving up with all the powers of our tired bodies, now, since well we knew that the minutes left to us were rapidly drawing to an end. All about us the great moon city lay in the shrouding dusk unchanged, the flying-circles massed still upon all the buildings about us, but we knew that within minutes the three great signal notes from the plaza would be sounding to bring all the hordes inside those buildings, and inside the one up which we climbed, out upon their flying-circles and toward the plaza and the cylinders and disk beneath it. So it was almost frenziedly that we followed Carson on our strange and terrible climb upward, until at last he, the highest of us, was within a few feet of the great building's roof.

Pausing there, he motioned cautioningly down toward us, and as we listened we heard faintly from that roof the sound of deep bass turtle-creatures' voices—many of them apparently. Carson then raised his head slowly above the level of the roof, peering across it and clinging to the topmost bar he had just inserted. Tensely we waited while he gazed over the roof, for were we discovered, a single blow would send each of us to eternity. Then Carson gazed down toward us again, his eyes motioning us to follow; then he drew himself gently upward through the dusk and over the great roof's edge, over until he had disappeared from our view on that roof.

IN A moment Trent had followed him, and was soon peering across the roof Howland followed and I was moving up toward the topmost bar after him. I reached it and slowly raised my eyes above the level of the roof. Its vast expanse of hundreds of feet stretched away into the dusk before me, from the edge at which I crouched, and I saw that upon its surface were ranged scores of great flying-circles, that were partially overlapping or piled upon each other. They were loaded with instruments and equipment, and I saw that each had been fitted with four of the great ray-hemispheres, at regular intervals around each of the circles. In them were no turtle-creatures. Their crews, their forces, were still in the great building beneath us, but at the opening at the roof's center from which the stair led downward, there waited a full score of armed turtle-guards!

Carson and Trent and Howland had drawn themselves over the roof's edge and were crouching now behind a great mass of bulky mechanical equipment that lay between us and the flying-circles, between us and the guards at the central opening. Swiftly then, with a glance toward those guards, I followed their example, drew myself up upon the roof and crept stealthily and silently across an open space to the shelter of those mechanisms, crouching down behind them with my friends. Then, drawing us to him, Carson whispered to us tensely.

"We'll have to make far one of the flying-circles!" he whispered. "It will bring us out into view of the guards but in the dusk they may not see us, and we've hardly minutes left!"

"Try to get to this nearest one, then," said Howland, nodding toward it. "It's now or never!"

So, crouching for a moment there behind our shelter with our eyes meeting, we crept out from behind that shelter, out on the open roof toward the nearest of the great flying-circles. We were within full view of the guards at the great roof's center, I knew, even through the twilight dusk, and I prayed that they might not turn toward us as we crept on toward the great flying-circle's edge. The guards, though, seemed to be gazing intently down the opening into the building beneath, and in a moment we had reached the great flat craft's edge, were stepping silently over its low protecting wall, toward the central mechanism that controlled it. Heart beating rapidly, I led the way toward that mechanism, my eyes upon the studs in it that controlled the flying-circle's motive power, and in moments more, moments that seemed eternities to us, we had reached that low flat cylinder at its center upon which were the controls. Then my hands were reaching toward those controls, toward the starting studs, were—

Clang! Clang! Clang!

Deliberately, majestically, awfully, they had sounded out over the colossal moon city in that dread moment, the three great bell-notes from the plaza that summoned the moon hordes to the chamber beneath the plaza and the disk and cylinders within it. Three mighty clanging notes of doom, precursors of that last great note that would send the moon hordes flashing down to Earth! Three titanic notes at which we, upon the flying-circle's center, crouched transfixed, and at which there came a hurrying rush of many feet from beneath! Then in the next stunned moment there had burst up through the opening from beneath masses of turtle-creatures, hurrying toward the flying-circles. Even as they emerged upon the roof, they and the guards had seen us, all at the same instant. They stopped short, stared through the dusk at us, and then their metal hemispheres had come up and a score of green shafts of the deadly vacuum ray were stabbing across the roof toward us!

CHAPTER THIRTEEN
Howland's Way

IT WAS at the very moment that the moon-creatures had trained their hemispheres upon us that my hands had grasped convulsively the control-studs of the great flying-circle on which we crouched, and it was that alone that saved us in that moment. For even as the green beams drove across the roof toward us there had come the smooth powerful throbbing of the craft's mechanism and I had jerked the central control upward, sending the flying-circle leaping upward, just as the deadly beams reached the spot where we had been. The next moment there came terrific thundering detonations from beneath us as those rays and a score of others that stabbed toward us as we rose, created great vacuums beneath us. Then our flying-circle was above the roof and was driving upward in the dusk with a wild uproar rising from beneath and all around us.

For across all the mighty moon city, now, in answer to the summons of those three great notes, turtle-creatures in hordes were pouring up on the roofs, were filling their great flying-circles and slanting up in those circles all about us! And from those and the flying-circles on the great roof beneath, that were rising now after us, there came a dull roar of deep voices as they saw our own craft, we four crouching at its center, driving up through the dusk above the mighty city. Almost at once, it seemed, we had been seen by all those hundreds, those thousands, of great flat craft, and they were driving toward us, were flocking thickly from all directions upon us, great masses of the turtle-creatures visible on them!

"The plaza!" Howland was screaming above the great throbbing of our craft. "Make for the plaza—for the disk! It's a matter of minutes now till the end—till the last bell-note sounds!"

But already my hands had tightened on the control and at its full speed I was sending the great flying-circle hurtling through the dusk above the great faceted buildings, above the mighty moon city, to that plaza and that disk that was the objective of all the swarming flying-circles about us. Swiftly, as we shot on, I pointed to Carson the four green studs beside me that controlled the green beams of the four hemispheres at the edge of our great flying-circle, and he crouched tensely beside those studs, watching, as the flying-circles about us drove closer. Like hornets aroused from their nest they seemed, swarming up in countless throngs all about and beneath us, across all the moon city, and while it seemed madness to believe that we could reach the plaza and the disk with these hordes about us, yet with the recklessness of despair I sent the great circle splitting the air as it rushed toward the plaza.

Now flying-circles were closing in from either side, from below, and there came a hiss and flash of green misty beams from beneath and to the right, beams that drove past us as I whirled the circle to one side, and that detonated with terrific explosions about us, sending our craft reeling sidewise from them! And even as we righted ourselves and shot on again, from ahead three great circles that had caught our approach were rushing toward us and were whirling straight in our direction. I cried to Carson, dipped the great flying-circle suddenly downward, and then as we drove beneath them, our own beams had stabbed up and flashed across their surfaces as they sought to dip also, the massed turtle-creatures upon them swelling, scattering, from each other, exploding bodily as the green ray's detonation thundered about them!

NOW THE air about us seemed filled with flying-circles, circles that were rushing toward us from every conceivable direction, from either side and above and below, whose great green beams were whirling madly through the air in an endeavor to stop our great rush toward the plaza, their own objective. Impossible it seemed that any could whirl through such a storm of flying-circles and stabbing beams and live, yet only conscious of the thundering hell of battle about us, I drove the circle onward across the great city, Carson playing symphonies of death upon the green studs before him as he sent our misty rays whirling to right and left and above, sending masses of the flying-circles it struck tumbling aimlessly downward into the city below, where the throngs of turtle-creatures were rushing through its streets at sight of this terrific battle above them!

But now behind us there drove down toward us a close massed dozen of flying-circles whose beams, sweeping toward us, made me whirl our own craft lightning-like downward, down until we were rushing on over the moon city clearing its faceted buildings by but a few feet, the close mass of our immediate pursuers directly behind us! Again their beams stabbed about us, and then as I swerved from them, an idea shot through my brain and I turned, saw that they were close behind, waited until they were but yards behind. Then, before they could loose their beams, I had dived sharply downward, swiftly followed by them. In the same moment that I had dipped downward, though, I had curved sharply up once more, and before they too could curve up, their flying-circles had smashed full against the side of one of the mighty faceted buildings!

And now upward we were slanting again, at awful speed, throbbing madly upward with the myriad of flying-circles rushing still from over all the moon city toward us, up and on across that city toward the plaza that was our goal! The swift rush of our mighty craft, the myriad of flying-circles that swooped toward us from all directions, the stab of our green rays and the thunder of detonations all about us, the hoarse shouts of Carson and Howland and Trent, all these merged in my ears into one dull great roar as with a madness of battle strong within me I sent our great craft rocketing onward. Lightning-like we flashed ahead, the great moon city beneath us giving forth a vast insensate roar of anger and alarm as we shot across it, the flying-circles about us driving still toward us from all directions with beams wildly whirling. Then from ahead, other great masses of flying-circles, crowded with turtle-creatures, were flashing toward us, and before I could swerve our rushing craft two of those onrushing ones ahead were full before us! In that instant a collision seemed inevitable, but with a wild jerk I brought the control-lever upward, just in time to raise our flying-circle a foot above the level of the onrushing ones. And the next instant we had flashed across both of them at that height, our own metal circle mowing the thick-packed creatures from the surface of theirs as a scythe might do with grain! But now Howland was shouting hoarsely in my ear.

"The plaza!" he was crying. "There ahead—and the opening!"

But there far ahead now I saw it, the great clear flat circle with the great black-glittering disk set in it, the big opening near it, and I nodded swiftly. "We'll make it yet!" I cried to him. "We'll land beside the opening—beside the switch!"

For now our great flying-circle had shot forward from among the masses of thick-swarming craft whose beams were raking about us, and hampered as they were by their very numbers, we leaped ahead of them, rushed down toward the great plaza's surface, toward the opening at the side of which was the great switch. Upon the plaza itself and beneath there seemed to be no turtle-creatures whatever, since we knew that all had just started toward it from across the great moon city. When our escape had given the alarm, all had been diverted from their course and were coming toward us instead. And now, as we shot down toward it, toward the great opening, the myriad of deadly beams, that had thundered and flashed about us for the last moments in a hell of vacuum death, ceased abruptly, and I understood instantly that because we were so close to their great disk and switch, the turtle-creatures could not loose more rays upon us without fear of striking and destroying their own switch and great mechanism!

Down we shot and then the next moment the great flying-circle had come to the plaza's surface beside the big opening and we were leaping from it toward that opening. The air above seemed full of flying-circles now, all the great forces of the moon massing to flash down within seconds from the great disk on the mighty beam, and as they saw us rush toward the opening, their own disks shot madly downward, to land beside that opening and rush after us, still fearing to use their rays! But now we had reached the great switch at the opening's side, whose throw upward or downward sent the mighty beam upward or downward from the disk, and now Howland had laid hold of that switch!

"Down into the cylinder!" he cried to us. "The bell-note will sound in a second and I'll turn on the beam!"

CARSON and Trent and I hesitated a moment, even in that mad moment when from all about the plaza the moon-creatures were rushing in hordes toward us, from their landing flying-circles, then flung ourselves down the narrow stair and into the great chamber beneath the plaza, across the narrow metal bridge and through the open door of the mighty cylinder that hung still in the framework beneath the disk, poised above the great shaft. We threw ourselves inside it, Carson's hand on the stud that would snap the cylinder's door shut when Howland should turn on the beam and rush down into the cylinder with us, and then as we looked back up, we saw Howland's hand tightening upon that great switch, saw the moon-creatures, the turtle-hordes, rushing from all about, and almost upon him, and then the next moment had come the terrific clanging note of the great automatic bell-signal, marking the moment when the disk on Earth and this disk on the moon were in line! Even as that note clanged, Howland had flung the great switch. But as we saw him do it, we cried out hoarsely, heard the awful cries of the turtle-creatures throwing themselves upon him as they too saw, heard across all the mighty moon-world a great dull roar as though of utter tear!

For Howland had flung the switch upward!

In the next instant, the great disk above us had hummed with terrific power and then its beam had shot from it, but that beam had shot *upward!* Had driven up with all its awful power toward the great transparent roof—far above! There came in that instant, as it struck that roof, crashed through it, shattered it, a great roar of wind, a titanic thunderous roaring of all the air upon the moon-world, rushing out into airless space through that great puncture which the mighty beam had made in the roof! I saw Howland's hand flung down toward us in a supreme gesture even as the thunderous roar of the outrushing air came to us, heard Carson click shut the cylinder's door at the same instant in answer to that gesture, that agonized command, and then in the succeeding instant Howland had flung the switch back and downward!

There came again a terrific humming from the disk above us, our cylinder seeming to hang poised beneath that disk for an instant while the air outside it, the air in the great chamber and above it, the air of all the moon-world rushed out into the airless vacuum of space through the gigantic puncture in the roof far above. In that moment, through the great opening above, we saw Howland and the turtle-creatures about him swaying, staggering, falling, as with a thunderous roar as of riven worlds the airtight moon-world's air rushed forth above, asphyxiating all life upon it in that one tremendous moment! Falling singly, in groups, in masses, above and over all the great moon-world, over all the colossal city of the turtle-creatures, dying as all in the moon-world were dying in that moment!

Howland's way! I cried it aloud in that moment, as our cylinder hung poised beneath the humming disk, as Howland and all the millions of the moon hordes sank to death above us with the rush of the moon-world's air out into space. Howland's way! The way of which he had spoken there to us in our prison; the one by which the menace of the turtle-creatures could be removed forever! He had slain all the turtle-races on the moon with one great blow as they had slain the worm-folk eons before, using the great disk and beam, which they had meant to use to transport their hordes to the conquest of other worlds! The way that had meant the sacrifice of himself, yet out of which sacrifice he had reached at last to save us three, to fling the switch downward! For even at the moment that I cried out, that the moon-world above us sank down to one great death, the humming disk beneath which our cylinder poised shot forth its beam again but *downward* now, driving our cylinder down into the darkness of the great shaft!

Clinging beside Carson and Trent there at its bottom, I was aware through darkening senses of the cylinder clicking down through darkness with velocity inconceivable; of its bursting out into flaming light in another instant; of hurtling through spaces unthinkable, gemmed with burning stars, toward a tremendous brown sphere that was growing lightning-like before us. Then new dazzling light was breaking about us from ahead, I seemed pressed by a giant hand to the cylinder's floor as its awful speed slowed up, and then as the light vanished and the cylinder came to rest, I heard the click of its door opening. The next moment I could feel Carson's hands on me, could hear the voices of him and Trent beside me, and then complete darkness enveloped me, and I knew no more.

CHAPTER FOURTEEN
Epilogue

NIGHT LAY still over the face of the Earth when Carson and Trent and I finally reached the summit of the great mound, into whose shaft our cylinder had dropped. It had been hours before that we had shot down out of the gulf of space into that shaft, coming to rest upon the great disk from which we had started on our momentous journey. All, we found, was as it had been when we had shot outward into the gulf twenty-four hours before, the great disk unchanged, our rope-ladder hanging still into the shaft from above. And it was up that ladder, that Carson and Trent had revived me and we had rested, that we had come, until now we stood upon the great mound's summit once more.

Standing together there, motionless and silent, we gazed out. In the black vault of the heavens overhead there burned the brilliant tropic stars, but it was not toward these that Carson and Trent and I were gazing—it was toward the brilliant silver disk of the full moon, sinking down now toward the western horizon with the passing of night—a shining shield which we three watched in silence, gazing out toward it over the moonlit jungles. Toward its craters and seas and mountain ranges, toward that great central crater through which our cylinder had flashed on our mad journey through the moon to its other side in search of Howland, and back through which we had flashed to Earth, with Howland's hand driving us back through the moon and across the gulf to Earth at the moment of his own and the moon world's death.

"Howland—" Carson was breaking the silence at last, speaking his thought. "We did find him, didn't we?—but we lost him in the end."

"Not lost, Carson," I told him. "Howland went the way he desired to go—for the world."

"Had I known what he intended—" Carson began, and then could say no more.

"We could not know," said Trent. "We could not know that Howland meant to annihilate the moon-creatures forever with their own great mechanism, and to die with them doing so. But now that he has done it, we know—and the world will know, and remember."

Silent again, we gazed out toward that shining moon-disk. And in that silence, as our minds traveled out across the great gulf toward the colossal, airless city in which the millions of the turtle-creatures had met the death which they themselves had given eons ago to another race. Trent's words seemed echoing again about us. The world would know, and remember—yes. It would know, and would remember, how Howland alone it had been who had stricken down those turtle-creatures' millions even as they had gathered to pour down to the doom of Earth. It would know, and would never forget, what a mighty debt it owed to the man who had saved it, and who lay dead now.

THE END

If you've enjoyed this book, you will not want to miss these terrific titles...

ARMCHAIR SCI-FI & HORROR DOUBLE NOVELS, $12.95 each

D-91   **THE TIME TRAP** by Henry Kuttner
THE LUNAR LICHEN by Hal Clement

D-92   **SARGASSO OF LOST STARSHIPS** by Poul Anderson
THE ICE QUEEN by Don Wilcox

D-93   **THE PRINCE OF SPACE** by Jack Williamson
POWER by Harl Vincent

D-94   **PLANET OF NO RETURN** by Howard Browne
THE ANNIHILATOR COMES by Ed Earl Repp

D-95   **THE SINISTER INVASION** by Edmond Hamilton
OPERATION TERROR by Murray Leinster

D-96   **TRANSIENT** by Ward Moore
THE WORLD-MOVER by George O. Smith

D-97   **FORTY DAYS HAS SEPTEMBER** by Milton Lesser
THE DEVIL'S PLANET by David Wright O'Brien

D-98   **THE CYBERENE** by Rog Phillips
BADGE OF INFAMY by Lester del Rey

D-99   **THE JUSTICE OF MARTIN BRAND** by Raymond A. Palmer
BRING BACK MY BRAIN by Dwight V. Swain

D-100   **WIDE-OPEN PLANET** by L. Sprague de Camp
AND THEN THE TOWN TOOK OFF by Richard Wilson

ARMCHAIR SCIENCE FICTION CLASSICS, $12.95 each

C-31   **THE GOLDEN GUARDSMEN**
by S. J. Byrne

C-32   **ONE AGAINST THE MOON**
by Donald A. Wollheim

C-33   **HIDDEN CITY**
by Chester S. Geier

ARMCHAIR SCI-FI & HORROR GEMS SERIES, $12.95 each

G-9   **SCIENCE FICTION GEMS, Vol. Five**
Clifford D. Simak and others

G-10   **HORROR GEMS, Vol. Five**
E. Hoffman Price and others

If you've enjoyed this book, you will not want to miss these terrific titles...

ARMCHAIR SCI-FI & HORROR DOUBLE NOVELS, $12.95 each

D-111 **THE MOON ERA** by Jack Williamson
REVENGE OF THE ROBOTS by Howard Browne

D-112 **SON OF THE BLACK CHALICE** by Milton Lesser
SENTRY OF THE SKY by Evelyn E. Smith

D-113 **OUTPOST ON THE MOON** by Joslyn Maxwell
POTENTIAL ZERO by S. J. Byrne

D-114 **OUTPOST INFINITY** by Raymond F. Jones
THE WHITE INVADERS by Ray Cummings

D-115 **TIME TRAP** by Rog Phillips
THE COSMIC DESTROYER by Alexander Blade

D-116 **THE OTHER SIDE OF THE MOON** by Edmond Hamilton
SECRET INVASION by Walter Kubilius

D-117 **DANGER MOON** by Frederik Pohl
THE HIDDEN UNIVERSE by Ralph Milne Farley

D-118 **THE WAILING ASTEROID** by Murray Leinster
THE WORLD THAT COULDN'T BE by Clifford D. Simak

D-119 **THE WHISPERING GORILLA** by Don Wilcox
RETURN OF THE WHISPERING GORILLA by David V. Reed

D-120 **SPECIAL EFFECT** by J. F. Bone
WARLORD OF KOR by Terry Carr

ARMCHAIR SCIENCE FICTION CLASSICS, $12.95 each

C-37 **THE GREEN MAN RETURNS**
by Harold M. Sherman

C-38 **THE SHAVER MYSTERY, Book Five**
by Richard S. Shaver

C-39 **MARS CHILD**
by Cyril Judd

ARMCHAIR MASTERS OF SCIENCE FICTION SERIES, $16.95 each

MS-9 **MASTERS OF SCIENCE FICTION AND FANTASY, Vol. Nine**
Poul Anderson, "The Star Beast" and other tales

MS-10 **MASTERS OF SCIENCE FICTION, Vol. Ten**
Robert Moore Williams, "Time Tolls for Toro" and other tales

COULD THE MARTIAN INVASION BE STOPPED?

There was no question that the Martians wanted to annihilate the entire human race. After all, had Earth not totally devastated their planet over two hundred years earlier? And the Martians, though practically immortal, were nevertheless a dying breed, unable to procreate their own race. So the Martians, thirsting for revenge and in need of a new home, launched an insidious invasion—not fought with giant machines of war, but with a new method that seemed to transform loyal Earthmen into raving traitors. These traitors were called "Suspects" and it was the job of Earth's security force, Public Defense, to ferret them out and eliminate them. The problem was that no one on Earth really understood the enormity of the problem. Yet Earth had the power to wipe out the entire Martian race by simply pushing a button. The question was—would they have the courage to actually push it?

CAST OF CHARACTERS

JAMES GIDEON
He was a loyal Public Defense agent, firmly against the Martian threat, yet something deep in his mind seemed to beckon to him.

CHIEF McDONOUGH
The top man at Public Defense. He wasn't afraid to take tough actions—including wiping out an entire planet!

MEL-EL-ABEN
This famous Martian master-surgeon was as brilliant as they came—even if he did look like a walking tree.

DR. S. T. FELLBANK
He was a skilled surgeon, yet mild mannered and ever so friendly. Why then did he appear to be a traitor to his own race?

SENATOR BURBANK
There was no question what this politician wanted—a complete end to the Martian threat by any means necessary.

NICK RIDENOUR
He was one of the best agents Public Defense had, but being stationed on Mars meant his life was under constant threat.

HASTINGS
Another tough Public Defense agent. So why did the annihilation of the Martian race bother him less than others?

SECRET
INVASION

By
WALTER KUBILIUS

ARMCHAIR FICTION
PO Box 4369, Medford, Oregon 97504

CHAPTER ONE

THE STENCH of the rotting Galani corpse filled the air of the Interplanet Trust's warehouse. Its sickening fumes half-blinded the Planetary Defense agents that were hurriedly assembled for the court-martial, but James Gideon kept his spasmorod pressed against the Captain's nervously twitching back. His finger ached from the desire to press the trigger and kill the traitor. If spaceplane captains become Suspects, who could be trusted? Gideon's mind whirled at the thought of the Martian Galani succeeding in their determination to conquer the Earth.

"You may proceed," Chief McDonough, tough master head of Planetary Defense, said.

"I offer in evidence the customs declaration," PD Agent Ridenour said, his voice ringing hollowly in the darkened warehouse. Gideon watched him, so that his eyes would not look at the green tentacles sprawled crazily on the floor where a brownish mass exuded from the pus-covered gash in the blackened, tree-like body.

"It is signed," Ridenour went on, "by the three spaceplane officials, the Captain and the First and Second Mates of the Interplanet Trust. Each of them had examined the crate marked 'Medical Supplies' and each must have known it was being used to smuggle a Galani to the Earth."

The Captain moistened his parched, frightened lips. Gideon, who held the spasmorod pressed against his back, could feel the man tremble. "I am guilty," he said nervously, "only of gross negligence in not personally inspecting the cargo. I took the First Mate's word for the crate's contents and signed the declaration without thinking. In any event, I deny the jurisdiction of this court. A rocket-hangar and warehouse is no place for a trial; I demand counsel."

McDonough's brows bent and he pointed an angry finger at the Captain.

"There hasn't been a Martian on Earth since the end of the war in 2009, and that was about 250 years ago. This is the first case of a nearly successful attempt to smuggle a Martian Galani through PD customs inspection. The fact that it almost succeeded indicates a serious weakness in Planetary Defense."

The Chief looked around him—at Gideon, Hastings, Ridenour, and the other PD Agents, as well as the two Mates and Captain. He added quietly, "There are traitors among us."

"I—I am innocent," the Captain said, shaken by the knowledge that he was suspected of treason, and that either his First or Second Mates—probably both—were Suspects, in Martian pay. "I demand the truth serum."

"Request granted," McDonough said, as Ridenour opened his PD kit quickly, and took out the ready hypodermic. The Captain smiled weakly and rolled up his sleeves while the First and Second Mates watched impassively. The dozen or so PD Agents, who had made the arrests when the spaceplane landed in the hangar, stepped forward curiously.

That moment of negligence was enough.

The First Mate stepped forward and locked his arm around the throat of the Agent in front of him; the spasmorod slipped from the Agent's holster, and a series of needle-like shots ripped through the cavernous warehouse. The Captain fell forward, his throat slashed open. Gideon felt the warm blood splash against him.

"A Suspect!" somebody screamed; "kill him!"

Red force-lines leaped through the air, piercing through the First Mate and the Agent he held in front of him.

"Idiots!" McDonough shouted, "use spasms! Take him alive!"

Ridenour lay crumpled against the wall, stemming the blood that seeped from a shoulder wound. The Second Mate's body was on the floor, a gaping mass where his forehead should be. A PD Agent, trusted aide of McDonough's, stood by the body with a grin on his face and the hammer of the spasmorod cocked for full-explosion.

"Too bad," he said, raising the blaster to his own face; "we almost succeeded." He pulled the trigger. The smashing blow splattered the warehouse with blood.

Gideon turned his face away, struggling against an overwhelming sickness. His eyeglasses steamed, and he tore them away to look blindly at the scene about him. It was not the sight of the five dead bodies that made him pale, but the truth, which was not painfully evident. After 250 years of espionage, the Galani had at last succeeded in turning loyal PD agents into betrayers of the Earth...

"DEFEATED again," McDonough said bitterly, knowing that truth serum was useless when Suspects were quick to commit suicide. He turned to the remaining members of the PD court-martial.

"Hastings, you prepare a faked report of a boiler explosion to account for the dead, James Gideon and Nick Ridenour will take over the investigation with full authority, and responsible only to me. Find out every contact these Suspects had in common. Track them down until we know how the Galani espionage system works. Go to Mars if necessary—but get results! Report to me in Washington. Court dismissed."

James Gideon, ostensibly a news reporter for Telefax Screens, spent the next week tracking down the past activities of the three planetary-freight officers, and the two PD Agents who had turned traitor. Index cards, listing every known physical action of these Suspects were assembled and then put through the Cyberneticon.

Gideon was faced with no easy task; but years of training had made him one of the select few Agents who were implicitly trusted by Chief McDonough. As a boy, Gideon had long been ashamed of the thick-rimmed glasses that nature had thrust upon him, but his father had been a wise man. "Never let anyone judge you by your eyes, or by any physical difference. It's the brain that matters—nothing else is important. Study! Study!"

James Gideon studied, and it was his knowledge of Galani history that finally led him into the ranks of the PD—that semi-secret organization that guarded the Earth in its silent, never-ending, never-erupting tension-filled relations with the Galani of Mars.

Over two centuries ago the Galani, a Martian species that was virtually immortal, was defeated after a long atomic war that neither side desired nor provoked. Instead of submitting peacefully to the terms of a lenient treaty, Galani resistance continued until Earth lost all hope of peaceful collaboration between the planets.

The Treaty of 2009 provided for the dismantling of all Galani heavy industry and strict prohibition against interplanetary travel. Planetary Defense, the intelligence arm of the Earth's military forces during the war, continued to operate by keeping Galani activities under constant surveillance.

For several decades, PD activity was limited to customs-bases on Mars; but later, surprising things began to occur. Despite the obvious hatred that the Galani seemed to feel for Earth, an unusually large number of Earthmen and Earthwomen conducted espionage on behalf of Mars and the Galani.

These "Suspects," as the PD called Earthmen who sold out to the Galani—for money, or other reasons—were becoming a powerful threat; it was PD's job to find these Suspects and the links that bound them to Mars.

AFTER STUDYING the activity-tracings, which the Cyberneticon made on the movements of the four dead Suspects, Gideon found the lead he was looking for.

"The Captain was apparently innocent," Gideon said when he reported his findings to his immediate superior—Nick Ridenour—at the PD substation disguised as Ridenour's apartment, "but the two Mates and traitor-PDs must have formed a single Suspect cell; the Cyberneticon shows their spatial-time tracks to meet on five different occasions."

"That doesn't help any," Ridenour said, "what we have to find is their contact with Mars. And—most important of all—how they were recruited…"

"No children or close relatives who would be used as hostages," Gideon said. "If they joined it must have been of their own free wills. There doesn't seem to be any hold the Galani can get on them. However here's a lead that might be their contact with Galani."

"Not more of us in the PD? Oh no!"

"No," Gideon said. "McDonough has ordered truth serum for the whole corps; that should clean the traitors out. Each of the Suspects was a patient of an Earth-doctor, Dr. S. T. Fellbank."

"Coincidence?"

"Not when free medical service is available through PD, and there is a good doctor on every rocket."

"Fellbank, Fellbank," Ridenour mused, "just a minute while I check the files." He switched on the Microcard Index, a series of screens immediately lighting up on his desk. He scrawled the name on a piece of paper, inserted it in a slot; in Washington, three hundred miles away, the complete files of PD, photographically scanned by telebeams, flashed across the screens on Ridenour's desk. He stopped the flow, snapped the "Copy" button and a photostatic duplicate of the dossier inched out of a slot. He tore it off the roll, skimmed through it and passed it on to Gideon.

"Read that last paragraph," he said sourly.

The greatest threat to civilization is the human race. What does an objective study of our history show? In the 275 years of interplanetary travel, we have completely destroyed seven distinct species in aggressive war on Venus, and two on Jupiter. What is even more horrible is our record on Mars. Not only did we hell-bomb a peace-loving people in 2007, but we have virtually enslaved the greatest race the universe has ever known—the Martian Galani.

Excerpt from speech delivered by Dr. S. T. Fellbank at the Society for the Defense of Martian Culture, January 9, 2257

James Gideon fingered his spectacles as he read the report. "A Suspect, definitely; he's our man."

"He's *your* man," Ridenour corrected. "I'm assigning Hastings to help you; find all you can about him. Incidentally, have you ever been to Mars?"

"Definitely not, and you couldn't drag me there. My health is good and I wouldn't care to have those Galani doctors go over me, despite the miracles they've done."

"Well, when you contact Fellbank, your orders are to go to Mars."

"Now, Nick, have a heart!"

"Those are orders, Gideon. As a Telefax reporter, you may get leads that PD Agent Munnheim—operating at Deimosport—has been unable to find. When you get there, look into this matter of disappearing Galani. Munnheim reports that there's a suspiciously big increase in the accidental-death rate. These eight-foot monsters are practically immortal; when they start dying off, there's something wrong. It might be a hidden civil war between an aggressive, vengeance-minded group and a more intelligent segment that realizes that war between the planets would mean the destruction of one or the other. Latest disappearance is that military writer Sko—So—what's his name."

"Scho-La-Nui?"

"Right. He's about a thousand years old. I guess. He's the author of that military classic *Enemy Infiltration,* now being used as a textbook by PD. Find out if he's been murdered, or smuggled to Earth."

Gideon looked at him sarcastically. "You wouldn't have something else I could do—in my spare time?"

CHAPTER TWO

IN HIS ROLE as Telefax reporter, Gideon made an appointment to see Dr. Fellbank for an article on Galani surgical techniques being made suitable for use by Earth doctors. Fellbank was cooperative, and Gideon found it hard to believe that this mild-mannered physician was a Suspect— a traitor to his planet. Surely, Fellbank was intelligent enough to see through the hypocrisy of Galani propaganda. There was a possibility that he was operating as a Suspect against his will. A truth serum test was impractical, but Gideon hoped that the radio-jammer hidden in his briefcase would indicate electronic-wave thought-control. When the interview was over, Gideon turned the conversation to a discussion of general Galani medical skills.

"Would the Galani be able to handle advanced myopia cases?" he asked. "My vision is 20/900. It's not that I mind wearing glasses—but in my Telefax work, it's a terrific nuisance."

"The operation," Dr. Fellbank said, "is absurdly simple for a Martian. Microscopic tentacles are inserted through the eye-apertures; the muscles around the eyeball are tightened, so that the eyeball is shortened, bringing the retina nearer to the lens. I have examined dozens of such cases and all have been successful. Of course, the operation is impossible for an Earth surgeon, who must use instruments."

"Would it be possible for me to go to Mars for such treatment? I have tried contact lenses but I can't get used to them."

Fellbank shook his head as if surprised at Gideon's naivete. "There's a waiting list, two years long, of Earthmen seeking admission to Galani hospitals. They're very selective on Mars and usually operate only on influential and highly-placed people."

"I'd be willing to pay the added expenses in order to get treatment earlier."

Dr. Fellbank ignored the subtle bribe. "I'll pass your name on to the Admissions Committee on Mars, headed by my former professor, Mel-El-Aben, but I doubt if it will do you any good. Good-day, sir."

ON HIS WAY back to the office, following the interview, Gideon paused at the Ninth Incline, waiting for the express. A group of schoolgirls cluttered around him as they waited for the Sidewalk to stop. When he climbed on and walked towards a seat, the substitute briefcase was already in position for him; the two were swiftly exchanged, and he went on his way. The original case, containing the radio-jammer and other equipment, would be taken to a PD lab, and Gideon would have the report delivered to him at the next PD substation.

There was still the problem of getting a blood-specimen on Dr. Fellbank; one had to consider the possibility of drugs. Gideon did not dare risk a court order, requesting a complete checkup on Dr. Fellbank's medical-identity card. He would be alarmed, and his contacts warned—or he might end as a suicide, taking his secrets with him.

Towards noon, Gideon came to a Music Center and approached one of the uniformed attendants.

"Do you have the latest color-sensory symphony by Quinxon?"

"Saturn Dreams?"

"I'm not quite sure, but I think it is expressed algebraically."

"Of course," the attendant smiled. "M. C. Square. This way, please."

He led him to one of the many booths that lined the wall of the Center. Inside, where the sensory symphonies were induced by drugs, Gideon and Hastings sat down.

"Fellbank was a cold fish," Gideon said; "he didn't bite at my offer of a bribe to get me to Mars. Got any reports on his background?"

"Not much that PD files don't already have," Hastings said, dropping the guise of a sensory-image guider. "He visited Mars in 2243 as an Oppenheimer scholar. Spent six months at the University, where he studied under Mel-El-Aben. His closest Martian friend—strangely enough—turned out to be the Martian general, Scho-La-Nui."

"One of the Galani on our 'missing list.' Evidently Dr. Fellbank became a Suspect on Mars quite rapidly. What more?"

"After returning to Earth, he practiced internal medicine at State Hospital here. In three years he became State's finest physician, with a terrifically big private practice among Upper-Upper-Class people; he takes in pretty sizeable fees."

"Just a bright boy out to make good, huh? Any indication that he may be paid regularly by the Galani?"

"None whatever; that's the tough nut to crack. No vices; no hobbies; no interest in anything but his work. Never known to gamble. Frugal taste. Lives in a cheap four room apartment."

"With his prestige and position, he could afford the best. Is he a miser?"

"I had recordings of all his personal and telephonic conversations psyched by the cybernetic staff. Fellbank's quite normal outside a fanatic devotion to the Galani cause—as if he were a Galani himself."

"Yet, he's obviously not," Gideon said, perplexed by the paradox of an Earthman acting and thinking as if he were a tentacled Galani with a tree-like body eight feet high, and possessing a cellular-construction utterly alien to any species ever evolved on Earth.

"He has one bank account with 4,000 bilars," Hastings went on; "his salary is 2,000 a year and private practice nets him anywhere from 12 to 50,000 a year."

"What does he do with it? He has no big expenses whatever, unless the money is used to finance whatever Suspect cells are under his supervision."

A green light flashed in the small room. Hastings turned on the screen and Ridenour's face appeared. "The report on your trip to Fellbank has just come through," he said. "The equipment in your briefcase showed no indication whatever of electronic thought-control. No evidence of drugging, if examination of air exhaled from his lungs means anything."

"What about blood?" Gideon asked. Ridenour nodded. "We got a sample by faking a small accident. Completely normal; no drugs. Apparently Fellbank is a Suspect of his own free will. But wait a minute—there's an added notation on the report saying that the blood-sample showed an unusually high oxygen-content. No significance, though."

"Okay," Gideon said, sighing. He took off his glasses, and rubbed his eyes. "If the Galani can talk a man like Fellbank into betraying his planet, I think it's high time we swept the whole place clean. There must be 20 or 30 rocket-ports all set to do the job."

Ridenour scowled. "Project Victory is highly secret. Keep that big mouth of yours closed; if the Galani ever get information on the location of the rocket-platforms, and the central control room, they'll move the universe in order to sabotage them. Sign off."

"Sign off."

The screens cleared as Gideon and Hastings bent over the mass of reports, trying to trace the Galani network on Earth. It was a heartbreaking task for it meant looking for traitors among humans who seemingly had no reason whatever to betray their world. Gideon, in particular, found it hard to understand why Earthmen turned Suspect—despite the many years he had spent studying Galani history and psychology. The tentacled tree-men of Mars had always fascinated him. Perhaps this was the influence of his father, Tom Gideon, who was a spaceman at heart, though he never left the Earth's surface.

James Gideon was born and bred in an atmosphere impregnated with Galani themes. *"Reserve judgment on the Martian planet,"* his father had told him when James was still a boy. *"I want you to study the Galani, and take part in interplanetary politics. Inevitably there will be a judgment day in which one planet or the other must be destroyed. Be in a strong position on that day; but until it comes, reserve judgment."*

He had kept part of his father's plans for him. He had gravitated towards Planetary Defense, and rose high in its councils. In one thing alone did he fail old Tom; he did not reserve judgment. Familiarity with information gathered by PD convinced him that the Galani were merciless monsters, fanatically dedicated to the future annihilation of the human race. How could old Tom have failed to realize that? He shuddered at the implications...

DR. FELLBANK televised him on the following evening at his home.

"You've been quite lucky," the doctor said when his image cleared on the screen. "One of my patients suffered an accident, which will make it impossible for her to leave the planet. She had a reservation on the next rocket, and it's yours if you want it."

Gideon tried to appear hesitant. "I...think I can get a substitute to fill in my desk at Telefax. When is the flight?"

"The rocket is scheduled for tomorrow. You will have to buy your ticket through the port-agency, which holds the cancellation. I am afraid they will ask for a premium."

Fellbank stated the price, and it was quite high. It represented all of Gideon's savings in the bank under his working-name; apparently Fellbank's espionage-unit was in top form.

"You can earn it back," Fellbank said, "by writing some scripts on Galani surgery. I will give you a letter of introduction to Mel-El-Aben, one of the most famous Martian medics."

It was an unexpected prize. Galani surgeons kept to themselves, and a world that virtually worshipped their medical skill would be grateful for information on their working methods. Apparently, Dr. Fellbank was quite anxious for Gideon to go to Mars. On a hunch, when the connection broke, Gideon televised Hastings and had him check the fate of the woman whose place he was to take.

"It was an accident, all right," Hastings said when the PD agent reports trickled in; "she was pushed in front of a truck by an unidentified Earthman. The ticket automatically passed on to the next person on the waiting list, but was suddenly withdrawn on Instructions from Mars itself."

"Thanks," Gideon said hollowly. *They all seem quite anxious to get me to Mars,* he thought. He 'vised Ridenour to report, but his superior was already aware of the decision.

"You are to appear immediately for a truth serum test."

Gideon resented the implication. "Why?"

Ridenour coldly flashed a report on the screen. "This is a transcript of a teleradio report direct from Mel-El-Aben on Mars to Dr. Fellbank:

...as for the eye operation on James Gideon, it will be a simple matter. Expedite affairs so that he comes here as quickly as possible. I knew his father quite well. In time James Gideon will be one of us.

The transcript was whipped away and Ridenour's angry face was on the screen again. "PD agents will pick you up," he said; "if you are a Suspect, and manage to survive the truth serum, I'll take personal pleasure in killing you."

"BUT LISTEN, Nick," Gideon shouted as the screen faded away. PD agents were already at the door when he left the apartment. They stood on each side of him, paralyzers ready, and escorted him to the Sidewalk Express. The suddenness of the accusation had stunned him. Not that Ridenour lacked reason; the ease with which Fellbank secured rocket-passage was suspicious in itself. The meaning of Mel-El-Aben's instructions to Fellbank tugged at his mind, as if some forgotten memory were trying to assert itself.

"I knew his father quite well..." the Galani words said; yet that was a manifest impossibility—Tom Gideon had never left Earth, and to the best of his knowledge Mel-El-Aben had never left Mars. True, Gideon's father had once worked as a minor official in one of the rocket-ports built as possible bases for hell-bombers. If the Galani had established Suspect-cells on Earth some decades ago, it was conceivably possible that Mel-El-Aben had been smuggled to Earth and had 'converted' Gideon's father—if such conversion were possible.

But most disconcerting was the blunt statement. *"In time, James Gideon will be one of us."*

When they reached the PD sub-station in Ridenour's apartment, Gideon accepted the truth serum hypo with a mixture of fear and eagerness. If, subconsciously, he had been "converted" either by hypnotism or electronic thought-control—the serum would uncover the subterfuge.

Drugged, half-aware of the questions that Ridenour hurled at him, Gideon spoke mechanically, and without any effort at evasion. Name? Age? Political beliefs? Your opinion on the Treaty of 2009? Are you a Suspect? Have you disobeyed any PD orders? When? Why? What were the circumstances? In the event of war, what would you do? Why? Why? Why?

* * *

When he came out of the drug's control the relaxed faces of Ridenour and the two PD agents near him assured Gideon that all was well.

"No doubts," Ridenour said, suddenly relaxed as if he had undergone a great strain. "No evasions, and no doubts. You're as sound as McDonough himself."

"But the transcript of Mel-El-Aben's instructions?" Gideon asked.

"Apparently a plant, to cast suspicion upon you. The Galani must know that you are a PD agent and that we have tapped all of Fellbank's wires, screens, and radios. There's a slip up somewhere—perhaps in PD itself. I just checked them myself with this serum," he said, noticing the two agents in the room, "and they've checked me. We're all loyal, praise the skies."

"What about the trip to Mars?"

"Go through with it; maybe you can bluff your way. I'll give you truth serum equipment to use on Munnheim and our other agents there. The stuff is now foolproof; at last we've hit on an infallible system to uncover Suspects. Unfortunately, they're too strong now and have incensed public opinion against its general use. But that doesn't prevent us from using it ourselves."

Gideon's mind was on the dangerous mission to Mars. If the Galani knew that he was PD, and that their attempt to incriminate him had failed, he could not expect to accomplish much. Worse yet, he would be placing his life in their hands if he underwent the eye operation. As if sensing his line of thought, Ridenour said, "Use your own judgment regarding the eye operation. You can return to Earth whenever you choose. While you're on Mars, report directly to Chief McDonough. He has all the records, having taken a personal interest in the Galani threat—did I tell you, by the way, that one of his ancestors was tortured to death by Mel-El-Aben himself? Praise the skies, I'll be on a much-needed vacation in the meantime—unless Project Victory breaks and we blow up the whole damn red planet."

CHAPTER THREE

MARS WAS visible in the skies when Gideon arrived on the following night at the Taos launching platforms. When the guards filled out his passport, they automatically wrote in the word *"Therapy"* after the query, *"Purpose of visit?"*

Commercial and diplomatic travelers were rare; most affairs could be handled by teleradio. Since the treaty forbid the admission of Galani to Earth, the rockets were usually filled only with the sick and aged who sought the expensive services of Martian physicians and surgeons. The fact that from five to fifteen percent of the rockets failed to get through to Mars—blowing up or disappearing mysteriously in space—did not deter the long waiting lines of Earthmen and women whose only hope for life and health lay in the miraculous tentacles of Galani surgeons, who had perfected their techniques after thousands of years of practice. Who would undergo a knife in an old man's clumsy hands when practiced tentacles, each a microscopic mind in itself, could heal painlessly and effectively?

Gideon mingled in the waiting room with the other 35 hopefuls, all drawn to Mars by the lure of quick and easy surgery. He glanced at the passenger listing, amazed at the indication that most patients were chosen from the ranks of the rich or famous. Heading the list was Senator Burbank, a violent Galaniphobe, whose speeches in the Senate had long denounced any attempts to alleviate the conditions of the 2009 Treaty, Gideon approached him on the pretext of an interview for Telefax.

"No one is second to me," Burbank said—his face and words recorded in the Telefax receiver carried in Gideon's pocket—"in my regard for Galani skill. The very fact that I go to seek their aid for an unfortunate kidney complication, and cardiac troubles, which Earth doctors have been unable to correct, is proof of my faith in their genius. But this does not alter my determination that not one sentence of the Treaty of 2009 be changed. Two great cultures cannot exist side-by-side on the same planet; eventually there would be a clash of wills—the opinions of many misguided Earthmen— commonly called Suspects—to the contrary, I am unalterably opposed to any weakening of the barriers between the two worlds."

His words were broken off by the barked orders to take seats on the rocket. The men and women herded into the aisle were the usual assortment of patients bound for Martian hospitals. Here was a young man with blue lips, patently a cardiac case. Seated about him in the various padded compartments were nephritics, tuberculars, cancerites, ulcer-ridden businessmen, and scarred radiation-workers, all seeking aid.

Virtually everyone would return to Earth with bodies cleansed of disease. Gratitude alone, the PD Agent decided, could account for the growing number of Suspects.

"Strictly off the record, Senator," Gideon said after the acceleration of the launched Mars-bound rocket had lessened, "what do you think of the Suspects?"

The Senator's face hardened. "Traitors who should be shot. Let me tell you something, young man; they are growing increasingly powerful. A good one-tenth of the Senate is composed of Galani partisans, and before long their demands for Treaty-revision in favor of Mars will be met."

"Any idea what makes them that way?"

The Senator was puzzled. "I just don't know—and it worries me. I used to think it was misguided idealism, of the sort that once favored anti-vivisection legislation. But the

Galani make no secret of their intention to destroy the Earth when and if they get the chance. What motive can the Suspects have to aid the would-be destroyers of their own world? It is beyond understanding; perhaps a fresh mind like yours can solve this baffling riddle."

ON ARRIVAL at Deimosport, Gideon registered at Skyways Hotel. Its ornate entrance bore the words, which the Galani deeply resented: *"For Earthmen Only."* Its lobby was the crossroads for interplanetary routes that stretched from Venus to Jupiter. Import-export officials, consular representatives, planet-hopping vacationists, and cure-seekers filled its halls, their merriment ringing everywhere. A peculiar gaiety filled the Hotel. Most of it came by deliriously happy Earthlings, cured of lingering diseases, awaiting transport home. Underlying it, however, was a deep-seated understanding that all of them were living on a planet that would be blasted to nothing the moment Earth-Galani relationships were stretched to the breaking point. Project Victory, in which guided hell-bombs were already prepared in launching ports on Earth, was no secret to the men and women in Skyways Hotel.

PD Agent Munnheim, a commercial code-clerk at the Import-Export Bank, contacted Gideon in the Andromeda Lounge, where sensory-image perfume filled the air, evoking subtle sensations of the artificial Venusian luxury-world. They sat in a corner of the bar where opaque light-walls shielded them from observation. They exchanged credentials and a superficial truth serum injection, whose effect lasted long enough to check PD loyalty.

"For the world's sake," the ruddy Munnheim said, "get McDonough to send a few shiploads of the serum. The planet is loaded with Suspects. They've infiltrated into every agency and office in Deimosport. I can't trust my own

Agents here. Some of my closest friends have been holding secret meetings with Galani warriors. About one fifth of the PD agents here are known Suspects, and Galani sympathizers. How many of the other four-fifths are loyal to Earth, I don't know—at times I am afraid of finding out."

Gideon asked the question, which still baffled them all. "What makes traitors out of them?"

"Drugs," Munnheim said flatly, "every known Suspect has, at one time or another, been in close, personal contact with a Galani physician. Something is done to them that changes their conception of right and wrong, wipes out a lifetime of loyalty to Earth, and replaces that loyalty with devotion to the Galani and their ambition to destroy our world."

Gideon shook his head. "We've repeatedly examined Suspects. There's no trace of any drug in their blood, bodies, or air."

"But there *is* a difference," Munnheim broke in quickly, "the blood of Suspects has an abnormally-high percentage of oxygen. I've studied the reports. It's true also in the case of Dr. Fellbank, which you followed."

"It has no significance that our doctors can find."

Gideon recalled medical experiments on Earth, in which PD physicians tried to duplicate the blood-content of Suspects in an effort to discover the significance of the oxygen-rate; there was none.

"But it *must* be in medical treatment," Munnheim said, pressing his point, "else why have the Galani refused to permit Earthmen to watch their surgical operations?"

"They *have* permitted it. Hundreds of Earth-doctors have watched and studied such operations."

"Non-Suspect doctors?"

GIDEON stopped suddenly, as if trying to draw up some underlying thought deep in his subconscious. Munnheim's suspicions were correct. Dr. Fellbank had witnessed many operations—but he was a Suspect. If Suspects were produced medically, then obviously only Suspect-doctors would be permitted to become familiar enough with Galani techniques to understand the process. It followed, then, that the whole membership of the medical profession that ever studied on Mars, was Suspect. It explained, also, why the Galani never permitted Telefax camera-recording of major operations. Permission was freely granted for a few decades, following the Treaty of 2009—and then gradually withdrawn until it could not be secured at all.

"It's in their surgery!" Gideon said, elated at the discovery of a lead that might explain the strange hold the Galani held over its Suspects. "If we can secure a camera-recording of an operation performed on a non-Suspect we might get the secret. The record, studied by loyal PD physicians, might indicate the means."

"There'll be some stink," Munnheim said, captured by Gideon's enthusiasm, "but it's worth the risk. Maybe they install some sort of thought-control radio that defies our jammers. If so, a photographic-record of the operation might indicate how it's done. There's still enough serum to test a few of the PD's here. If they're loyal, I'll arrange to plant ourselves with a camera in one of the operating rooms; we'll get the evidence..."

The evidence, Gideon thought ruefully, *will provoke war if it is found that the Galani are forcing Earthmen and women to turn traitor against their will.*

In that case, he would feel no compunctions in urging Project Victory. The Martian Galani would be destroyed, but the future of the human race would be saved. To his own surprise he felt a wave of secret admiration at the skill and persistence of the tree-like Galani, waging their hopeless cold war against the Earth. They knew they would be destroyed the moment Earth discovered what was being done; but still they fought back by secret infiltration into Earthling's loyalty. If there actually was such a secret invasion—made possible by Galani medical skills—Mars would be annihilated.

*   *   *

It was several days before Munnheim was able to arrange for the secret observation of a case of Galani surgery. Blueprints of the Galani hospital, open only to patients and sympathetic Earth-physicians who had passed a screening board, had to be secured. Tapping of teleradios, wires, and management offices produced the schedule of operations; the names of the patients and doctors; and the rooms in which the operations would be held.

Gideon ran his finger down the list.

"There's our man," he said suddenly. "Senator Burbank is due for heart and kidney surgery. He's been on record for many years as being steadfastly opposed to any revision of the Treaty of 2009. If he turns Suspect, the Galani will have won a powerful ally; millions of people would say that if Burbank is in favor of admitting Galani to Earth, then it must be all right."

"You figure the surgeons will try to make a Suspect out of him?"

"There couldn't be a better ally for them. The operating surgeon is listed as Mel-El-Aben; he's Dr. Fellbank's immediate superior in the Suspect espionage group."

Gideon remembered the transcript of Mel-El-Aben's instructions to Dr. Fellbank. *"I knew his father quite well. In time James Gideon will be one of us."* Of course, it was a countermove to discredit him in the eyes of the PD—but a doubt still lingered in his mind. What if the words had more meaning than he thought? Coldness swept up within him and clammy fingers encircled his heart; a pain began to beat in his head. He shook the feeling away. Of course they would try to make a Suspect out of him—but he knew that he would never undergo any Galani surgery. Thick eyeglasses or not, he preferred freedom with myopic eyes over good sight as a Galani suspect-slave.

The momentary feeling of panic eased away as he and Munnheim made their final plans to secretly observe Galani surgery in action.

CHAPTER FOUR

ON THE NIGHT before Burbank's scheduled operation, Gideon and Munnheim entered the hospital through the fuel-chambers. For several hours they waited, cramped in a packing case, until the guard schedule permitted them to reach the third floor without observation. The individual rooms were filled with Earthling patients, but the main offices were staffed entirely by Martian Galani. Their giant tree-like figures rolled eerily down the hospital hallways, casting quivering shadows.

Once in the operating room, they set up camera and rope-guards in the shaftways used for the disposal of laundry. It was an uncomfortable position, hanging on a rope with a loaded camera perched precariously on shoulders. "It'll be safe enough," Munnheim said, "unless one of the Galani decides to look down this shaft."

The circular doorway of the laundry shaft swung open slightly, so the camera lens could emerge, Gideon could see nothing but the hall doorway opposite them, and a crescent of space that would be occupied by the surgeon and patient.

* * *

At noon, the red doors swung open and Mel-El-Aben, Galani Surgeon, First Grade, rolled in.

Gideon had seen many Martians, but each sight was virtually a new shock, Aben was monstrously tall and heavy. The main trunk of his body, some eight feet high, resembled a blasted, ivy-colored, deformed oak tree. Green tentacles emerging from two main branches, hung over him like blossoming foliage.

Millions of years in a constantly changing environment had produced this complicated species, which embodied features of both plant and animal life. In the struggle for survival on a hostile world, the life expectancy of the individual Galani had been tremendously increased—but at a frightful cost. Though the life span had reached as high as 700 years, the Galani had their Achilles heel in a declining birthrate. Simple creatures reproduced without difficulty, but the incredible complexity of the Galani structure made the newborn death rate a source of terror.

For several hundred thousand years, the Galani had known they were a doomed race; their entire science had been concentrated upon medicine, biology, surgery, and the other physical fields of knowledge in an effort to find an answer. In addition, racial memory, whereby each individual Galani held the instincts, thoughts, and aspirations of his ancestors, made the future fate of the species a highly personal tragedy to each Martian Galani.

The operating chamber, red throughout as if to complement the green tentacles, had no furniture but a concave diagonal chair upon which the pillaring form of Mel-El-Aben leaned. The patient, Senator Burbank, was wheeled in on a pink stretcher by another Galani and set before Aben. The second Galani left and Mel-El-Aben remained alone with the quietly breathing, but unconscious, Senator Burbank.

Gideon shifted the camera lens so it would be directed at the Senator's chest. "Hypnotic suggestion," Munnheim whispered. "All anesthesia is strictly local. I understand that the Galani manufactures it himself in his own brown-blood vessels."

ABEN'S TWO tentacles rested upon the bare chest. The green branching appendages divided into two, then, four, eight, and sixteen parts, dividing again and again until a gossamer filament seemed to envelope the Senator. Each of the microscopic needles was like a living, intelligent pinpoint knife, able to push through tissue, curving and wending through bone and muscle. In a few minutes the Senator's chest was infiltrated with several hundred spidery threads, each one under the absolute precision control of Mel-El-Aben's brain. They severed nerve, anesthetized, seared, and healed with such infinite care that virtually no one died of internal hemorrhage.

Gideon's camera ground away silently, taking pictures of the operation, which would be studied with minute cue by PD. The outer technique was obvious, but nothing could record what those miracle-working tentacles were doing under the skin. The Galani produced drugs from his own body and there was no way in which the camera could record the process. Within an hour surgical treatment of the heart was over; the Senator was then rolled over on his back, a portion of the tentacles removed and then placed over the small of his back. This was the kidney operation. As yet, Mel-El-Aben had made no move in which a thought-control device could conceivably be planted in the Senator's body. When Aben's tentacles were lifted from the body there were no marks but a slight bluish discoloration; the quiet, measured breathing of the Senator continued.

"He hasn't done a thing that would affect the Senator's willpower or character," Gideon whispered to Munnheim as he twisted about for a better hold on the rope. "Maybe we made a mistake in thinking that hypnotism has been ruled out; there seems to be no answer, surgically."

The door of the operating room opened again, but instead of one Galani who should come to remove the patient, several green-enveloped Martians entered. They filled the room quickly; their bodies, pressed upon the laundry-chute door, slamming it shut. Munnheim cursed softly, but Gideon shushed him for the muffled sounds of the Galani could be heard.

"O mighty Mel-El-Aben," a husky, grating voice, made by the rasping of two tentacles rubbing against each other, cut through the air in Martial Galani syllables. Munnheim, his mouth held toward Gideon's ear, quickly translated, "Surgeon without equal, and devoted patriot, is this worthless carrion alive?"

"The Senator from the putrid third planet," Mel-El-Aben's voice answered, "is well; his body is healthy, and no damage has been done."

"General Scho-La-Nui, now serving our species on Earth, reports that this Burbank holds a strategic post in the Senate; we have need of Earthmen in his position."

"It shall be done, my friends. Let the operation proceed."

The Galani were now silent, nor could their actions be seen by the two Earthmen hiding in the chute. Gideon waited impatiently, hoping that one of the brown bodies with green tentacles would move so that he could photograph the operation. When at last they did leave, several hours later, nothing could be seen but a hasty shifting to the doors as the Galani rolled away from the scene of the operation. Burbank's body was gone. At night Gideon and Munnheim crawled out of the storage room and escaped safely to town, angry at their failure to discover the means by which Earthmen became Suspects.

That such means existed was now beyond doubt.

ON THE following day Gideon scanned the current issue of the facsimile *Deimosport News* on his desk. Munnheim ruefully pointed to a lead article.

Scho-La-Nui, noted War Veteran, killed in rocket crash. Nineteen Galani, including General Scho-La-Nui, whose military exploits during the late war earned him immortality in the hearts of the Galani, were killed in a rocket crash in Revenge Desert yesterday noon. All bodies were burned beyond recognition. Intimations that Planetary Defense agents—Earth's terroristic organization—were responsible for the crash have been stoutly denied by Earth-authorities. Several motors were tampered with, investigators declare...

Gideon angrily crumpled the facsimile and flung it away. "A set of deliberate lies," he said, "to stir up hatred against Earth. What was it the Galani said in the operating room? 'General Scho-La-Nui, now serving on Earth.' Evidently the crash was deliberately caused by the Galani to throw off suspicion regarding Scho-La-Nui's activities and location. If we think he's dead, the PD won't search for him on Earth."

Munnheim read the passenger listing. "Nineteen dead," he said, "and fifteen of them were war veterans formerly involved in information-work—or espionage, as we call it."

"They've all been smuggled to Earth," Gideon said, "and a mass of dead Galani bodies put on the rocket and destroyed. Try to get our own PD agents there—though I'm certain not a single body will be identified."

The telescreen glimmered on the table and Gideon turned on the switch. The face of an attaché in Earth's consulate office swirled on the screen. Munnheim backed away to be out of the field of vision.

"The Galani Government," the attaché announced, "has formally asked us to recall all PD agents on Mars, on the grounds that their activities constitute a menace to Earth-Mars relationships."

"My name is on the list, of course," Gideon said.

The attaché, a loyal PD, shook his head. "No. Funny thing is that the whole Earth-colony here knows you are PD. It's impossible that the Galani are unaware of the fact, yet you are not listed. Do you want a copy of the diplomatic letter?"

"Put the name-list on the screen."

Munnheim, having recognized the voice of the speaker, leaned forward with Gideon to study the listing of PD agents requested to leave Mars. All of them were loyal, and none had ever undergone treatment in Galani hospitals. PD agents, the Galani charge read, acted as brutal conquerors in an occupied country. Their continued presence could be regarded as an unfriendly act, contrary to the spirit of the Treaty of 2009.

"The diplomatic maneuver," Gideon said, when the attaché's copy of the request cleared from the screen, "will force a showdown in the Senate. Apparently they have become quite confident that enough Suspects in the Senate will vote in their favor. I think I'd better go back to Earth before the big blow-up—but first I'll have a word with Senator Burbank."

THE INTERVIEW was easily arranged, on visitors' day in the hospital. One of the Galani led him to the bedside where the pale Senator greeted him.

"Just feeling tired," he said, "but apart from that I'm perfectly fine. These Galani doctors can perform miracles."

"I'm glad to hear that, Senator; when will you return to Earth?"

"As soon as they permit me—which will be in a week or so, I imagine. I am anxious to get back to the Senate in view of the critical Earth-Mars diplomatic relations."

"Are you referring, Senator, to the Galani request that PD agents be recalled to Earth?"

"Yes. The record of Planetary Defense is a foul one. Our agents, instead, of representing the best that Earth can offer, have been recruited from criminals, perverts, and other debased character groups. They have amassed great wealth for themselves by abusing their positions of trust. Through them we have insulted and abused a great people, the Galani. Young man," he said, pointing a finger at Gideon, "when you return to Earth you may quote every word I say to Telefax; and what is more, I will give you an unquestionable scoop."

He leaned back with a satisfied smile on his face. Gideon felt cold, remembering some ancient proverb that said if you must tell lies, tell gigantic ones. Gideon knew the work of the PD, having read the Martian agents' reports. The Senator's outburst was sheer fabrication.

"What is this scoop, Senator?"

"Having met the Galani, and having studied conditions here first hand, I have reconsidered my stand on the Treaty of 2009. I am in favor of immediate revision, and I hope that all my many friends in the Senate will vote with me for the abrogation of all limits upon trade and immigration between our two great planets."

Gideon thanked him and after a few more words, walked away with a pain that clutched at his mind.

Senator Burbank was now a traitor-Suspect.

A Galani nurse, evidently a female—the trunk was shorter, and the tentacles brighter in color—met him in the corridor. "Please enter this doorway," she said, her tentacles slurring the unfamiliar English words. "O mighty, noble news-correspondent of Telefax, this doorway please."

He entered a small, bare room—empty but for the massive figure of a brown-and-green Galani who stood in its center.

He whirled the sound-producing tentacles. "I am Mel-El-Aben."

"It is an honor," Gideon answered, "to meet the surgeon, whose skill is renowned throughout the solar system. This poor, unimportant…"

"Dispense with the formalities," Mel-El-Aben's voice said sharply; "between us, there need be no hypocrisy."

THE GALANI'S tentacles twitched as if with great emotion. It was said that their feelings could be read in the changing tints of their tentacles, but Gideon found no clue to the meaning of this strange meeting. It was best to be silent.

"You have delayed submitting to surgery. Why?"

"I have reconsidered," Gideon said; "wearing thick lens glasses is not such a handicap."

"You do not trust us. You think perhaps that we will kill you on the operating table, because we know you are a highly-placed agent in Planetary Defense's espionage-corps."

"The surgeon is mistaken."

"Mel-El-Aben makes no mistake. In any event, the operation will not be performed. In its place we have other treatment planned. It may interest you to know that all reports sent to McDonough in Washington have been intercepted by us. In their place we have sent your conclusions that the Suspect-organization on Earth will be abandoned the moment the Senate votes for treaty revision. We have also included your considered opinion that peace with the Galani is not only possible, but quite essential, and that self-seeking PD agents in the past have sent false reports. Since we know what your actual opinions are at the moment, you realize that we cannot permit you or Munnheim to return to Earth."

Gideon turned abruptly and ran to the door, intent on escape. A jab of pain shot through his shoulder, twisting him about so that he could see the raised Galani tentacle plunged like a needle in him. He grasped the wiry branch and pulled. His whole body was wrenched from within.

"Fool," Mel-El-Aben said. "I can kill you by producing poison at the tip, but a strong sedative will serve the purpose as well."

Gideon lunged, kicking at the brown mass, hoping to free himself. Mel-El-Aben reeled back, but the tentacle held. A numbness grew in Gideon's back; with his fists, he hammered at Mel-El-Aben's body and felt a weakness grow in his arms. The world blackened but before unconsciousness swept over him he dimly heard the door bust open and the loud report of paralyzer-guns rip through the suffocating air.

CHAPTER FIVE

HE AWOKE to see Munnheim's anxious face hovering over him. There was the jab of a hypo-needle, and his mind suddenly cleared. They were in a copse of reddish trees; in the distance could be seen the vague outlines of the hospital.

"I followed you," Munnheim said, "and entered the hospital on the pretext of visiting another patient. When I saw you enter the small room, I simply listened at the door."

Gideon shook his head, clearing away the last traces of Aben's drug. "They've framed the whole PD," he said, "made us appear like devils, faked our reports to Washington, and misled headquarters as to the true state of affairs here."

"I should have killed him instead of using a paralyzer," Munnheim said, helping Gideon to his wobbly feet. "No one saw me drag you out, but when Mel-El-Aben comes to within the hour there will be a dragnet put out for you."

They crawled through the bushes, away from the hospital and in the general direction of the hotel and the launching-port. They hid behind some abandoned rest-cottages as a busload of Earth patients rode out from the hospital to the Earth bound rocket. They watched the red dust settle and then walked on the road.

"Passports for the patients," Gideon said, "have all been cleared. If I could substitute for one of them..."

"...and ride back to Earth today?" Munnheim concluded. "Good, if it can be done; but they're all Suspects by now, and each identity is known. Better try the stowaway trick."

The rocket for Earth gleamed in the faint evening light, the long row of passengers lining up to present their passports at the main gate. In the rear of the rocket, husky

Galani lifted the baggage racks with steel-like tentacles, and shoved them through, between the jets.

"Baggage room," Gideon whispered. "There's only one Galani on duty; keep him busy for ten minutes while I crawl into one of the crates."

"You'll never pull through the acceleration."

"The chance has to be taken. I'll be arrested by customs on Earth, but I'll manage to get in touch with Ridenour. Get going, Munnheim, and wish me luck!"

They shook hands quickly, and Munnheim walked to the front of the baggage office. When the Galani's body was turned, Gideon stepped into the back and hurriedly walked to the rear door, where a truckload of rocket-bound crates and luggage was assembled.

"I beg your pardon," he could hear Munnheim's voice saying, "but I left some bags here yesterday and lost my ticket."

The crates were locked, but Gideon swiftly opened one with the aid of a crowbar, and hurriedly flung out the assortment of clothing and personal effects. He kicked the material away and then climbed into the crate, pulling down the top over his head and holding it in place with the crowbar. The rumble of a hand truck was heard and a few minutes later he felt the crate juggle as if clutched in the tentacles of a Galani. He felt himself raised and flung across another crate. The crash ripped the top out of his hands and sent him flying against the crate wall. It was dark inside the rocket's storage section. He heard the faint roar of the motors and a Galani call out, "All set with baggage! Lock doors!"

The lone door closed, and the rocket shook as it gained power for the long voyage back to Earth. A sudden blast told him the rocket had set off; a few minutes later, blood came rushing through his nose and mouth and darkness set its claws upon him.

HE AWOKE some hours later, weakened by loss of blood and the shock of acceleration. No bones were broken and his eyeglasses were miraculously intact. A sharp headache persisted but this too seemed to be passing.

He hammered upon the bulkhead door until a surprised steward opened it. Gideon surrendered himself, knowing that passenger-rockets did not dare turn back in mid-space and that, come what may, they would get to Earth. He knew that the patients were all Suspects, but the pilots may still be loyal; their presence would save him from instant execution. It would be an easy thing to say that he had been killed during unprotected acceleration.

"Name and rank?" the Second Mate asked when he had been led to the control rooms.

"James Gideon, Agent, Planetary Defense, Intelligence Corps. Here are my papers."

The Second Mate glanced over them hurriedly. "For all I know, you're a Galani spy like the rest of the traitors among the passengers. The PD will find that out soon enough; consider yourself under arrest. Customs officers and PD will be teleradioed, and informed of your presence on the vessel. They'll meet you when we land. In the meantime get the hell in the back, among the rest of the passengers."

Gideon sighed. For the time being, all was well; he leaned back in a passenger seat, pressing his hands upon his pain-wracked forehead. He hoped he would reach Earth in time to save Munnheim and the rest of the loyal PDs on Mars. Only evacuation would save them,now; the Galani had become brutally direct in their hidden war with Earth. They possessed some secret that made them supremely confident of victory; the hate-campaign in their facsimile papers was reaching a new height of arrogance. On top of strained diplomatic relations was the knowledge that traitor-Suspects had become increasingly powerful on Earth. If every man who had ever visited Mars for medical treatment was a traitor, then Earth's position was precarious indeed.

Earth still held the upper hand, Gideon knew, and this thought gave him hope. Project Victory—in which atomic warfare could be unleashed in one minute from a building near Washington, and thus destroy Mars in one sweep—was ready if needed. The threat to use this secret weapon would stop the Galani once and for all. The thought of the planet Mars, blasted and ruined forever, made him uneasy. But if Gideon had to choose between the survival of the human race or the Galani, would there be any doubt where his loyalties belonged?

When the rocket landed on Earth he was promptly arrested, placed in a cell, and held incommunicado. His identification papers were taken by the local PD officer, but this was to be expected; the prints, descriptions and signatures would automatically be checked with the main files in Washington.

For three days he lay in his cell, watched by the overhead observation lens, without seeing or hearing any man. His food trays, without knives or forks, came sliding through slots that opened and closed mechanically. The dishes were of paper; he had no razor or glass, and his face began to grow haggard.

ON THE FOURTH day he was brought forth before the PD tribunal, a weakened, exhausted figure.

"I demand to know on what charge I am being held," Gideon said, "and that my PD superiors Nick Ridenour, and Chief McDonough, be informed of my arrest."

The presiding officer leaned forward across the judge's stand. As he did so his hair fell over his eyes and he pushed back the toupee angrily. Gideon wondered for a moment why one so young was bald and needed a wig.

"The charge," the judge said, "is murder. You are accused of strangling Planetary Defense Agent Munnheim. Three witnesses saw you commit the murder and attempt to escape through the baggage room of the Earth rocket. In addition you have been charged with treason, with the attempt to kill Mel-El-Aben, one of the greatest, noblest surgeons the mighty race of Galani had ever produced."

"You—you are a Suspect!" Gideon blurted suddenly. He looked wildly about him, but saw only suspicion and hatred in the eyes of the judges and guards. "I demand the truth serum," he shouted, feeling walls close in upon him. If a PD court was Suspect what hope could there be? "I demand that my case be brought before the attention of Nick Ridenour and Chief McDonough, or the President."

The judge rapped his gavel. "Both Agent Ridenour and Chief McDonough are occupied with other duties. A transcript of the testimony given by the witnesses on Mars has already reached us. In view of the delicate interplanetary situation Chief McDonough has authorized each Court to deal out immediate justice in cases of treason. Such a case is now before me.

"On the basis of the evidence before me, and by virtue of the authority invested in me by Planetary Defense, I sentence the accused, James Gideon, to death in the gas chambers at Alamogordo. The execution is to take place tomorrow at noon; court dismissed."

GIDEON spent an uneasy night in his cell. There was no doubt that the PD court was ruled by Suspects; evidently they were quick to pass sentence before it could be overruled by Ridenour or McDonough. He had no way of knowing what was happening in the outside world. If the Senate was infiltrated with Suspects, treaty-revision would be voted; and in a few short days, the Galani would overrun the Earth and rule it through the Suspect organization. His mission to Mars had been a failure, for, despite proof of Galani determination to wage the cold war, he had no knowledge of the means used to convert loyal Earthmen into traitor-Suspects. Such means did exist and he was convinced that the answer lay in surgery. But how? Why?

A guard hammered on the iron door and then walked into the small cell. It was early afternoon and the execution was set for evening. The guard carried a pressed suit of clothes and toilet implements under his arm.

"You can shave and wash up," he said. "I'll be back in a half hour."

"Thanks," Gideon replied, grimly. At least they would permit him to die decently. The suit was surprisingly a good fit and his own was stained and tattered. He washed and shaved slowly. He felt no fear but his heart pounded; his face flushed, and the dull ache, which troubled him since the rocket flight, throbbed again in his head. When he was finished, the guard came and escorted him out of the prison to a waiting PD truck. They walked past armed guards, all of them hostile, hatred and contempt in their eyes whenever Gideon stepped near.

In the truck he was manacled to the wall. There were no windows within and he could not guess the general direction in which they rode. The guard beside him sat silently.

An hour later the truck stopped and its rear door opened. This was not Alamogordo, he knew. "Am I to be shot while 'attempting escape?' " he asked bitterly. Apparently they did not dare execute him officially, so illegal means would be chosen. When the truck rode by, leaving them in the field, he recognized the desert-surroundings of the Taos Airport. A black jet, unnumbered and with no identification, stood in the center of the field.

"The sentence has been suspended," the guard said when he led Gideon to the plane. His voice was almost respectful. "The judge almost made a mistake, but everything will be settled now."

"Am I being released?" Gideon demanded. "Where will you take me?"

"The court decided that you were ill on Mars, and not responsible for your actions; it has committed you to the care of Dr. S. T. Fellbank."

Feeling the prod of the paralyzer, Gideon stepped into the jet.

HIS APPARENT docility convinced the guard, for when he entered the jet, Gideon was ready for him. He jammed his knee into the guard's belly, then brought his fist against the man's mouth. The guard crumpled and fell upon his face. Gideon leaned down, picked the paralyzer from the holster and turned to face the pilot's seat. There was no one there, but the jet soon roared and set off, acceleration flinging him against the wall. "Pre-set automatic," he muttered when he made his way to the control board and tried to take over the flight.

The instruments would not respond, and he knew that any effort to tamper with them would warn the control agent in Taos. Jets from other ports would launch and intercept him no matter what route he took. He had no choice but to stay where he was until the jet reached its destination.

Gideon turned to the unconscious guard and rummaged through his pockets. Aside from PD identity cards with the name and descriptions of Agent Barrows, there was nothing that would indicate where the jet was going or who would meet them at the destination. Barrows was about his general build and appearance. Gideon stripped him of his clothes, and dressed in them. He slapped the guard's face until he was conscious, and then forced him to dress in Gideon's clothes.

"Where is the rocket going?" he demanded.

"New York," Barrows answered, apparently easily resigned to their changed roles.

"Will anyone meet you there?"

The guard seemed to consider this and then shook his head.

Gideon slapped his face. "Don't lie!" he said, "if there's anyone waiting for us I will kill you and say that you attempted to overcome me."

"No one is there," Barrows replied, wearily. "I was to take you to Dr. Fellbank's office."

"For surgery?"

The guard looked up sharply. Their eyes met and Gideon felt as if the man were probing into his soul. Gideon turned his eyes away.

"Don't look at me," he warned, "or I will kill you. Remember that I have nothing to lose. Why does Dr. Fellbank want me?"

"To keep you under observation. You have been ill; you were hurt in the rocket and now you feel fevered. Thoughts are running through your mind; your head aches, and the blood seems to pound and pound and pound..."

"*Stop!*" The guard's voice was hypnotic in its effect. Gideon slapped him again. He dared not look at the man's eyes or listen to him. Was be actually ill? Did he really kill Munnheim on Mars, and was it his imagination that the Galani were a monstrous race who hated the Earth? Ideas swirled through his mind and he tried to shake them away.

"You are a Suspect?"

"Yes."

"You know that the Galani want to destroy the human race. Why do you betray your native planet and aid an alien species of vicious tree-like friends?"

Barrows' eyes flashed angrily. "The Galani were a civilized race when homo sapiens lived like vermin in dark caves; they explored the stars when humanity was still fettered with superstition and ignorance."

"That may be true," Gideon said, speaking earnestly as if to convince the guard—even though it was his own doubting heart that needed the words—"but is it not better to serve your own species than a set of monsters who will wipe out your kind, and everything that your children and children's children may yet be able to achieve? You are human like myself; you have arms, legs, a heart, and mind like I have, and not a brown-bark, green tentacles and a foul putrescent body. Why betray your own people and serve the Galani?"

The guard shook his head in exasperation. "Dr. Fellbank will explain it to you."

"No! He will explain nothing! The Galani have discovered some way whereby the human will can be destroyed and made subservient to an alien race. He wants to treat or operate on me so that I, too, shall become a traitor-Suspect. No, my fine Galani-lover, neither Fellbank nor Mel-El-Aben will make me act like anything but an Earthman. I am human. I was born so, and I will die so."

Barrows said nothing but stared ahead into the darkness.

CHAPTER SIX

As BARROWS said, there was no one to meet them at the port when the jet landed. "This must be," Gideon said, as he brought down the butt of his paralyzer upon the guard's head. The man fell, and Gideon tied his body with sheets torn apart from his clothing. Stepping out alone on the field, Gideon walked calmly away.

From a small paybooth he televised Ridenour's apartment and told him of his whereabouts.

"Evidently the Martians think I am important enough to be worth framing. Was Munnheim really killed?"

"As dead as they make them; it doesn't look too good for you. Where are you now?"

"At the Airport Rest Room. There's probably a dragnet out for me—or there will be as soon as they find the guard's body. Can you send me a group of trusted PD's so I can get to your apartment without being picked up by some Suspects?"

"Sure. Stay there; I'll have some of the boys on the way. Learn anything on Mars?"

"Not much, but I think if we take a few Suspects by force, and even dissect them if necessary, we might find out how it's done. See you later."

He switched off and then walked out into the waiting room. The excitement of the escape must have damaged his better judgment; it was a mistake, he realized suddenly, to make a direct call to Ridenour's apartment. Since the Suspect organization was so extensive, they would undoubtedly tap all PD wires; they might even reach him before Ridenour's men could. How could he tell, anyway, whether the PD who approached him were loyal or Suspect? It was a foolish, dangerous move; he would have been wiser to go to Ridenour's apartment directly, and he could still do it.

He left the waiting room, stripping off the PD chevrons on the guard's suit, and took the bus to the city. The apartment was not being guarded; he walked into the hallway and headed for the elevator.

RIDENOUR was alone in his room. "About time," he said, looking up. "We couldn't locate you at the Port."

"Couldn't help it," Gideon said. "The wires might have been tapped by Suspects and I thought it safer to come here straight. Where can I get in touch with McDonough? My reports to him were intercepted and forged by the Galani; they are probably loaded with misinformation regarding Galani plans. There's no doubt about it, this time, Ridenour; the Galani are out to destroy us."

Ridenour looked thoughtful. "The new menace from Mars, eh?" he said. "Are the monsters all set to take over the Earth?" He pulled open a desk drawer and rummaged through some papers.

"Yes, at any moment," Gideon said. "They've succeeded in some surefire way of making Earthmen think and act like Galani; even Senator Burbank, who knew the menace for what it was, has become a Suspect. There might be millions of them on Earth!"

Ridenour kept his hand in the desk drawer. "You see them everywhere? These Suspects who are plotting to destroy the Earth?"

"Yes. They're in the Senate and they have infiltrated the PD. Munnheim was killed by a Suspect, if not by the Galani; the judge who sentenced me in Taos is a Suspect; and so is the guard who brought me to New York. The danger is great! I don't know what their immediate plans are, but their ultimate goal is to make Earth subservient to the Galani."

"I see," Ridenour said, "and when is this great calamity to take place? Tonight?"

"Perhaps not tonight, but..." Gideon stopped suddenly; and a sickening, fearful sensation swept through him as if his whole body had been stabbed with a thousand pain-inflicting knives. "You—you, Ridenour, don't believe me! You, too, are a Suspect!"

"I see," Ridenour said, "so I, too, have become part of this great conspiracy to destroy the Earth. It is very interesting, Gideon..."

Gideon stepped forward blindly, unable to grasp the full meaning of the disastrous feeling that gripped him.

"Stay where you are," Ridenour said, pulling out a paralyzer from the desk drawer; "make no move toward me, or I will shoot."

"You—you a Suspect! I should have known! I should have demanded a truth serum test immediately, instead of walking into this trap!"

"No trap," Ridenour said, his firm hand not moving as he held the paralyzer, "but for your own good." He raised his voice. "Will you come in now, Doctor?"

The curtains leading to Ridenour's apartment rooms were pulled apart. Gideon turned his head to look into the smiling face of Dr. S. T. Fellbank.

"Good evening, gentlemen," he said. "I was most interested in our friend Gideon's comments on these Suspects."

Gideon was silent. With Ridenour a Suspect, there was virtually no hope. Ridenour was one of a small handful of men who knew the location of Project Victory control room. If men like him had been turned into Suspects, there was no hope for Earth but the complete atomic destruction of Mars.

The Galani needed no war industry to conquer the Earth; their secret invasion was made by twisting the minds and loyalties of Earthmen. Against such an attack there was no defense but the total annihilation of the planet, which controlled and produced such traitor-Suspects. This was the beginning of interplanetary war, which would continue until one race or the other would be destroyed forever.

"Do not pretend," Gideon said, "for I know that both of you are Suspects."

Ridenour turned slightly to Dr. Fellbank, but he still held the gun firmly. "Your opinion, Doctor?"

"Schizophrenia, obviously. Delusions of persecution, probably accompanied by violent headaches. Do you feel any pain at the base of your skull? Any spots before your eyes?"

Involuntarily Gideon reached for his glasses and ran his fingers quickly across his forehead. "No," he said, lying. "No pain, whatever; none at all! Stop trying to pretend that I am ill!"

THE SMILE dropped from Fellbank's face. "Let us drop the pretense," he said to Ridenour. "I don't think it would be possible to persuade him to surrender to treatment peacefully. Apparently, James Gideon, you saw and understood quite a bit of what is happening on Mars and Earth."

Gideon did not affirm or deny. The truth was that he did not understand; but he hoped that Dr. Fellbank could be tricked into revealing the facts.

"Unfortunately your father did not prepare you for the truth," Dr. Fellbank went on; "if he had, you would realize what we are trying to do."

"My father was not a Suspect!"

"He should at least have given you a thorough grounding in Galani history and psychology. If you knew as much as we do, you would not be opposing us; you would be serving us."

"I am not a traitor to my people and my world," Gideon said coldly.

"If there were time," Dr. Fellbank said, "I would force you to grow up overnight, and understand things, which are now obviously above your level of comprehension. Mel-El-Aben, however, has specifically warned me against tampering with your opinions. That is why we shall do nothing to you but put you in confinement until you realize, and accept, what we are trying to do."

"I will not change," Gideon said. "You will try to convince me that the Galani are superior to homo sapiens, and that we must choose the stronger and destroy the weaker. I reject that basic premise! I am an Earthman, first, last, and always; my destiny is with Earth. It is for my race and my people that I fight, regardless who is superior or weaker."

"Take him," Dr. Fellbank said to Ridenour.

Ridenour stood up. "Do you have any weapons?"

"Yes. In my back pocket."

"Don't reach for it." Paralyzer in hand, Ridenour slowly encircled Gideon, while Dr. Fellbank looked on idly; his free hand reached into the back pocket. With a precision made possible only by years of constant practice in PD gymnasiums, Gideon grasped Ridenour's gun-hand and jerked the trigger finger. The blast rocked the walls of the room. Continuing the same motion, Gideon brought Ridenour's arm over his shoulders and bent forward so that Ridenour's body flew in a flying mare, striking Dr. Fellbank. Both fell backward. Ridenour rolling away and Fellbank drawing the blaster held in his jacket. Gideon drew his own paralyzer and fired twice at the Doctor. Fellbank gasped; a streak of blood ran from mouth and nose and he fell backward, gun hanging loosely in his hand. The third shot of the paralyzer lashed at Ridenour whose face paled; his body leaned weakly against the desk and then collapsed upon the floor.

Gideon stepped closer to the bodies and leaned down to feel the pulses. Dr. Fellbank was dead, killed by the additional paralyzer shot. Ridenour was still alive, though considerably stunned. When he fell against the desk, a toupee slid from his scarred skull.

HOLDING Ridenour under the armpits, Gideon dragged him to the next room and placed him upon the bed. In one of the desks he found the truth serum narcotic kit and hurriedly prepared the solution. The shots had probably been heard and if Ridenour and Fellbank were both in the same apartment, it was evident that it would be used as a Suspect base. He had to work quickly before other members of the Suspect unit came to report to Ridenour.

He plunged the hypo needle into Ridenour's flesh, and waited for the drug to take effect. He had never known Ridenour to wear a toupee, and glanced curiously at the man's head. He was not bald, for new, strong hair was evident. Around the circumference of the skull was a series of fresh scars, barely covered by the toupee.

"Can you hear me?" he asked when he felt Ridenour's body trembling upon the bed. His heart beat strongly and it was clear that Ridenour would live through the combined shocks of paralyzer and truth serum.

Ridenour's lips moved clumsily. "Yes. I can hear you."

Gideon paused before asking the next fearful question.

"Are you a Suspect?"

"Yes."

"When did you become one?"

"Three weeks ago."

"How?"

"Surgery."

"Who performed the surgery?"

"Mel-El-Aben."

"You were on Mars?" Gideon asked, surprised.

"Yes. I was ordered to report to Earth for duty three months ago. The operation was performed by Mel-El-Aben four weeks ago."

Ridenour's answers confused Gideon; his identity was not clear. Apparently Ridenour considered himself a Galani. Who was he in reality? Were Ridenour's answers given by Ridenour's brain or by some telepathic Galani on Mars?

"What is your name?"

"General Scho-La-Nui, Ninth Division, Mars."

"Where is Nick Ridenour?" he asked softly.

"Dead."

Gideon sat down. His knees suddenly weak.

"Tell me in detail why he died, and how it is that Scho-La-Nui, Galani, speaks through the lips of an Earthman."

"Brain-transplantation. It is impossible to remove a human brain from its casing without destroying vital tissue; my own body has also been irrevocably damaged in the process. Being only a soldier, and not a surgeon, I know nothing but that the insertion of a Martian brain in the skull-cavity formerly occupied by an Earthman's brain unavoidably destroys the human brain and the Martian body. The transfer is permanent."

Gideon struggled to push down the growing sense of horror. He looked at Ridenour's human body and thought of the tentacled monster's mind that now occupied it.

"What are the Suspects?" he asked, his mouth and lips suddenly dry.

"Galani minds, which are now permanently occupying human bodies."

"Where are these operations performed on Earth?"

The body that was Ridenour's twisted, as Scho-La-Nui struggled against the drug that forced him to tell the truth.

"I—I do not wish to answer. Mel-El-Aben has said that the truth regarding the Suspects may be revealed to you, but not military information. I will not answer."

"I can spare your life if you tell me where the operations are being performed."

"You will tell the PD," Ridenour's lips said, the man's face contorted, "and they kill our most valuable surgeons."

"Tell me! Where are the operations performed on Earth?"

"The drug—" Scho-La-Nui said, apparently fighting its effects, "I will have—have to cease living—else I—I betray…"

The lips stopped as the mind of the Galani brain contracted the muscles of the human heart and brought it to a stop. Gideon felt for the pulse. There was none. There was an ominous silence about him. He stepped to one of the windows, and looked out from the side so that he would not be seen. The streets were empty. Further down could be seen police lines that prevented cars from passing. City police, their uniforms glistening in the evening sun, rode through with armored cars and stopped in front of the apartment house.

HE TURNED away and rushed towards the main entrance door. It was locked, apparently under mechanical control from police on PD orders. Unable to escape, he pushed the desk and other furniture in front of the door. There was not enough to hold them back, but a few seconds might be gained. He stepped to the telereceiver and dialed the number of the PD Headquarters in Washington.

"Chief McDonough," he said to the secretary's face. "PD Agent Gideon speaking. Vitally urgent. *Quick!*"

Whether the call came through or not he could not tell. The fumes from sedation gas, released by the police, filled the corridors, poured out from under the doorway. Gideon staggered toward the window and punched his fist through the glass. It was too late for he had breathed a draft of the sedation gas and felt his senses reeling. He could see the city before him, suddenly bathed in a brilliant flash of light. In the far distance a giant black mushroom filled the horizon. He stepped back to avoid the death-dealing radiation of the atomic explosion and then he felt himself falling into a deep, dark whirlpool.

CHAPTER SEVEN

CONSCIOUSNESS returned to Gideon, and he breathed it in like a man who had been suffocating. He lay upon a hard cot and beside him was a white table with an empty truth serum hypodermic laying upon a few sheets of sterile gauze. At the foot of the bed was the vague outline of a man.

"Here are your eyeglasses," a deep voice said. "I guess you'll feel better with them."

Gideon put them on and looked into the iron-lined face of Chief McDonough, head of Planetary Defense.

"You were not alone on the case," McDonough said, raising his hand to still the flood of questions, which he knew, would come from Gideon. "Other agents corroborated your findings. Our loyal PD's moved in with the local police when we found the Taos office to be Suspect. We've been using truth serum everywhere, for at last we've been able to produce it in quantity. Now we have a way of finding out Suspects, and we will exterminate them. The construction of Galani brains is quite different when compared with ours. Simulation is impossible and X-rays of the skull will show immediately who is a Suspect. Mass X-rays, and the use of the truth serum on all captured Suspects, will smash once and for all the secret invasion of the Galani."

Gideon got to his feet. There was still some weakness in his legs and a heavy, dull sensation surged through his brain. The effects of the sedation gas were wearing off and strength returned.

"I even took an X-ray of your head," McDonough said, with a faint smile; "we cannot afford to trust anyone until we are certain that they are not Galani intelligences occupying human bodies. You, my friend Gideon, are a human being! Thank the skies for that. Considering the strange interest Mel-El-Aben had in you, I often felt doubts."

Gideon reached for his clothes and quickly dressed. "That atomic explosion," he said, "the one I saw as I passed out in Ridenour's apartment—what was it?"

The Chief's face darkened. "The Newark pile blew up."

"Accident?"

"Sabotage, of course, but what proof can be found in radiating ruins? The possibility of accident has already been planted and nurtured in the Suspect-controlled press and Telefax. There has been a wave of sabotage in strategic factories and headquarters. One truth serum plant has been lost; X-ray film factories and machines have been smashed. Now that we have the means for locating Suspects, the Galani are desperate. If they are to strike, this is the moment."

This is the moment—the words flashed through Gideon's mind. It meant final, conclusive war; for, if the secret organization of Suspects on Earth were smashed, Galani strength would be ended forever. Never again would their physicians and scientists be permitted to approach Earthmen. Every factory, and every Galani city, would be kept under the strictest surveillance.

The proud Galani, whose ancestors had wandered across the skies when Earthmen were savages, would be reduced to museum specimens in carefully controlled reservations. Their proud spirit broken, they would soon die—for their scientific efforts to keep the race going would be hindered and restricted.

This was their last chance. Whatever forces the Galani had would strike now.

"Project Victory," Gideon said, "is it ready?"

"The Senate is debating the fate of Mars now. We are due there in a few moments, and I wait for the second when I will pull the levers that set the atomic vessels sailing against that damned planet!"

WHEN THEY arrived in the Senate chambers they found the very walls lined with armed PD agents, their faces drawn and haggard. Several bodies lay slumped over their desks, blood flowing from blaster-wounds. Rows of Senators, some trembling and some unconcerned, stood behind a series of X-ray machines. As each man stepped through, the negative was instantly developed and a white-faced doctor pronounced the verdict. If the cranial photograph indicated a brain construction different from that of normal Earthmen, the Senator was arrested and bound; those who struggled were shot. Apparently, the Suspects in the Senate knew their danger; when the X-ray machines were rolled into the chambers, they made a break for freedom and were shot down by the armed PD agents that encircled the walls.

Gideon saw with horror, when the examinations were finished, that one-fourth of the Senators, the most powerful body of men in the world, had been shot or arrested. Senator Burbank's body sprawled in the aisle until a guard came and dragged it away.

The President, his face aged twenty years, walked to the officiating desk and gently tapped his gavel. The silence was like that of the grave.

"The bodies among us," he said quietly, his voice sometimes breaking, "while appearing to be those of dear friends, house the minds of the Galani, whose professed intention it is to destroy the Earth and the human race. Their plan, discovered when we were on the brink of disaster, has been to not only murder us but to take over our bodies as well by transplantation of their minds. Trapped by the knowledge that Nature has decided their race to be unfit for perpetuation, they have attempted to take over human bodies in a final effort to preserve their dying species. That the human race has been saved from such extinction has been due in main part to the valiant work of PD agents McDonough and Gideon—who are still with us—and Ridenour and Munnheim, who have lost their lives in the service of Earth."

He paused for a few moments, unable to continue. When he spoke again, it was with the dull, set tones of a man who knows the inevitable result of the thing he must do.

"I will ask the Secretary," he said, "to review briefly the acts performed by the Galani in the last twenty-four hours."

The Senate chambers were silent as the Secretary walked to the speaker's desk. He leafed through the papers with trembling hands and summarized them.

"Seventy PD armored rockets were seized at Deimosport and occupied by Galani forces. The PD garrison at Marsalene has been taken by sedation gas and all its members taken to Galani hospitals where, according to the Telefax espionage screens still operating, operations removing and destroying their brains are being performed.

"Suspect groups in the largest Earth cities have taken over control. Los Angeles, Paris, and Shanghai have fallen overnight and declared themselves for the Galani. In eighteen other major centers battles are now taking place between PD and Galani forces. PD victory is assured in these skirmishes, but the War Department declares that if vessels operating from Mars bomb our production-centers, the ultimate issue of this struggle may be in doubt. Confused by Galani propaganda claims, many loyal Earthmen are joining the ranks of the Suspects."

A SUDDEN rumble shook the building and one of the walls split. The distant roar of jets and rockets could be heard. Uneasily the Senators looked about them at the shaking walls.

"It will not be necessary," the President interrupted, "to continue the summation of aggressive Galani attacks. Suffice it to say that the Capital itself is now under attack by Suspects."

Through the Senate chambers could be heard the labored breathing of the Senators and PD agents. The temporary lull was broken again by the roar of guns and the swish of bomb-laden jets over the Capital. A few moments later another explosion rent the air, cracking the walls. The bombs were coming nearer.

"Why aren't they using fission bombs?" Gideon whispered to McDonough. "It would take only one to destroy the Capital and most of the PD leadership."

"They either want to use our bodies," McDonough said softly, "and therefore must preserve them, or they feel we will be needed to act as collaborators and Quislings for Mars."

A messenger delivered a note to the President's desk. The wearied head of the Senate read it and then turned to the assembled people who sat waiting for the inevitable decision.

"Our Telefax espionage screens," he said, "have reported the assembling of a huge fission-bomb fleet on Mars. These vessels constitute our entire fleet, which has been captured by traitor-Suspects. The fleet is being reconditioned and manned by Galani. It will be ready to sail against us in a few days."

"Mr. President!" a gray-haired man, a virtual patriarch among the Senators, rose to his feet. "Mr. President! I move that Project Victory—the atomic destruction of the planet Mars—be released immediately!"

"Aye! Aye! *Aye!*"

A deafening roar swept up from the Senators. Even the calm PD agents lining the walls gave loose to hoarse shouts and cheers. Dignified men stood upon the desks and yelled.

Gideon was swept along in the mass hysteria and shouted with them. One or the other race had to be destroyed. Since the Galani attempted such an insidious invasion, they could never be trusted again. With the destruction of Mars, the main base of the fighting Suspects would be smashed; in due time, isolated resisting bands would be wiped out and the threat of the Galani destroyed forever.

"Death to Mars! Destroy the Red Planet!"

The President hammered with his gavel upon the stand.

"It is so moved!" he declared. "I order Project Victory!" Turning to the white-faced McDonough he yelled, "Do your duty!"

Wordlessly McDonough turned away to the doors. Gideon followed him, pushing through the mob and listening to the cheering of the Senators and the Agents.

"Free us from the Martian threat! Destroy the Galani threat! Victory! *Victory!*"

The Senate became a turmoil as the yells of its people filled the air. A great weight seemed to be lifted from their minds. Pale faces were now flushed with joy. The threat, which would have made monsters of them and their children, was about to be destroyed forever.

"Death to the Galani!"

CHAPTER EIGHT

THE STREETS of Washington were littered with bodies along the hastily erected barricades. The jet-attack of the Suspects had failed and regiments of the loyal PD were mopping up isolated Suspect bands.

McDonough and Gideon commandeered tanks and sped towards the Virginia hills, which housed Project Victory's control station. An armed escort followed them, their guns firing warning salvos to every nearing plane or truck.

"Suspect bands are already attacking," Agent Carlisle reported as they neared the simple terra cotta building, which housed the controls.

"Attack immediately," McDonough ordered. "Apparently they do not know its importance, or fission bombs would have been used. Gideon, Agent Hastings, and I will head for the controls; the rest of you will fight off any attacks that may come."

They left the tank, machine-gun blasts exploding overhead, and ran towards the building. A tank salvo had smashed the camouflaged doors and the group struggled past overturned building blocks. They fled towards the control room, camouflaged among the machinery-filled sections of the building. The air around them was ripped by gun-flashes from snipers. The hurrying Agents accompanying them were put to swift use, for at the doorway of the control room they faced a rudely built barricade.

They fell downward as the first enemy volley blasted above them. A band of Suspects, apparently including one actual Galani, had attempted to break through the door. Finding this impossible, they had decided to defend it against any Earthmen until additional Suspect reinforcements were able to penetrate the PD defenses.

"Sedation gas!" Gideon yelled.

An Agent crawled forward, gun-tube in hand, and fired the fumes. The gas swirled upwards, and then pushed forward by fans, rolled clown upon the Suspect barricade.

"Hold fire!" McDonough said; "they'll try to stop breathing for a few minutes, but one whiff should be enough."

Several of the Suspects jumped up from the barricade, guns in hand.

"Fire!"

They fell, their hands feebly clutching at gashed open stomachs and lungs. A minute passed and then there was silence.

"Sterile gas!" McDonough shouted. It burst behind the rude barricade, its pink streamers flowing downward and cleansing the air.

"All clear!" McDonough said.

They ran forward and jumped over the machine stacks that made the crude Suspect defense. "Have them all shot," he said, pushing aside blast equipment that had been placed against the door to the control room.

"The Martian, too, sir?" an Agent asked.

Gideon turned swiftly. Crushed among the battered machines, his tentacles still and a brown mass exuding from his mangled body, was the Galani surgeon, Mel-El-Aben.

"This crude gas," his tentacles rasped, "while dulling our senses is not sufficiently effective for the Galani. You have slain my associates; will you complete the task?"

The guard's finger tightened on the trigger.

"Spare him," Gideon said, surprised at his own decision. "Bring him into the control room with us; we may need to question him."

MCDONOUGH looked at him curiously but said nothing. "Be sure to tie him up," he ordered curtly and then bent to the control door, which opened mechanically to the word-control commands given it by the PD Chief.

McDonough and Gideon entered the control room, which could decide the fate of a whole world. Agent Hastings dragged the body of Mel-El-Aben in after them and then shut the door, leaving the PD Agents on guard.

Once inside, Gideon was surprised by the simplicity of the room. Legend had given it many sizes and shapes; in reality it was completely bare but for the series of screens lined against the wall, and a plain set of levers in the center.

Project Victory had been in existence for 200 years, constantly being enlarged and strengthened. Dispatch-ports around the world were controlled from this room. Mechanical computators made corrections every second in the controls of all hell-bomb vessels in the ports, so that no matter when they were released, they would head immediately for their predetermined target on Mars.

"Twenty launching ports," McDonough said, his voice awed despite his familiarity with the construction and nature of Project Victory. "Each one is completely ready, and only a handful need reach Mars to wipe out the planet forever…"

Mel-El-Aben, his tentacles mercilessly strapped down by Agent Hastings, uttered an oath. Gideon walked over to the Martian on the floor and helped him up to a sitting position. He felt a wave of nausea as he touched the shifting scales and the tentacles. To hide his revulsion he turned to Hastings.

"Draw your gun," he said bruskly, "if anything goes wrong, shoot to kill."

"In the years to come," Mel-El-Aben said, his voice thick because he could not move his tentacles freely—"in the years to come, James Gideon, you will regret this action; and remorse for the murder of the Galani will pursue you to the end of all time."

McDonough stood over the controls, working them and checking each against the screens that showed the rockets in their port cradles. He did not listen to the Galani.

Gideon resented the words: he, Gideon, was not a Suspect. His heart, flesh, bone, blood, and brain were Earth and his loyalty was only to the human race.

"How many thousands of us did you murder?" he demanded, in order to break off this strange feeling of guilt, which Mel-El-Aben sought to force upon him.

The Galani made a gesture, which might have meant the same as the shrugging of shoulders. "It was necessary," he rasped; "did you not slaughter us by the millions when you first came to Mars?"

"But that was an insane war, and it was ended. Why begin again?"

"Begin? It never ended. Our technology was liquidated by Earthmen and for many years we bided our time, practicing the only skill you encouraged in us—surgery and medicine."

"But to attempt to take over a complete species!" Gideon interjected. "That meant giving up your bodies and living in a physical setting that must be as repulsive to you as your bodies are to us. Surely there could be some other solution."

MEL-EL-ABEN said, as three Earthmen in the control room watched him, "If there was, we did not find it. Our race is ages old. Through endless mutations we have come to our final end-bodies of such complexity, and such perfection, that by your standards we are virtually immortal. But in achieving that end, Nature has betrayed us by rendering birth and the continuation of our species extremely difficult. In seven births out of twelve, both parent and child die. Despite our individual ages is there any hope for the Galani race as a whole? None!"

"Metal robot-bodies! With them you would *actually* be immortal!" Gideon said; "that would have been a solution!"

"No!" Mel-El-Aben exclaimed. "You keep thinking in individual terms, while our concern is with the species as a whole. Remember that, through our ancestral memory—a thing foreign to you—each of us bears the conscience of our species. Individual Galani are important. Our task is to find a way to preserve the species when nature has dictated that we can no longer propagate at all. Occupying your bodies, we could reproduce and carry on the Galani traditions. Surgical transplantation of our brains to your bodies was the solution to our desperate problem."

"But you have lost," Gideon said, "lost completely."

"Have we?" Mel-El-Aben said.

There was an inflection in his tentacle-created voice that Gideon did not understand.

"The controls are ready," McDonough said stiffly. Hastings stood by his side as if to give him courage in the execution of his task. The realization of the enormity of the destruction, which would be unleashed upon Mars, swept over the three Earthmen.

"There is no other, acceptable choice," Gideon said, suddenly remembering his father's words to him when he was still a child: *Do not condemn in advance the actions of the Galani. There will come a time when you will understand your part in world history. Reserve judgment!* He had not understood his father then and he did not understand him now. How could he reserve judgment when the horror and guilt of the Galani was so clearly evident?

McDonough breathed deeply. "May the future races of the world forgive me," he said, his voice shaken.

He reached for the first lever, which would send an atomic-armed vessel to Mars. The lever came down savagely and with a clanking finality clicked in place.

All of them fastened anxious eyes upon the first group of telescreens. A huge rocket, monstrous in size and shape, twisted crazily in its cradle and then lurched sideways. A bright flash of fire burst upon the screen, which then died and went blank. The second and third screens showed a pillar of smoke rising from the valley in which the rocket had been hidden.

"Score one for the Galani!" Mel-El-Aben said victoriously. "There are more of us placed in strategic positions than you imagine!"

MCDONOUGH'S face was suddenly white.

"Sabotage!" Hastings gasped.

Gideon knew well the meaning of the struggle that now cut lines upon the bomb-ports. By pulling the control-levers he would only be setting off the bombs upon the Earth itself, and destroying countless millions of Earthmen.

"Delay!" Hastings cried. "Have the rockets examined for sabotage before you release them!"

McDonough shook his head. "Galani vessels are already assembling on Mars. If they leave the planet, our weakened and infiltrated PD forces could not cope with them. They would overrun the Earth, and the aid they could give the Suspects would be decisive."

Each of the rockets had been adjusted, first to spray disease-dust over a designated area, and then to crash its atomic load upon a pre-selected industrial center. The explosion of a rocket in its cradle on Earth would wipe out the disease-load, but the atomic destruction was still tremendous. Every last precaution had been taken to save the ports from infiltration by Suspects, but it needed only one traitor to smash the controls.

"The Fifth Port," Aben said, almost crazily, for he was on the brink of seeing his native planet annihilated. "The Fifth Port," he went on, "is only fifteen miles from New York City. Do you dare pull the lever and risk destroying the city? Our Suspects, remember, have been everywhere—even in the highest ranks of the PD and the Senate! If we had planted only one in the Fifth Port you will destroy New York. Do you dare pull that lever?"

McDonough's hand was upon the lever. Beads of sweat formed on his brow.

"Use the truth serum on him!" Hastings said. "He would know which ports are sabotaged and which are not."

"I can order my mind to cease functioning," Mel-El-Aben replied coldly; "the serum cannot work on us, for we know how to die willingly. Answer, McDonough! Do you dare pull the levers?"

"What are your terms for peace?" McDonough said brokenly, his hand lying limp upon the switch.

"I am only a physician…" Mel-El-Aben began.

"Not true," Gideon replied, angrily; "each Martian is possessed of racial memory; and each one, despite his occupational or educational status, can speak for the whole planet."

Mel-El-Aben turned his tentacles toward Gideon so that the light-sensitive tips were focused at him. "True," he said. "Each of us has inherited the knowledge and experience of millions of years. What is hard-won knowledge to you is but instinct to us. Instinct, Gideon, remember that word!"

"What are your terms?" McDonough repeated weakly.

CHAPTER NINE

MEL-EL-ABEN said, "To show our sincerity we will destroy each of our laboratories on Earth. We vow never to effect another brain-transfer to a human body, as long as our race survives."

"What do you ask in turn?" McDonough demanded.

"Nothing but this: free immigration and free trade between the planets. Reaffirm the 30th amendment guaranteeing personal privacy against every sort of examination, physical, and mental. Destruction of all existing medical records."

"It sounds reasonable," Hastings muttered uneasily.

"Reasonable hell!" McDonough exploded. "Gideon, you tell him what it means."

Gideon nodded. "It means that we promise not to hunt down, or even attempt to locate, the Suspects planted in our race. They will intermarry, without our knowledge and become one of us; their children will be Galani in heart and mind. With free immigration, and the Suspects already living on Earth and occupying positions of power, Earth's supremacy is over forever. Within a decade, their technology would sweep over ours; whatever their secret invasion had not done, their weapons would finish."

"Accept our terms," Mel-El-Aben said, "and you will have peace."

"Peace as slaves!"

"Peace! What is your answer?"

McDonough paused and looked at Mel-El-Aben whose tentacles twisted and strained in excitement. In McDonough's eyes was revulsion and horror.

"This," he said savagely, "is our answer."

He reached across the control board and pulled down one lever after another, blindly. They clicked angrily in place.

"You'll destroy the Earth!" Hastings gasped.

McDonough turned away from the board, haggard and worn. Mel-El-Aben was impassive. The tentacles were still, and there was no sign of what he thought or felt.

They all turned to stare at the screens. Each of the plates burst into activity. The third flashed and was silent.

"Another city gone," Hastings said quietly; "that was the port near Chicago."

The fourth screen turned dim, its surface clouding; then the fifth screen faded, too. They stared, tense. Would these screens too become suddenly blank, indicating an explosion caused by Suspect-made sabotage?

"It cannot—it cannot," Gideon said, trying to reassure himself and still the growing sense of panic.

The screens suddenly cleared. The enormous launching cradles that held the rockets were empty. The vessels had escaped from Earth, unharmed, and were now carrying their loads of devastation to Mars.

A sigh came up from the three Earthmen.

"It was a bluff," Gideon said to Mel-El-Aben, "a gigantic bluff. You didn't get through all our defenses."

McDonough sat down, hands trembling. His eyes fell upon the blank screens, which indicated ports that had blown up on Earth. The majority of the screens were clear, but a few showed that the Suspects had succeeded.

"WHAT A PRICE to pay," McDonough said wearily, looking at the blank screens that indicated sabotaged ports. "But we have won after all."

Have we? Gideon thought. Now that the bombing-flights had been launched, he realized the tension he had been undergoing. His hands were moist and his head and body ached. The destruction of an entire planet with a culture a million years old *was* a terrible price to pay...

Mel-El-Aben faced the screens, silent and unmoving. The color had drained from his tentacles and he appeared dead. Gideon felt a surge of pity, which shocked him. He had no right to feel any sympathy for the Galani for he knew what their intentions were. The Galani were monsters who had to be destroyed.

"There are still the Suspects," Hastings said.

"We will finish them," McDonough sighed. "Without reinforcements from Mars, we will annihilate the armed bands. If there are any still hidden among us, X-rays fill find them."

"Once the bombs have landed on Mars," Gideon said, "and destroyed the planet; they will have lost the war. The psychology of the Galani is such that, once they realize the inevitability of defeat, their confidence in victory shaken, they will lose all hope. Isn't that correct, Mel-El-Aben?"

The Galani waved his tentacles in agreement. "When we lose all hope, we shall die," he said simply; "now that you know the surgery we have used to transplant our brains to human bodies, you will search out our laboratories on Earth and kill the few tentacled-Martians that remain. We expect this."

"How long before the screens show the explosions of the bombs on Mars?"

McDonough glanced at the figures, which raced in a band across the control board. "An hour at the most," he said, raising his hand to his forehead. "The thing is done, but I have a strange feeling of regret—almost of sadness. It was as if, for a moment I could see things from the Galani point of view." He saw Gideon's quizzical look. "Nonsense," he said, as if aware of what Gideon was thinking. "I am not a

Suspect, and neither are you—else we would not have pulled these levers. This feeling I have is just—just—strange..."

Gideon's heart began to hammer. He could feel the pulse-beat in his fingertips and the back of his head. For one startling moment he knew what McDonough had been trying to say. A vast picture of Martian life and history seemed to suddenly beat through his brain and then die away slowly.

He looked at Mel-El-Aben, tied there so securely, and wondered. He lifted his fingertips to his forehead and felt the line between hair and scalp. No, he had not been operated on without knowing it. He felt reassured; he was an Earthman—of that there was no doubt. It was only the overwhelming nature of the catastrophe they were about to witness on the screens that made him so uneasy. One does not see the destruction of an entire planet every day.

Mel-El-Aben's sight-tentacles were turned to him. "I observe," the Galani rasped, "that you are no longer wearing your eyeglasses."

GIDEON brought his hand back and forth before his face. The thick lenses that he had worn ever since childhood were no longer there. His mind jumped back and the events of the preceding hour—the rush through the streets, the fighting around the control room, the lifting of the barricade—somewhere in those hectic events the glasses had slipped or fallen from his face and—miracle of miracles—instead of seeing a hazy, fog-ridden world, he saw with clarity and precision. His eyes were perfect.

A terror swept through him. "You operated on me without my knowing it!" If this had been done, perhaps other changes were also effected.

"No," the Galani said, "we have not touched you. Your body has merely overcome a physical, muscular disability. We Martians have long studied the operation of racial memory and instinct, and have come to understand such matters, which are utterly beyond the comprehension of Earthmen. Life—whether Martian or Earthian, or other— strives constantly for perfection, and for the evasion or postponement of disintegration. The long life of the Galani is due not to any peculiar structure of our cells, but to the fine control that our minds have over our body. You Earthmen had often approached the secret in the religious cults that believed that "sickness is error; there is no death," but your undeveloped brains were unable fully to master your physical constituent particles. In your case, Gideon, your brain came to your aid in a critical moment when you needed sight so badly. Just as men under pressure find increased strength and endurance, so in the same way your mind can control and shape your body, when urgently necessary."

Mel-El-Aben's words fell on deaf ears for the eyes of the three Earthmen were fastened upon the screens. They waited, in fascinated horror, for the bombs to land upon Mars. Would that hour never end? The red globe of Mars shone so hugely upon the screen.

"Zero hour minus ten minutes," the mechanical voice from the control board rang out.

Gideon felt the nape of his neck quiver with excitement. Mel-El-Aben was still talking about instinct, but Gideon did not listen. It seemed that the Galani was trying to tell him something—to prod his memory and bring out knowledge forgotten or not yet remembered.

"The newborn child," the Martian said, "possesses all the instincts of his species—but these do not manifest themselves at once. As the body grows, so do the instinctual capabilities. Some instincts, for example, will lie dormant until maturity; are you listening to me, Gideon?"

The rocket-bombers were nearing their destination and in a few minutes the rain of death would fall upon the planet.

Gideon felt a surge of excitement, and his head began to ache. He reached for some aspirins in the medical chest near the control board; a stabbing pain jabbed through his skull, from forehead to back and dipping down in the center as if reaching for his soul. The shock sent him gasping.

"Zero minus five."

Gideon leaned weakly against his seat. McDonough's eyes were also closed as if in pain. Mel-El-Aben's sighted tentacles turned from one to the other, while Hastings stared at the screens showing Mars' huge red form waiting for the bombs.

THE PAIN came in shocking throbs. Brain tumor, he thought. He had read enough to know the symptoms.

It was hard to think clearly. Ideas flashed through a pain-wracked mind. They were confused ideas and images, wordless thoughts seemingly without meaning and then suddenly a strange significance. He thought he saw the beginnings of life from primeval slime, and the long, long drive of the cell to shape itself and to fight against a hostile world. He saw the cell split and become two and then four and eight. He saw this mathematical progression through the ages of life struggled to develop and to master a world that sought to destroy it.

The evolution and growth of a species began to have a meaning and a purpose he had never suspected. He began to feel one with the primeval cell and the millions and billions of living forms that stretched across the panorama of endless centuries. The drama of life spanned untold years and new suns grew old while the struggle for life continued.

"Zero minus four."

Gideon shook himself. Only one minute had passed but it seemed like uncounted years. Something clawed at his brain as if unformed thoughts were striving for expression. He looked at McDonough. The Chief's face was drawn and lines of pain were marked on him—as if he, too, were going through some inner struggle. Only Hastings was serene and confident as he watched the screen and saw the rockets maneuver over Mars for their pre-calculated positions. In a few minutes the flashes would come and the surface of that red world would be wiped clean of its civilization.

"The Galani have lost forever."

Mel-El-Aben, dying member of a doomed race, glanced from McDonough to Gideon. "Have we?" he asked.

Gideon tried to ignore the pain in his head. "What do you mean?"

Mel-El-Aben paused, watching the screen.

"Zero minus three."

"Is it not strange," Aben said, "how vanity and conceit form so large a part of Earthian psychologies? Could you not guess that the racial memory each of us have would make it forever impossible for any of us to accept Earth's rule over our planet? Was it not clear that eventually our superior minds would find some way to destroy your race and make ours survive—no matter the cost?"

"You did find the method," McDonough said; "the transplantation of your minds into our bodies. We have discovered that and will now destroy you. We have won the battle."

"Zero minus two."

"*But have you!*" Mel-El-Aben said triumphantly. "How long," he demanded, "do you think we have been in possession of the technique for transplantation?"

"Twenty years," Gideon said hesitantly. There was something here that cast a shadow over his soul. Uncertainty gripped him as he waited for the answer.

"No! No! No!" Aben said, his weakened tentacles quivering from excitement: *"not twenty years but for two hundred and fifty!"*

"That's a lie!" McDonough answered sharply; "we would have known! We would have found the Suspects sooner."

"Vanity and conceit!" Aben said. "You cannot accept the fact that we had made long-range plans for your destruction and for the inevitable victory of the Galani way of life. It was only when we began to enlarge our operations—to include the smuggling of Galani physicians on a large scale to Earth that you discovered a secret that we kept for over two Centuries!"

"Zero Minus One!"

MEL-EL-ABEN said, "For two hundred and fifty years, we have eaten away at the core of the human race. We have transplanted our brains and souls into your bodies. How could you recognize those of us who become Earthmen in every outward visible form? We lived your lives; acted your lives; even thought like you. We even bred children!"

"Stand by for explosions!"

"Yes! Suspects bear children and these sons and daughter are Galani! The God-given gift, which will save us from annihilation, is ours at last. Two hundred and fifty years— eight generations of births, deaths, and marriages. Those of us who earned transplantation to human bodies became mortal and died as you died—but they had children whose brains and instincts are Galani!"

The words were like bullets aimed at Gideon and McDonough. Gideon realized at last why Mel-El-Aben had been so interested in him, and why his own father had repeatedly told him to avoid passing judgment on the Galani. *"I knew his father quite well..."* Mel-El-Aben had said to Dr.

Fellbank. James Gideon's father was a Suspect; that human body he knew and loved possessed a Martian Galani brain.

"You know what hybrids are," Mel-El-Aben said, "but do you know which characteristics can be inherited and which cannot when a Galani brain occupies a human body? We know! Neither your X-rays nor your truth serums will work on the children of Suspects but we know!"

"When does instinct manifest itself? When the species is in danger! The racial memories, which lie dormant in all the children and all the descendants of Suspects will come to the fore when needed. You, Gideon! You, McDonough! You, the billions throughout the world who think yourselves Earthmen! Listen to this: our racial memory is in you. It will come to each man and woman when he and she reach maturity. You, who are the children of Suspects—and there are billions of you—you who are the descendants of this new hybrid—half-man, half-Galani, listen to me! *You are Martian! Martian! Martian!*"

"*Bombs away! Bombs away! Bombs away!*"

THE SCREENS turned a brilliant red as the planet met the deadly barrage of atomic weapons. The Galani cities were blasted and the surface scarred by the terrible, shattering explosions. One by one, the death-dealing mushroom clouds spread over the crimson planet and radioactive dust covered the fields spreading ever wider. The holocaust smashed the cities and erased life from the plains. Mars, Mars the Eternal, was dead.

Gideon's thoughts sped back to childhood. He remembered the sad voice of his father, alone among Earthmen whom he did not understand: "*Remember me when you realize what you are and what I am. There will be millions like you. You will not be alone.*"

He knew now that the invasion was complete. The shock of the destruction of Mars would rouse the latent instinct of every man and woman who, like himself, was descended from a Galani-occupied human being. The knowledge of the history of Mars—incredibly old—swept over him, and the acquired knowledge of Earth—hurriedly gleaned from dull books—faded away.

He looked at the red, hellish screens that showed the death of the world. With pity he turned his eyes to the body of Mel-El-Aben, who had died. In McDonough's eyes he saw friendship and understanding; both of them now shared the racial memories of a species countless millions of years old. They looked at Hastings, poor weak Earthman, ignorant and useless. *Let us spare him,* Gideon thought, *for there are few like him now.* They, the Suspects, would destroy the minority of Earthmen.

"We have won," he said to himself, "despite the destruction of our native planet, Mars."

"I," said James Gideon, in whose brain now flooded the memories of long dead ancestors, "am proud to be a Galani."

THE END

If you've enjoyed this book, you will not want to miss these terrific titles…

ARMCHAIR SCI-FI & HORROR DOUBLE NOVELS, $12.95 each

D-51 **A GOD NAMED SMITH** by Henry Slesar
WORLDS OF THE IMPERIUM by Keith Laumer

D-52 **CRAIG'S BOOK** by Don Wilcox
EDGE OF THE KNIFE by H. Beam Piper

D-53 **THE SHINING CITY** by Rena M. Vale
THE RED PLANET by Russ Winterbotham

D-54 **THE MAN WHO LIVED TWICE** by Rog Phillips
VALLEY OF THE CROEN by Lee Tarbell

D-55 **OPERATION DISASTER** by Milton Lesser
LAND OF THE DAMNED by Berkeley Livingston

D-56 **CAPTIVE OF THE CENTAURIANESS** by Poul Anderson
A PRINCESS OF MARS by Edgar Rice Burroughs

D-57 **THE NON-STATISTICAL MAN** by Raymond F. Jones
MISSION FROM MARS by Rick Conroy

D-58 **INTRUDERS FROM THE STARS** by Ross Rocklynne
FLIGHT OF THE STARLING by Chester S. Geier

D-59 **COSMIC SABOTEUR** by Frank M. Robinson
LOOK TO THE STARS by Willard Hawkins

D-60 **THE MOON IS HELL!** by John W. Campbell, Jr.
THE GREEN WORLD by Hal Clement

ARMCHAIR SCIENCE FICTION CLASSICS, $12.95 each

C-16 **THE SHAVER MYSTERY, Book Three**
by Richard S. Shaver

C-17 **THE PLANET STRAPPERS**
by Raymond Z. Gallun

C-18 **THE FOURTH "R"**
by George O. Smith

ARMCHAIR SCI-FI & HORROR GEMS SERIES, $12.95 each

G-5 **SCIENCE FICTION GEMS, Vol. Three**
C. M. Kornbluth and others

G-6 **HORROR GEMS, Vol. Three**
August Derleth and others

If you've enjoyed this book, you will not want to miss these terrific titles…

ARMCHAIR SCI-FI & HORROR DOUBLE NOVELS, $12.95 each

D-61 **THE MAN WHO STOPPED AT NOTHING** by Paul W. Fairman
TEN FROM INFINITY by Ivar Jorgensen

D-62 **WORLDS WITHIN** by Rog Phillips
THE SLAVE by C.M. Kornbluth

D-63 **SECRET OF THE BLACK PLANET** by Milton Lesser
THE OUTCASTS OF SOLAR III by Emmett McDowell

D-64 **WEB OF THE WORLDS** by Harry Harrison and Katherine MacLean
RULE GOLDEN by Damon Knight

D-65 **TEN TO THE STARS** by Raymond Z. Gallun
THE CONQUERORS by David H. Keller, M. D.

D-66 **THE HORDE FROM INFINITY** by Dwight V. Swain
THE DAY THE EARTH FROZE by Gerald Hatch

D-67 **THE WAR OF THE WORLDS** by H. G. Wells
THE TIME MACHINE by H. G. Wells

D-68 **STARCOMBERS** by Edmond Hamilton
THE YEAR WHEN STARDUST FELL by Raymond F. Jones

D-69 **HOCUS-POCUS UNIVERSE** by Jack Williamson
QUEEN OF THE PANTHER WORLD by Berkeley Livingston

D-70 **BATTERING RAMS OF SPACE** by Don Wilcox
DOOMSDAY WING by George H. Smith

ARMCHAIR SCIENCE FICTION CLASSICS, $12.95 each

C-19 **EMPIRE OF JEGGA**
by David V. Reed

C-20 **THE TOMORROW PEOPLE**
by Judith Merril

C-21 **THE MAN FROM YESTERDAY**
by Howard Browne as by Lee Francis

C-22 **THE TIME TRADERS**
by Andre Norton

C-23 **ISLANDS OF SPACE**
by John W. Campbell

C-24 **THE GALAXY PRIMES**
by E. E. "Doc" Smith

If you've enjoyed this book, you will not want to miss these terrific titles...

ARMCHAIR SCI-FI & HORROR DOUBLE NOVELS, $12.95 each

D-71 **THE DEEP END** by Gregory Luce
TO WATCH BY NIGHT by Robert Moore Williams

D-72 **SWORDSMAN OF LOST TERRA** by Poul Anderson
PLANET OF GHOSTS by David V. Reed

D-73 **MOON OF BATTLE** by J. J. Allerton
THE MUTANT WEAPON by Murray Leinster

D-74 **OLD SPACEMEN NEVER DIE!** John Jakes
RETURN TO EARTH by Bryan Berry

D-75 **THE THING FROM UNDERNEATH** by Milton Lesser
OPERATION INTERSTELLAR by George O. Smith

D-76 **THE BURNING WORLD** by Algis Budrys
FOREVER IS TOO LONG by Chester S. Geier

D-77 **THE COSMIC JUNKMAN** by Rog Phillips
THE ULTIMATE WEAPON by John W. Campbell

D-78 **THE TIES OF EARTH** by James H. Schmitz
CUE FOR QUIET by Thomas L. Sherred

D-79 **SECRET OF THE MARTIANS** by Paul W. Fairman
THE VARIABLE MAN by Philip K. Dick

D-80 **THE GREEN GIRL** by Jack Williamson
THE ROBOT PERIL by Don Wilcox

ARMCHAIR SCIENCE FICTION CLASSICS, $12.95 each

C-25 **THE STAR KINGS**
by Edmond Hamilton

C-26 **NOT IN SOLITUDE**
by Kenneth Gantz

C-32 **PROMETHEUS II**
by S. J. Byrne

ARMCHAIR SCI-FI & HORROR GEMS SERIES, $12.95 each

G-7 **SCIENCE FICTION GEMS, Vol. Four**
Jack Sharkey and others

G-8 **HORROR GEMS, Vol. Four**
Seabury Quinn and others